SIRKI'S CHILDREN

SIRKI'S CHILDREN

KYT WRIGHT

www.blkdogpublishing.com

Other titles by Kyt Wright

Sirkkusaga

Love Bites

The Journals of Professor Guthridge

Sirki's Children

Further adventures from the continuing story of Sirki Da N'tan (nee Vigsdottir) in two parts
By Kyt Wright

It is nearly thirty years since the attempted coup.

Sirki has married Bren and had two further children, Bren has become Thegn following his father's death but Sirki is reluctant to leave her New Winchester home forcing him to divide his time between there and Scartho.

Sirki is now Thegnestre but prefers to be known as Fro Scartho. She has given up her show business career and tries very hard to act respectably as befits her title, something at which she occasionally succeeds!

Her three children, Freya, Aelfred and Sari are now adults, with her youngest daughter having had two children, Willa and Bern.

The story picks up at a particularly bad point in her life.

BOOK ONE

CHAPTER 1 - VISITING MUMMO

What did I do wrong my love to make you fly away?
What was it I should have said to make you turn and stay?
I'm falling to pieces now without you by my side
So I wear a brave face though I want to run and hide
Our bed saw so much of our love but now I lay alone I lay
You only have to call me and I'll take you back this day
I've put on a brave face but I want to run and hide
Don't you know, not being here is killing me inside?
(Excerpt from Brave Face – music Guthric, lyrics Vigsdottir.)

"*Mummo*, can you fly like mummy and Auntie Freya?" asked the small child.

"Juu, but *mummo* just doesn't feel like it anymore and it's not flying it is called le-vi-tay-ting" answered Sirki spelling out the word. Her granddaughter was a very curious four-year-old.

"Do you not feel like it 'cos you're sad?" inquired the little girl, determined not to give up.

"Why do you think *mummo* is sad *lapsi*?" asked Sirki curiously.

"Because sometimes when mummy and Auntie Freya talk without words I can hear them" she answered. "They think you're sad about *their* daddy."

Sirki was astonished by Willa's admission. Thought reading at such an early age was unheard of. "Well, sometimes I am sad because he's been away for such a long time, but he will come back one day and then you'll meet him and he'll be so pleased to meet both of you," the grandchildren were one of the few joys she had left.

"Mummy, stop filling Willa's head with nonsense!" Sari path'd in sharply, she had come back inside with Bern her youngest, he had wanted to see the blue-beaked ducks in *mummo's* pond. Aloud she said. "Willa, play with Bern while I talk to *mummo*."

The little girl sat quietly with her brother to play with his plastic bricks.

"Do you know she can read thoughts already?" Sirki began a telepathic conversation.

"Yes I know, she's only just started but I wasn't going to tell you just yet!" Sari Penelopy was Sirki's youngest daughter, tall and blonde with classic Beta looks. *"Mummy, dad's not coming back, it's been years now and we've all accepted it."*

"Freya still believes in me, your father will return, our wyrd is linked so I know he will return!" retorted Sirki. Bren had vanished over five years ago and she could not let him go, he was the only man she had ever loved and his disappearance had broken her heart. She had put on a brave face at first but as the years passed Sirki had sunk into a very deep dark pit, her refusal to give up based on a feeling deep inside.

"Of course she says she believes in you, she's the chosen one, wouldn't want to change that would she?"

"Sari, how can you say that?"

"Freya humours you because she believes you will get over it eventually but you're not! There are dark circles under your eyes, you've lost weight and you're wearing the same clothes all the time, and talking of the chosen one when was the last time you saw her?"

"A month ago I think, Freya is very busy at the moment she'll visit when she has time," replied Sirki quick to defend her older daughter. Sirki had three children by Bren; Freya, the double of her mother, a Flytgealdor in the RAF"s fledgling

Star-Wing with hopes to be the first person to walk on the moon in over three hundred years. Her son Aelfred, an Alpha who chose to be a *Huscarl Rihtleech* rather than follow the warrior's way, currently stationed in Southwest Frankia. Sari, at twenty-four was the youngest, a feisty ex-*Huscarl*, war-widow and mother of two.

"Freya only agrees because she doesn't want to hurt you" continued Sari.

"But you, it seems, have nej problem with that!" Sirki retorted.

"I just hate seeing you shutting yourself away like this, you need to face up to the fact that dad is gone and isn't coming back!" it was hard seeing her mother desperately clinging to hope while watching it destroy her.

"Your father is not dead! He and I have a link, made when we first met and I know he is only lost. He will come back!" path'd Sirki. *"This is my belief lapsi and I have to have it or I will go insane, you don't understand."*

"I don't understand?" Sari was incredulous. *"I lost Stig while I was carrying Bern and I received very little support from you because you were such a mess. Oh, Fri and Alfie made the right noises but we've never been that close. Even though I have your enhanced psionic powers I'm still a Beta and my Alpha was taken from me. I was torn in half, how do you think I coped?"*

"Lapsi I…" began Sirki.

Sari was now in full swing. *"I had no choice but to get on with my life, the only support I got was from mummo and grandma, oh and Ani too!"*

"Oh, Sari I'm so sorry," Sirki was crestfallen, her daughter had lost her husband two years ago and she had been too wrapped up in self-pity to be of any use. "I just find it hard to think straight sometimes."

"It's alright mummy I was just letting off steam, I can never be angry with you for long" replied Sari. "Look, I have to go now but I'll be back at the weekend *and* I will make Freya visit!" she threw her arms around her mother hugging her tightly before gathering up the children.

Sirki made light of Freya's absence as they walked to the flyer with Anya, the granddaughter of the redoubtable Mrs Jensen, carrying little Bern on her shoulders. Sirki noticed how Sari and Anya touched hands as she helped her son into the flyer and the lingering look they exchanged. *"Well, I never!"* thought Sirki raising a rare smile.

The flyer lifted off and after setting the auto-*helmward* for New Winchester Sari decided it was time to contact her sister. *"Freya!"* she path'd to no avail. *"FREYA!"* there was still no response, so she telepathically generated an irritating drone.

"Mummy that's horrible!" shouted Willa from the rear seats.

"Horbul," parroted Bern.

"What do you want, Cuckoo?" came an angry response.

"What are you so angry about?" her sister only used that name when she was annoyed with Sari. She had taunted her with it with as a child.

"Mind your own business, I'm busy!" retorted Freya.

"Too busy to see our mother obviously, I can't get through to her sus but she'll listen to you. You must go and see her and try to coax her to let go of dad" suggested Sari. *"This conviction that he's still alive is making her ill and she's worse every time I visit, mummy hardly ever leaves the house and if it wasn't for Ani she wouldn't eat properly."*

"Saz, I can't just yet…"

"Why not?" interrupted Sari.

"Alright, I will come and visit soon, does that check?" she reluctantly replied.

"Check, and make sure it is soon! So, what are you doing that's so important?"

"I'm in Scartho on official business," Freya path'd back somewhat guardedly, her temper flare-up now subsided.

Sari knew she was hiding something. *"I imagined all your official business would be at New Winchester Airdock?"*

"I er, have to fight a duel at the anwighus," answered Freya hesitantly.

"What? Sus you're a shit fighter, what's it about and why in Scartho?"

"Petronius picked the place, he's stationed here at the moment and I think he wants to humiliate me on my home turf."

"If he picked the venue that means you issued the challenge, why?"

"A matter of family honour Saz," replied her sister.

"You should have seconded me to do it I've always been a better fighter than you," suggested Sari.

"Yeah, I remember, how many times you were threatened with expulsion at school and how old were you, twelve?" sneered her sister.

"I only picked on older kids," replied Sari defensively, despite a mutual enmity she didn't want her sister to suffer further humiliation in the arena. *"Don't put yourself through it, sus."*

"I have to Saz, it's important, now leave me be!" and with that Freya broke contact.

Sari sighed, if her sister wouldn't listen to her, there was someone at Scartho who would.

"Sari dahling, I don't know what you expect me to do, Freya dislikes me enough as it is and if I interfere it will only make things worse?" she had path'd Penni Anderson who was now Campaeldor of the Scartho garrison.

"Can't you stop it, Auntie Penni? It's taking place in Scartho after all."

"Na, I'm only the Huscarl Campaeldor, the RAF does not come under my jurisdiction."

"Can't you at least watch to make sure she doesn't get hurt or make too big a fool of herself?" pleaded Sari.

"Check, I'll see what I can do" Penni answered somewhat reluctantly. Of all Sirki's children Sari was her favourite, and she found it hard to refuse her anything.

CHAPTER 2 – THE CONTEST

Freya Da N'tan strapped on her bright green body armour and hefted the composite training *seax*. Although designed principally for sparring it could still cause serious damage in the right hands. She wore a power shield on her left hand and her open-fronted helmet was equipped with a similar device to ensure a blow to the face did no damage, her opponent was similarly attired but his armour was red.

The *anwighus* comprised of a circular pit encompassed by tiers of seats with a sprung wooden fighting floor at the bottom. The combatants now stood in the centre of it facing each other and waiting for the Pit *Demend*, a grizzled old Tithengealdor whom little would surprise, to join them. "You have called Flytgealdor Petronius to task on the grounds that he has insulted your family name and you feel obliged as a matter of honour that it must be settled by combat?"

"Yes *Demend!*" affirmed Freya.

"Flytgealdor Petronius, are you willing to withdraw the remark Flytgealdor Da N'tan finds so offensive?" the umpire inquired.

"Nay *Demend* the remark was made in jest, I feel Flytgealdor Da N'tan's challenge is unjustified and it is for my honour that I fight," he replied, Freya and Petronius harboured a long-standing enmity, she found him boastful and arrogant, he, in turn, disliked Freya for her privileged upbringing.

"Then if there is nothing more to be said let the contest begin!" and the *Demend* withdrew to the edge to watch for any infringement of the rules. Norms and *novae* were allowed to face each other in the arena so quickspeed and psionic power were strictly forbidden.

After turning on their shields each took up a fighting stance. "Da N'tan is it true that your mother and father used to take turns with Campaeldor Anderson?" suggested Petronius slyly, an important part of the bout was to goad the other until their temper broke and they attacked without thinking clearly. White noise generators ensured all comments were muffled from the audience above.

"At least I know who my father is, bahstard!" it was a weak counter and Freya knew it.

"Your mother is such a *hore* my father may very well be yours!" he retorted.

Anderson watching from the darkened entrance tunnel could hear everything quite clearly, *don't bite, Freya.*

"If your father had a cock as small as yours, I doubt he could have even managed it." Freya spat, her anger rising.

"Your mother's kitty is so big I doubt any man could manage it, is that why she fucks women?" His comment hit home causing Freya to lunge but he parried the blow easily and swung for her neck but Freya caught it on her shield and thrust at his chest.

A green light came on and a bell rang.

"First blow to Da N'tan." shouted the *Demend* and a cheer rang out from Freya's supporters in the seats above. Petronius began a furious assault forcing her into a defensive position and stumbling backwards she allowed him to strike her on the side of the head, the red light came on and the bell rang again. "First blow to Petronius, the next will be the decider." There were fewer cheers from the gallery at this.

Petronius helped Freya up and they resumed positions, she didn't wait to start and landed a fierce blow on his shield sending him reeling backwards.

Go on Freya, follow it up!" thought Penni.

Freya leapt for his exposed chest but her opponent managed to parry and their seaxes clattered noisily. Pushing back with his shield he struck again at her neck but Freya, ducking under his attack went for his chest again. Spotting this Petronius brought his shield across in time spinning her around and exposing her flank as an easy target for a side stab. "Final blow to Petronius" the umpire called as the light shone crimson with its accompanying bell. "Red wins!" a slight ripple of applause followed. It was not a popular victory.

As the spectators began to disperse Marcus Petronius removed his helmet and extended his hand. "You nearly had me there Da N'tan, no hard feelings eh?"

Freya grunted in reply and shook it briefly.

Anderson, deciding it was time to make an appearance, stepped into the arena. "Officer on the floor!" yelled the *Demend* and both combatants jumped to attention.

"Good day to you both, a fine contest indeed… a word however Mr Petronius, I could not help but hear what was being said. Do you honestly believe I was once some kind of plaything for the Thegn and Fro Scartho?" she asked staring in his face.

"No, Ma'am!" he replied nervously.

"Furthermore, Flytgealdor Da N'tan's mother is a respectable lady and is not and has never been a *hore!*" she continued. "I am making myself clear, ya?"

"Yes, Ma'am, it was only barrack-room humour ma'am!" he hadn't realised the Campaeldor had been listening.

"Good, now we have that clarified I suggest you leave. Da N'tan, stay, I want a word with you!" she regarded her friend's daughter seeing Bren in the set of her jaw but otherwise she was Sirki's double.

Da N'tan regarded Anderson with scorn written on her elfin face. "What did you want ma'am?"

"Freya, you know you can call me Auntie Penni when there's no-one around."

"And?" she snapped.

"You mustn't let your anger get on top of you" Penni was trying to be helpful. "If you can channel your aggression into your attack you would be a much better fighter.”

“Is that it, can I go now?” snarled the young woman.

“Freya, why do you dislike me so much?”

“You know why. A lot of that crap Marcus said was true!” her short temper was rising again.

“Oh dear child, we were in a loving relationship, it was not something sordid and I was not passed around like some kind of toy. You grew up with this we never tried to hide it, your mother is a dear sweet woman and that idiot’s other comments were just plain insulting” answered Penni.

“But you have a secret, one you think I don’t suspect!” countered Freya sharply.

“What?”

“Is my suster your child?”

“How is that even possible?” Penni appeared anxious. “You were five when your mum was carrying her, you must remember that? You know I can never have children and why, please stop this, it’s ridiculous.”

“You’re hiding something Aunt Penni and I can feel it, why is Sari so much like you?”

“She has a Beta physique, we all look similar, your dad is her father and your mum gave birth to her… and she has incredible Psi ability far more than me I’m just a regular Beta!” she answered quickly.

“Oh, there is something of mum in there but she resonates mostly like you, I think she is your child somehow!” Freya was starting to simmer.

“You need to speak to your mother about this, I can’t say anything more,” Anderson could feel Freya’s temper boiling and made to walk away as the *Demend* returned.

“I challenge you, Campaeldor Anderson!” she shouted.

“What? Why are you doing this?” Penni was astonished. “I do not accept it!”

“I challenge you again, you are hiding the truth from me and if I win you will reveal it.”

“Na, I will not fight my best friend’s daughter!” *this was not going to end well, why had she listened to Sari?*

"Ma'am that was her second challenge" cautioned the umpire in concern, *to decline a third time would be unthinkable.*

"Campaeldor Anderson, meet me in combat or live with dishonour as a coward!" Freya made the final challenge.

"Ma'am, you are the superior officer, if the Flytgealdor strikes you she could be subject to court-martial" warned the *Demend.*

And yet if I refuse I will be seen as a coward, it was now a matter of her honour. She would have to fight very carefully as she could easily kill Freya who had little more resilience than a norm.

An outrageous idea occurred to her. "Very well I will meet you here and now in unarmed combat!" she began to remove her clothing until she stood before the astonished pair in only her underwear. "*Demend,* will you please note for the record that I am not in uniform."

"This is unprecedented Ma'am and I'm not sure it changes anything?" he replied.

"Fine by me" stated Freya who began to remove her body armour.

"You keep that on!" ordered Anderson. "You can't fight *me* without armour."

"I meet you at the same level!" Freya now wore only her tight fighting suit, having gone this far she was determined to see it through.

Some of the late leavers in the seats above were witness to this and sat back down calling others to see the Campealdor in her cups and pants. "Well are we doing this?" asked Penni accepting the inevitable and walking into the middle of the arena. "The usual rules, best of three."

Freya followed her wondering if she was doing the right thing. Although Anderson was in her early fifties she looked twenty years younger, her body was finely toned and the unpleasant scar above the waistband of her pants was a visible reminder of the wound that had almost killed her leaving her sterile.

"Come on Flytgealdor, don't worry about my state of dress it's not the first time I've stripped off for a Da N'tan!" She was an old hand at goading.

"You old *haeg*, there's little wonder my mother doesn't fancy you anymore!" retorted Freya.

"She's a better person than you'll ever be, you Psi weakling!" Penni made a feint which Freya easily dodged.

"Is that all you have, old woman?" Freya, getting the hang of this sprang, forward to punch her *aunt* in the stomach but it was like hitting a tree and she danced back shaking her right hand. Penni launched a kick at Freya who grabbing her foot pushed upwards, the Campaeldor fell on her back and the younger woman quickly pinned her shoulders down.

"The first point goes to Da N'tan" the *Demend* called, there were some cheers above.

Penni sprang up then making a feint grabbed hold of Freya to throw her over easily.

"One point all!" shouted the umpire.

She waited for Freya to stand before closing but Da N'tan, as quick as any *nova*, rained several blows on her opponent and she staggered back under the fusillade. Anderson hooked Freya's leg tripping her only for the younger woman to spring up and launch herself at Penni and drive her head into her stomach. The Campaeldor doubled up to be knocked to the ground by a two-handed blow to the shoulders. The older woman rolled onto her back to lay there winded. *She beat me, she actually beat me!*

But before the *Demend* could announce the result, Freya, now in a red rage, kicked Anderson viciously in the ribs before attempting to stamp on her exposed throat but Penni instinctively rolled clear while at the same time driving a heel into the younger woman's abdomen.

Freya howled in pain and fell to the floor to lie in a foetal curl. Penni leapt to her side. "Gods, *lapsi* I'm sorry." the young woman was moaning through gritted teeth, face screwed up in pain.

"Campaeldor I've called for *haelers*!" called the *Demend*. "Ma'am, if I were you I would get dressed before they arrive, I'll look after the Flytgealdor."

Anderson travelled with Freya in the *scethewaegn* and waited while she had emergency surgery for a ruptured spleen then sat outside her room head in hands. She had seriously injured a junior officer and would undoubtedly have to face an inquiry but far worse than that it was her best friend's daughter, her attempt at help had turned into disaster. Upon hearing familiar footsteps in the corridor she looked up to see Sirki striding towards her with Sari in tow.

Penni stood up, "Sirki, forgive me, I'm sorry…" she didn't have time to finish as Sirki slapped her hard across the face. *I deserved that.*

"You hurt my baby, how could you, *you* of all people?" she yelled as Sari half pushed her mother into Freya's room then she looked in askance at Penni before following her inside.

Anderson returned to the *camphus* to wait at her desk and as anticipated an *Aelicgealdor* arrived shortly after with Cempa Rika. "Campaeldor Anderson, henceforth you are temporarily relieved of command and are summoned to attend an inquiry into the incident this afternoon which resulted in serious injury to an RAF officer, namely Flytgealdor Freya Mia Da N'tan. The hearing will be held tomorrow at 10 am in the Moot Hall and until further notice, Cempa Rika, being the most experienced of your subordinates will assume the role of Acting Campaeldor."

The legal officer, having finished his discourse nodded once and left. Penni got up and moved away from the desk holding out her hand to the chair. "It's all yours Hal, I can't think of a better person for the job."

"I didn't want this, Pen, and certainly not like this!" he replied. "Loge, how did it happen?"

"I was fucking stupid, Hal, I could have killed her!"

"Go home and try to relax, do you want me to come round later?" he asked. They were keeping a burgeoning relationship under wraps.

"Na, I wouldn't be good company tonight, I just want to be alone," what she actually wanted was to be able to crawl into a hole and disappear.

Penni was lying on the couch in her quarters going over events time and time again in her head when Sari contacted her by telepathy. *"Hei Auntie Pen, mummy's calmed down and I've explained that it was my fault that you intervened. Freya has responded well to surgery, and is in recovery so I'm staying at the*

Haelinghus with her. I have made mummy go to the Hall to rest and I'm not suggesting that you go to see her but if you wanted to apologise in person?"

CHAPTER 3 - WHERE IS BREN?

With a low whistle, the silver vehicle expanded from a point of blue light. Insect-like with four stilt-legged gravity drivers it resembled the Flying Beetles used by the forces, the highly mirrored surface, however, would be ill-suited to a combat situation. The vessel alighted on the snowy ground light as a feather while moisture froze on a hull colder than the wintry air around it.

Da N'tan looked through the forward port. "It looks like Yuletide out there! The landing area wasn't like this on Skuld's records, do the seasons change rapidly here or something?"

Craeftwitan Llewelyn joined him at the window. "Hmm, we won't know until we get out and have a look around?" he regarded the snowy landscape. "At least we packed for every eventuality," he remarked, Aesh and Trevithick were entering the airlock dressed in Fimbulwinter suits.

Singh closed it behind them and watched through the tiny window as they opened the outer door, they did not bother to cycle the lock as the sensors had detected a breathable, if cold, atmosphere outside.

The two bulky figures moved to the underside of the vessel where a smaller version of itself was attached. "Aesh here, Skuld appears to be intact and undamaged."

"Check, stand clear I'm sending her out," replied Flytgealdor Pravin Singh. The ice around the clamps holding the small vessel cracked as the probe was released, and it glided smoothly out to settle at a predetermined distance from Sleipnir.

"In position," announced the small vehicle. It had been named Skuld after one of the *Norns* from the sagas and had been given a feminine voice by its designers.

"It's minus fifteen out here!" exclaimed Aesh, looking at her wristband. A snowball hit her. "Stop being a twat, Kawaro!" she chided the large Kernowek, who merely grinned in response behind his faceplate. They had landed on a flat snow-covered plain and in the distance could be seen high hills but there was no sign of life other than the landing party.

"Are you two clear?" asked Llewelyn. "I'm sending Skuld back to tell the pad we've arrived."

"Both clear" confirmed Aesh.

The smaller vessel lifted from the ground slightly and with a low whistle that descended slowly to a hum shrank to a tiny point of blue light before vanishing.

Psi Bella Fordyce, the sixth member of the crew glanced worriedly at Da N'tan. "Something's not right sir, I didn't expect to be able to path to anyone but there's no background noise, it's like all psionic contact has stopped."

"Are we in a flat zone?"

"No I have full use of my psionic power but telepathically I'm completely alone."

It had taken fifty minutes to transfer from their home dimension and as expected, the probe returned exactly one hundred and four minutes later but it carried no message from mission control and the landing area recorded by Skuld's cameras showed a desert landscape.

"The pad's not there!" Da N'tan turned to Llewelyn in alarm. "Can you explain this?"

"I can't, Thegn, I'll need to go over the calculations with the atellan."

"Should we jump to where Skuld just returned from?" asked Bren.

"I think it's best to wait it out here for a while until I can work out what happened," replied Llewelyn.

Aesh and Kawaro returned and the crew made themselves as comfortable as possible. There wasn't a lot of room inside Sleipnir, it was as big as a Flying Beetle but half of the interior was taken up with bunks, crates of supplies and of course, the airlock.

When the ACG had been forcibly disbanded thirty years before, the PRW had inherited its research and discovered an incredible experiment that had achieved something even the most powerful Psi could not. While testing prototype psionic distortion generators a method of physically accessing the Helm was discovered, ACG *craeftwitan* hypothesised that by utilising experimental gravity drivers in conjunction with the new distorters it might be possible to go *somewhere else* from there. Their research had been initiated in an attempt to further understand and control psionic power but instead had stumbled upon a means of proving one of the most outlandish Q-theories correct, the existence of parallel dimensions. Recognising that the actual realisation of this would require a great deal more study the ACG put it on the back burner in preference to their more immediate concern, the overthrow of the hated *novae*.

With the war against the Dominion finally over and Reignweald forces helping to maintain their borders against the Ket, peace followed enabling the Palace Research Wing to divert resources to more esoteric projects, and possessed of a more favourable outlook towards the Helm they followed this research path with vigour.

It took two decades to develop a viable probe able to enter the Helm, radio and microwave communication proved to be impossible there so full autonomy was built in. The probe was to enter the dimension and after spending a designated time return by reversing the field to *pull* itself back to its point of origin, the idea seemed simple enough but several probes were lost before the technique was perfected. It quickly became apparent that the gold-speckled, blue nothingness of the Helm, previously known only to the Psi, was quite benign despite its daunting appearance and there was no obvious clue as to it being the source of *novae* power. One odd thing noted was the slight time variance between dimensional planes, anywhere between a few seconds and an hour.

A highly advanced and powerful probe called Skuld was built and sent into the Helm, it *jumped* forward for fifty minutes to another dimension, and when the vessel returned one hundred and four minutes later it had recorded a bucolic landscape of grassy plains with large grazing animals in the distance, the air registered as breathable and the temperature suggested a temperate climate. The probe had visited a viable parallel universe to return unscathed but once again, there was the time anomaly, an extra four minutes had elapsed at the starting point when compared to Skuld's onboard chronometer.

Having safely repeated the journey twice, a second probe was sent with the same success and the decision was made to send a manned expedition.

Craeftwitan Geraint Llewelyn, who had spent a score of years working on the project was the obvious choice for mission specialist.

Bren Da N'tan, had spent almost as many years kicking his heels as Thegn and since Scartho had put a lot of resources into the project he appointed himself as Mission Campaeldor. Sirki was not best pleased to say the least, and he was made to promise this would be his one and only mission.

A Psi was considered an absolute necessity so a Magus, Bella Fordyce, one of Bonnie Ashby's protégés was duly appointed.

The other norm in the crew was Pravin Singh, regarded as one of the best fliers in the RAF, he was appointed as *Helmward* with *Huscarl* flier, Kawaro Trevelyan, as co-pilot.

Da N'tan, remembering Tithengealdor Elke Aesh, had approached her to act as Security Officer and having been a weapons instructor for years she jumped at the chance to see active service again.

Sleipnir had taken four years to construct using the design of the ubiquitous Flying Beetle as a template but given a mirror-like surface which had proved to provide smoother travel in the Helm.

The mission had set out over five years ago with the original Skuld slung underneath to act as a messenger pigeon, flitting between dimensions as required if telepathic communication proved impossible.

The mission was scheduled to return after two days.

The allotted time passed and they did not return.

One week later and there was still no sign of them, *perhaps Sleipnir had developed a fault?* The vessel had been equipped for every conceivable environmental condition and had ample provisions onboard, sufficient for many weeks, and they could possibly hunt the grazing animals seen on the recordings.

Two weeks passed and still nothing so a second probe, called Urdr after another *Norn*, was sent to explore the proposed landing site but it was unable to locate them. The Highest, along with Bonnie Ashby and Sirki herself projected their minds deep into the Helm but no trace could be detected.

A vigil was kept for over a year before the operation was reluctantly wound down to a skeleton staff. Sirki, who like her husband only gave lip-service to the gods, found herself begging Thor to keep her husband safe and even appealed to Sif, his golden-haired wife, to return him before the corn rose again.

After a further year, a commemoration service was held in the New Winchester Hearg, until then Sirki had until then put on a brave face as befitting a Thegnestre but now she publicly broke down in tears burying her head on the shoulder of Campaeldor Anderson. This was not good form and caused consternation among some in polite society but Sirki didn't care.

Completely unaware of any anxiety caused by their absence, the crew of Sleipnir were using Skuld as a test-bed, experimenting with dimension jumping using new coordinates arrived at by Llewelyn and the ship's atellan. It was determined that the energy used to jump Sleipnir, fifty times greater than the amount required for Skuld, was far in excess of what was required. This quantity had been arrived at using a power-to-weight ratio in the belief it would propel them to the same destination but Llewelyn now realised the original calculations were wildly incorrect. Only a small percentage would have been required to jump the larger vessel, and Sleipnir had overshot its destination by an astronomical amount to leave them an untold number of dimensional planes away from home.

It also became apparent that the further from their starting point they travelled, the further they went back in relative time meaning Sleipnir had materialised during the ice age of a world roughly twenty thousand years behind their own. A reverse jump made using only forty times the energy brought the ship to a desert-like environment inhabited by large primordial mammals where they set up a basecamp enabling Skuld to make a series of small exploratory jumps. Aesh meanwhile, had proved remarkably adept at hunting, providing them with a regular supply of fresh meat from the local fauna. After staying for several weeks they jumped to a newly discovered world, a lush rain forest that was home to many species having a distinctly modern look about them. It was also damp and humid, they were plagued by insects and most of the larger wildlife was predatory or hostile so the decision was taken to move camp when a better habitat could be found.

After an uncomfortable fortnight Skuld found a more promising location, a marshy environment remarkably similar to the fenlands of Aenglia…

Sleipnir dropped out of nowhere to settle on the largest area of firm ground available in a dank landscape with a misty sun. It was an incredibly humid environment, almost as bad as the rainforest but with half the insect life and no obvious predatory animals so overall it seemed a healthier place to stay and since they were already wearing shorts and tees there seemed no reason to change the dress code. On an optimistic note, Fordyce could feel a faint psionic background hum but as yet could not establish any telepathic communication. Bren and the other *novae* also felt more at ease here than any previous landing site. The rain stopped upon their arrival and the sodden ground had begun to dry up, it seemed a good omen.

After setting up camp Skuld was sent off on her way yet again. The little vehicle, now looking slightly the worse for wear, was regularly overhauled by Llewelyn and Singh. The expedition's chances of returning home were reliant on the little probe.

Da N'tan watched Aesh unrolling a tent from its carry-bag her right leg gleaming in the watery sunlight, the woman was attractive and buxom, seeming to thrive on adversity and positively enjoying the experience. Bren had been there when she was injured and after pledging to look out for her had lived up to his promise. Elke had been fitted with the most advanced mekhanikal limb the Thegnweald could find, and having been upgraded several times over thirty years the leg functioned like a real limb even having a rudimentary nervous system linked to her own. The only thing she could not do was run at quickspeed.

Llewelyn, sitting at the campfire, passed Da N'tan his flask while expounding his ideas about parallel dimensions. Bren had heard it all before but let the Brython *Craeftwitan* ramble on. "You see if we think about the dimensional universe like a giant onion with infinite layers then we can just push our way through to another layer which is slightly younger than the one we live in. We pushed far too hard you see and went a lot further in than intended, we went in so far that mankind hadn't established itself," he took the flask back to take a swig. "This is good stuff, shame we're running out."

"Do you think we will find our way back?" asked Bren.

"I'm sure, it's just a matter of time, if not we'll have to start a new branch of humanity somewhere. Do you think Fordyce and Aesh fancy being the mothers of a new human race?" he joked.

"I hope you're fucking kidding!" Aesh had turned up. "I'm too old to think about having any more kids and as for Bella, well the Psi' don't do that sort of thing" she took the flask and drew on it herself.

Bren thought about her comment, typically Psi never married and supposedly couldn't have children, the exception being his beloved Sirki but she could hardly be called typical! Against her wishes his rightwife had been awarded the category of Omega which, of course, she refused to acknowledge. He missed Sirki, remembering how she had exploded into his life and how they clashed when they first met, she behaved like a spoilt child and they had *words* before she attempted to seduce him using her unique powers only for them to both fall in love.

Bren wondered how she was coping.

Aesh broke into his reverie. "I was saying, Thegn, I'll see if there's anything edible around here tomorrow, some waterfowl perhaps or some large aquatic mammal?" she had proved very proficient with the crossbow she had brought in her personal belongings.

"Check, Tithengealdor don't forget your Sterlinger, just in case."

"Check sir, I am a *Huscarl* remember?" she replied with a grin.

CHAPTER 4 – APOLOGIES, PAST AND PRESENT

You can't know what it's like 'til you feel it for yourself
I'm not gonna sit around to be put upon your shelf
I found me a brand new love who's completely off this world
And rides across the firmament her golden locks unfurled!
I'm loving the Waelcyrie, she's got room in her heart for me
Yeah, loving the Waelcyrie, it's plain for all to see.
(Excerpt from Loving the Waelcyrie – music Dunne, lyrics Vigsdottir.)

Anderson stood before the sturdy doors of Scartho Hall and cast her mind back thirty years to when she had been a newly promoted Cempa stationed at the East 3 base. Penni was showing Campaeldor Da N'tan the new construction work when a Ket barrage sent them diving for cover and she had fallen on top of him into an air-raid bunker. Her resonation immediately began to synch with his, it had happened a couple of times before but Bren had always broken away to prevent her linking. This time he did not and feeling his arousal she kissed him, he returned it with passion but quickly pulled apart upon hearing movement outside, the barrage was over and the all-clear was sounding.

"That was close," he remarked as they left the shelter, *too close, I wanted to hump you,* he thought guiltily of Sirki and his infant daughter in New Winchester.

"Bren, what happened just then, I couldn't help myself."

"I think we should try to avoid each other for a while, check?" he suggested.

"Check," her sad reply.

Da N'tan returned to Slote next day enabling Anderson to put the incident behind her but a month later the cohort returned to Slote to prepare for shipping back to Scartho. She was billeted in Sari Hof's old quarters, opposite Bren's, and coming out of her room spotted him in the corridor.

"Hei Penni, looking good!" he observed, she was wearing a red stretch dress, short to the point of decency, with matching heels and her corn-yellow hair was tied in high bunches. She reminded him so much of Faedra.

"I'm just going down to The Queen's Arms, want to come?" she asked.

He smiled. "You know, I don't mix socially with my officers often enough." They went to the hostelry on North Avenue A where they met several other Elite Guard officers and a good many drinks later they staggered back to stop outside Bren's door. "Good-night Cempa Anderson," he slurred.

She waved uncertainly in the direction of her room. "I'm just across there if you need me?"

"It's a long way, do you want me to walk you back?" he joked, both were a little worse for drink.

Penni woke up in the middle of the night fully clothed and laying across Da N'tan, her shoes were on the floor but her underwear was intact and her dress wasn't in too much disarray, *thankfully, nothing had happened.*

"Pen, how much did we drink?" her movement had woken Bren.

"I don't know..." she giggled. "You know, it's not often I spend a night in bed with a man and keep my knickers on!" her resonation was starting to synch with his once again as her genetically engineered body sought its compatible Alpha mate.

"And I didn't get to see them?" teased Bren.

She fumbled about then waved a pair of red pants in front of him.

"Well, I guess you haven't got them on now?" her frequency now almost matched his and it was affecting him in a similar way to Sirki's charisma, not as intense but even so his desire was growing. "Penni, we mustn't do this." she sat up and slowly peeled the dress off over her head to reveal her naked body. "Gods, I'm married now Pen!" it was as perfect as he'd imagined and she looked so much like Faedra, he tried hard not to give in to the urge.

"Bren, I've wanted this ever since I met you. You're my Alpha and I thought I had a chance until Sirki turned up," she began to unbutton his shirt and he did not resist but instead ran his hands over her toned figure. Her skin was smooth to the touch and she had the petals of a daisy tattooed around her right nipple giving it the appearance of a flower, he had never realised she was a Freyan until now and cupping her breast he sucked on it to make it erect before moving to the other.

Despite all his misgivings he wanted her badly. "You mustn't link to me," he warned helping her to unfasten his trousers. "You know how this has to go?"

"Ya dahling, I have to go on top," she replied before straddling him and pushing herself down onto his erect penis, an Alpha and Beta could have sex without linking provided the latter assumed dominance but her resonation was still cycling to match his.

"Penni, what are you doing?"

"I don't care, Bren, fuck me!" she cried grinding her hips against his. It was just too much so giving in he put his arms about her to roll their coupled bodies over so that she was now underneath. "That's more like it!" she cried then locking her ankles over his back began biting at him as they made love in an aggressive, almost animalistic way.

Penni synchronised with Bren at the point of climax to experience the most explosive orgasm she had ever known. Almost painful in intensity it coursed from her finger-ends to the tips of her toes seeming to last an eternity. This was the trigger to fix her link to him.

When it was over the urgency and passion of the Beta lure died away and he was no longer in her thrall, *what had he done?* "Pen, how do you feel?"

Her face and breasts were flushed and she had a dreamy look on her face. "I thought it would never stop!" she whispered breathlessly.

It was the last thing he wanted to hear, Faedra had said virtually the same thing when she had linked but they were in love and he'd promised to always be there. Now he had betrayed his wife and ruined this young woman's future into the bargain, *I'm a bahstard!* Then he realised her resonation was cycling back towards its normal frequency.

He touched her face gently. "Penni, are you alright?"

Her beautiful face lit up with a smile. "Nothing's changed *lufiend*, I'm still me."

"But we synched and to my shame I didn't try and stop you, are you sure you're alright?" It was unheard of, when a Beta synched to an Alpha the link should endure until death.

"I'm fine, really I am, Bren!" she laughed. "I don't have any compulsion to be your undying love-slave or anything but I am up for a second round!"

He bent his lips to hers and as she raised her face to kiss him Bren took Penni in his strong arms and they made love again.

Bren woke late in the morning with a nagging feeling of guilt, he had promised Sirki he would always be faithful and had broken his word so easily.

Penni was already awake. "We shouldn't have done that should we?" in the years since Freya's birth Sirki had stopped flirting with her and they were on quite good terms.

"Penni, it's my fault, you just lost yourself in passion." *this was a mess!*

"Na, I wanted it as much as you, more if I'm honest," she answered.

"Sirki's going to kill me when I tell her," *would she forgive him?*

"You're going to tell her?" asked Penni in surprise.

"I have to… at least I haven't *literally* fucked up your future, something to be thankful for I suppose." The Legion was shipping back tomorrow and he would tell her face to face. Before they were betrothed he had forgiven Sirki for something similar, *perhaps she would be as kind to him?*

Da N'tan drove straight to their New Winchester home, upon his return, intending to confess all but as he walked in Sirki ran to embrace him, crying. "I've missed you so much *rakas!*" The she stiffened and stepped back with a look of horror upon her face. "Nej, Bren, you haven't?" her lilac eyes widened. "Thor's Hammer, I can feel her on you, *sinä vitun paskiainen!* Of all the women on Nerth, why did you have to fuck her?"

"It just happened, Sirki, I came to tell you face to face and it was just the one night." he pleaded.

"Oh that's alright then!" yelled Sirki. "I thought you were the one, Bren, I had your baby! I became your rightwife for Thor's sake… how could you do this to me, how could you hump that Kernowek *bicce* behind my back?" she fumed. "Get out of my house *kusipää!*" The front door opened by itself and Da N'tan felt an unseen force pushing at him. "Get out or I'll throw you out!" her powers had grown considerably since their daughter's birth.

"Sirk, I did a stupid thoughtless thing, I don't want to lose you like this, and what about our daughter?"

"You should have thought about that when you were humping the *hore*." Sirki was incensed. "We made a deal remember? I leave her kitty alone and you keep your cock out of it, go away, I don't want you near me at the moment!"

When he had left Sirki cast her mind back several years to when she was in Slote recovering from the attempt on her life. She had gone to the officer's *aethus* with Bren and Bonnie and Penni was already there.

Sirki could feel her resonation, warm and inviting.

Anderson, for her part was confused at how she felt drawn to this woman, she had always believed she was hetero but now found herself imagining what it would be like to have sex with the glamorous singer. She pushed the idea to the back of her head, Sirki and Bren were in a relationship, *it was the talk of the base and she must not get in the way.*

"Undercempa Anderson is replacing Sari Hof as my S in C while she's at the firebase," Bren had explained, Sirki picked a salad from the menu and Bren went with Bonnie to join the queue.

Sirki regarded the Beta with longing, the woman was beautiful in a storybook way *and I'm with Bren* she'd told herself as her interest in the goddess rose again. An awkward silence had descended so she asked. "Were you sorry Colm had left by the time you got back from the March?" her old band's guitarist had a brief liaison with Penni.

"Na why?" she asked.

"I thought you two hooked up?" Sirki had replied. *I know you did, the cocky sod bragged about it.*

"It was just a bit of fun, I wasn't looking for anything serious" she looked at Sirki curiously. "Bren has told you about Betas, hasn't he?" The girl had a pleasant Kernowek lilt to her voice.

"Jaa, it must be pretty shit for you sometimes."

"It can be very difficult that's why I stick to going with *norms*, there's no danger of me linking to them."

"Only men?" asked Sirki, eager to know.

"Ya, *only* men!" *had she stressed that a little too much?*

"You're missing out on so much," said Sirki with a grin.

"You're with Bren now aren't you?" Penni had asked pointedly.

"Oh, I'm not coming on to you!" *she was hard work.* "I can be a bit flirtatious at times I guess, didn't mean to upset you.

"I'm a bit overawed by you if I'm honest. I'm a massive fan, got all your recordings including those with Star Hammer." Penni confessed.

"You're kidding me? Star Hammer only had two decent songs" Sirki laughed.

"Ya "Message for you" and "Loving the *Waelcyrie*" and you wrote both of them." Penni seemed to have relaxed slightly.

"Well, "Tank" Dunne had a hand in writing "Loving the *Waelcyrie*"," recalled Sirki.

Bonnie and Bren had returned and they talked while they ate their meal…

What if I had made a pass at her back then, would Penni have betrayed me with Bren?

It was a ridiculous thought her *wyrd* had been to bear the *Huscarl's* child regardless of the consequences.

Her crestfallen husband meanwhile had driven back to Scartho and gone straight to the Officer House instead of the Hall. His parents would want to know why he wasn't staying at New Winchester and he couldn't face that at the moment.

On spotting his return Penni came round to his quarters curious to discover what had happened. "It's as much my fault, I did throw myself at you after all!" she admitted. An idea came to her. "I'm off duty for a few days, I'll talk to Sirki."

"No Pen, I'm to blame for this, do not go to see Sirki, she is very upset, check?"

"Check!" She lied.

Penni drove to New Winchester the very next day and Sirki answered the door to stare silently at her. She had dark circles under red-rimmed eyes, her wild chestnut hair, grown long since Penni last saw her, was held back by a large golden fillet. "You've got a fucking nerve," she said at last. "Have you come to steal my daughter now?"

"I came to apologise Sirki, please listen to me."

Sirki had thought briefly about slamming the door in the Beta's face but decided to hear what she had to say. "I've just put Freya to bed so we'd best go on the music room, it's soundproofed so she won't wake up if I start screaming!" she explained tersely as she led her in.

"Sirki, if anything I'm more to blame than Bren, I came on to him and my Beta lure did the rest. I've always wanted him Sirki, ever since I joined the 3rd Elite, please forgive him," pleaded Penni.

"Why are you so bothered, surely it's to your advantage that I don't?" snapped Sirki in reply.

shuddered as its three massive anti-gravity drivers began to cycle.

A low hum began vibrating the hull.

"Control, drivers are up and running" reported Dexter.

"Check, Sparrow, we confirm drivers running, start cycling the coils."

"Spinning up" Freya input another sequence, the hum rose to a roar and there was a slight movement as Sparrow became weightless. The star-boat was now merely sitting on its anti-gravity fields. "Control, we are free" announced Dexter.

"We confirm you are free, you may lift when ready and may the gods grant you safe passage."

"Lifting!" shouted Freya over the roar, she increased power to the fields and the teardrop-shaped star-boat leapt from the ground to hurtle skywards, a boom following it as it went supersonic, pushing the *steorrafarae* into their seats.

"Sonic plus 10" called Freya. "Plus 15, 20, 24, 27" they were approaching the point where they had failed previously.

"Plus 28, 30, 29, 28, 29," Dexter Sartorius picked up the count as the drivers struggled against gravity.

"Control to Sparrow, initiate boosters," came the command from the *steorhus*.

Freya put her finger on the ignition and they were thrown back into their seats once more as the solid fuel rockets fired. "31, 32, sonic plus 33, Control, we have reached escape velocity, our ceiling is 120 miles and rising."

"Approaching maximum dynamic pressure," shouted Dexter over the roar inside the cabin.

A few seconds passed then. "Control to Sparrow, we confirm D-Max."

"Booster cut off in 3, 2, 1." they were jerked forward in their harnesses as the acceleration cut off abruptly. Freya touched an icon on her display. "Boosters released."

Sartorius looked in the mirror on his side of the cabin to see three thin cylinders floating away with balletic synchronicity against the background of their blue world. "Booster release confirmed."

A few tense minutes later came the message they had been waiting for. "Congratulations Sparrow, you have achieved a distance of 165 miles above sea level, you are the first to achieve Nerth orbit in over three hundred and fifty years!"

Now in free fall, the two *steorrafara* made great play of floating a toy troll around the cabin for the cameras.

Freya could see Selene's crescent in the starry vista to the right then rotated the craft along its length to see Europa spread below, Aengland was far to the west and they would not see it until completion of their first orbit when, provided everything had gone well, they would be allowed make a second before returning to the ground.

She could just make out the coastline of Frisha below with the island of D'an Mark and the long coast of Sweorice clearly visible but further to the north, her mother's homeland of Soomi was obscured by thick cloud. Far to the northeast was a vast desert of scorched rock and fused sand once home to the **Rus-Canton** Federation and Freya could see it was slowly being reclaimed by nature as fingers of green vegetation reached in from Frisha. When they approached the eastern borders of Europa the night terminator quickly came upon them to shut out any chance of seeing the Ket homeland but Sparrow's cameras, recording on various wavelengths would reveal the mysterious land below. Freya switched to her night vision briefly but found it unrewarding although several bright areas suggested habitation. Sparrow then continued in darkness over the unfortunately named Peaceful Ocean which had separated the two main combatants of the Q-war, it was once home to the sub-continent of Zeeland and many smaller islands of varied and vibrant cultures but all were now reduced to a widespread scatter of rocky islets and volcanic caldera. The starfarers had seen it all before on satellite imagery but to regard it with their own eyes left them awestruck at the harm wrought by the Q-weapons.

Freya had stayed telepathically linked to Fordyce at the launch facility but now found it difficult to maintain a connection, it was at its worst when they were on the same latitude as Zeeland as if the planet's core was blocking Psionic communication like a massive flat zone. *If she was at the exact antipodal point to Fordyce would they have been cut off from each other completely?* Sparrow itself maintained radio contact by bouncing signals off the defence ring that had been put in orbit to destroy Ket missiles.

During the ocean crossing a collection of lights could be seen at the coordinates for Hawai'i, life it seemed had survived there against all the odds. The coastline of West Hispania was easily spotted, marked out by many active volcanoes glowing redly against the dark landmass.

"It looks like Surtr's realm, Muspelheim!" remarked Freya aloud.

"Mithrans would say it was the inferno where the unworthy are punished" countered Dexter, the old Roman religion was well established in southern Aengland and he wore a Miles pendant under his spacesuit.

The journey across the Ocean of Atlantis was uneventful until Sol's brilliant glow burst out in a man-made sunrise as they crossed the terminator once again, they were heading back to Aengland and it had taken them a little over eighty minutes to circle the entire planet.

"Control to Sparrow, everything is looking good, you have clearance for second orbit" announced the voice over the radio and the two star-farers grinned at each other behind their visors.

There was a sudden powerful burst of noise over their headsets. "Sparrow to control, did you send us a signal just now?" asked Freya.

"No Sparrow, we did not send a signal?" the reply.

"The origin was somewhere on the Frishan coast." Dexter checked the recording. "It seemed to come from around the Oostende region."

Freya frowned on hearing this. "That's odd, Control, the signal came from somewhere near Oostende can you confirm there are no military operations taking place there?"

"Check Sparrow, we will look into it, we register your observation as at twelve hundred hours Reignweald Standard Time but we still require your confirmation for second orbit"

"Check Control, we are good for orbit number two" asserted Sartorius.

The second orbit went as smoothly as the previous one but this time around the *Steorhus* ordered them to make a landing and with a feeling of disappointment they rolled Sparrow over to orientate its rounded rear to the correct angle for re-entry and begin braking the vessel's speed using the gravity fields.

Freya could feel the G-force through her chest as they re-entered the atmosphere and it took a little more effort to breathe but it was nothing she couldn't handle as a display of sparks and glowing plasma rushed past the cockpit windows which was both frightening and spectacular.

She reached out to Dexter, who taking her gloved hand squeezed it slightly. "Nearly there Fri." he said.

"One small step to landing on Selene!" she affirmed her driving ambition.

As anticipated, radio contact was lost to hull ionisation during re-entry but Freya's telepathic link to Fordyce remained unbroken. Re-orientating the ship once more they began the approach to New Winchester Airdock while on screens across the Reignweald and Europa people watched as Sparrow dropped to within thirty feet of the ground before halting in mid-air and float gently to a landing. Da N'tan and Sartorius had just become household names and the Selene project assured of its future, next time they would build a more powerful vessel,

There was just the little matter of the rogue signal, who was sending scrambled messages into the firmament and where were they being sent to?

CHAPTER 12 – PARTY

In honour of Sleipnir's return and Freya's successful flight Sirki organised a party that sprawled through the entire lower floor of her large home. The usual caterers had been hired and virtually everyone she and Bren knew had been invited including most of her old musician friends. Bren had shown concern over security but as she pointed out, half of the guests were Elite *Huscarls* or serving in the other forces so security wasn't likely to be a problem. Even Geraint Llewelyn had been coerced into coming and was presently regaling her with his theories on time dilation between dimensions. Sirki had heard most of it from Bren several times already.

Aelfred Da N'tan, spotting his mother's eyes glazing over, came to the rescue. "Craeftwitan Llewelyn, it's such a pleasure to meet you in person. I've heard all about your theories on time travel."

He turned his attention on her son. "Oh it's not time travel Dr Da N'tan, it's time dilation, see?"

"Thanks so much dahling." path'd Sirki as she slipped away.

"You owe me, mum!"

The Queen arrived with a pair of Palace Guard in tow and smiled at her old friend, Effie had aged more obviously than Sirki with pure white streaks in her corn blonde hair and fine lines tracing their way around her brilliant blue eyes.

They embraced each other warmly. "You *bicce*, you look younger than ever, how do you manage it?"

"It's simple, now Bren's back he's humping me senseless every night" laughed Sirki.

"That's not funny, even thinking about that makes me jealous" joked Effie.

"Who are you jealous of, me or Bren?" she fluttered her eyelashes. A waitress proffered a tray of drinks and she eagerly helped herself.

"Both of you if I'm honest," answered Effie. "Now that you're back in circulation will you consider working for me again?"

"Doing what?" Sirki drained her glass.

"The same as before you went reclusive, sweetie. By being there at functions and using your gift to make people agreeable while eavesdropping on them. Say yes, Sirki I do miss your company" her expression changed. "There's something else and we could really do with your help."

"Serious?" asked Sirki curiosity piqued.

"Psi business but it'll keep for now. Will you come to the Palace tomorrow morning?"

"I'll think about it dahling, I might have a bit of a hangover though." Sirki glanced around and spotting Colm Murphy in the gathered throng realised she had slept with a fair percentage of the people here *Effie included* and there was her husband talking avidly to Elke Aesh. She was wearing a short skirt showing off her shapely legs, one flesh and one shining metal, a low cut blouse displayed her other assets. "Excuse me dahling I'm just going to pour cold water on Bren" and she swayed over to them. "Tithengealdor Aesh, how nice to see you and to see *so* much of you too!" she remarked pointedly.

"Fro Scartho, please excuse me I was just about to go and talk to Kawaro" she bowed her head and gave Sirki a lingering look before moving off.

Tall, strong and fine-featured, just my type! Sirki watched her walk away feeling slightly aroused at the thought of the metal limb pressed against her body. "That's a very shiny leg she has there dahling and I hear they are quite realistic to the touch, almost like real flesh, is hers?" demanded Sirki with a quizzical look.

"Sirki, I've looked out for Aesh for years and you know I feel responsible for what happened to her? We're just friends!" Bren tried to explain.

"Hmm, I hope you scooped your eyes out of her cleavage before she left and I do hope you behaved yourself when you were *lost* with her for all that time?" she teased.

"What? Sirki, you were never far from my thoughts and… hej, you slept with Penni while I was gone!"

"Aesh is a very sexy woman and I'm just protecting my man." She replied.

"From who exactly?" asked Bren, he had to admit Aesh did look different out of uniform.

"Why, from himself dahling" she sat next to him. "Anyway, have you thought anymore about us having another baby?"

"Do you really want to go through all that again? Nine months of discomfort then all that crying and yelling and that's just me" he quipped.

"We can start trying, doesn't mean I'll get pregnant straight away."

"Erm…" Thankfully for Bren salvation turned up in the form of Adrian Barnet, her old studio manager.

"Now then Sirki you old tart, is your piano in tune?" he asked.

"Jaa, I always keep it tuned."

"Good, get your pretty arse in the music room and give us a song, no party is complete without a song" he chided.

"I haven't been a *sangestre* for nearly fifteen years, I doubt I can sing?" Sirki had, of course, practised virtually every day of those fifteen years, even during Bren's absence.

She stood by the piano while Adie played and ran through several of her old songs including "My Love is the Moon" and "Harvest Flowers."

Seeing her daughters watching she waved them over and they joined in on the harmonies, they had been part of the entourage while children and knew all her old songs by heart.

It was turning out to be a good party.

Sirki suddenly became seized by the idea that someone may be plotting against her, *how ridiculous, I'm surrounded by family and friends.*

"Have either of you considered following your mother into show business?" Adie asked the younger Da N'tan's.

"No, I may look like mum but I croak like a frog," confessed Freya. "Sari can sing though."

"Fri!" exclaimed Sari.

"Go on Saz, you know you can." goaded her sister.

Sari reluctantly agreed to sing "My Desperation" it was one of Harvest's lesser-known numbers loosely based around an old Soomi folk song and Sirki had to play the piano as Adie didn't know the tune. She belted it out in a powerful voice and writhed quite suggestively during the emotive verses, when the song finished the room was silent for a moment before everyone broke into spontaneous applause.

"You are coming to the studios as soon as fucking possible. Sirki, where have you been hiding this girl?" asked an enthusiastic Adie. "I've found the new star I was looking for."

"What do you think mummy?" inquired Sari.

"Wow, *lapsi* even though I'm your mother and quite obviously biased, I think you sang brilliantly." the strange mood seemed to have passed for now.

Spotting Penni with Hal Rika, Sari asked excitedly. "What do you think mum…er Aunt Penni?"

No-one noticed her slip except perhaps one of the catering staff.

"I think you should go for it, you're much better than your mother ever was," Penni answered in jest.

"Thanks for that, *bicce!*" interjected Sirki and Penni blew her a kiss.

Spotting Dame Scartho nearby, Sari asked. "Hei mummo what did you think?"

Hilly rebuffed her. "It's grandma or grandmother south of Soomi, dahling. I think your singing is very good but that hip wriggling stuff is a bit much!" she glared at Penni. "Still what should one expect from that sow's changeling?" she imagined that only Penni had heard, but the attentive waitress was there again.

"What's up with Bren's mother?" asked Rika.

"Oh, she still hasn't forgiven me for hurting Freya. Hal let's go back? We have to leave for Scartho early tomorrow anyway and I'll think of something exciting to do in our hotel room" Penni felt uncomfortable after the pointed remark.

"Enjoying offending my friends Hilly?" enquired Sirki. "I don't know what you said to Penni but you've clearly upset her, she's talking about leaving?"

"I'm not going to pretend to like her because you contrived a child between the three of you!" she turned to the ever vigilant waitress. "Is there something you want, girl?"

"Sorry ma'am, I thought you might like some more wine?" she replied brightly.

"The Dame has had more than enough thank you, you may go" Sirki waved her away angrily. "Would you like to stand on a chair and tell everyone the family secrets, would you like me to fetch you a microphone?" she said it a little louder than intended and people around busily pretended not to be listening.

"I believe in plain speaking Sirki, you know that!" retorted Hilly.

"Please, we are celebrating the return of my husband, your son *and* your granddaughter's successful space mission so could you try to be less plain speaking, just this once?" asked Sirki a little drunkenly. "Say sorry to Penni!"

"Very well fetch the woman back and I'll apologise" she answered gruffly.

Hilly was as good as her word and Penni agreed to stay, Hal seemed a little disappointed but she whispered something into his ear to cheer him up.

Sirki spotted her son chatting to the attentive waitress who seemed quite interested in him. Sirki hoped the girl wasn't a media spy, *they were probably watching her children as well!*

Hilly buttonholed Sirki again about returning to the hall with Bren to take on her role as Fro Scartho. "Please give me a bit more time Hilly. I want to help Sari's singing career for a month or two then we'll see?" she felt reluctant to leave her lovely house for the dreary old Hall, her life was in New Winchester, *anyway why should I do as that harridan asks? The old bicce was probably spying on her anyway.*

Freya was out by the pool with Dexter, she liked him a lot but he was a norm and could foresee problems with both families if they got together. Nevertheless, she had steered him out here to be alone with him and out of the way of everybody, *especially Sari, who would undoubtedly take the piss.*

"I can't get over how much you look like your mum," he said.

"Dex' that is not a good way to impress a girl especially if you follow it by saying your dad used to fancy her or even worse, that you used to fancy her as a kid. Have you got the point?" she asked in mock contempt. He smiled, put his hands round her waist and leaned in for the kiss. Freya reached up to his face then…

"Oh sorry Fri, I didn't mean to er…" Aelf had come outside with a certain waitress, who stalked off shamefaced.

"Oh really Alfie!" snapped Freya, he'd ruined the moment and she was not best pleased. "Picking up on the hired help are we?"

"Well, she is rather cute and… ahem, I'd better go" he understood his sister's expression only too well.

"Well that's killed it!" lamented Freya after he had gone.

"Not for me Fri, I never fancied your mum when I was a boy and I don't think my dad has even heard of her." replied Dexter before kissing her slowly.

"It's a warm night, fancy a swim?" she asked with a smile.

"I don't have a costume?"

"I'm not planning on wearing one" she slipped the dress off her shoulders.

"What if anyone else comes out here?" he asked.

"The only people I'm interested in *coming* out here are you and I!"

Telekinetically locking the patio door, Freya let the dress fall to the floor to reveal she was wearing very little underneath.

Sirki sat down and put her arm affectionately around Selene Guthric, her friend, ex-band member and ex-lover. The older woman was still striking but her red hair was now mostly dyed. Sirki often forgot that her old band were *norms* and aged faster than she did, Dag, the most senior of them, had crossed the bridge two years ago, his death helping tip Sirki further into a black mood. "How are you Selly dahling, it's been so long since we last met, do you need anything?" they embraced and kissed, the two women had spent many a happy hour in each other's arms.

"I don't want for anything Sirki, dahling" she replied. "Dag made enough silver to last me and I still see lots of the old musos, Harry and his family still keep in touch and Colm and Ife come round every now and then."

"Fancy Colm settling down with Ife" remarked Sirki. "I should have come and seen you long before now."

"I remember you singing so beautifully at Dag's funeral, best I ever heard you."

"I owed him everything, he created me. He made me lead singer of Harvest and wrote most of the songs, there would be never have been Freya without Dag Guthric and I'd probably still be Sirki Vigsdottir, failed rocker, joiking and busking Soomi folk songs on the guitar while dreaming of what could have been."

Selly grinned. "Remember how the dirty old sod used to like watching us together?"

"Jaa" confirmed Sirki as memories of their relationship flooded back, they seemed so clear and vibrant.

"You've fell on your feet with the Thegning though, despite all that drama."

"I've not done too bad, have I?" Sirki snapped back to reality and smiled, she was feeling woozy and her mind was all over the place, *how much had she had to drink?*

Then Sirki spotted her older daughter scurrying in from the pool with a young man and smiled upon noticing that both had wet hair. Her mind began to wander again, this time to darker places and feeling tightness around her throat as a memory of struggling to breathe and falling into nothingness rushed back to haunt her. She stood, swaying slightly. "Forgive me, Selly, I need some fresh air."

Sirki staggered into the night to find herself on the patio with no clear idea of how she had got there then realised she was not alone, for in the pale light a figure could be seen staring at the crescent moon. The planet Freya was shining above it as if waiting to be clutched in its embrace and Sirki, seeing the gleam of silver, knew instantly it was Aesh, completely unaware of her presence. Watching the Alpha discretely Sirki thought of her old love song to Selene and remembering the older woman's gentle arms about her, sighed loudly.

Aesh turned in surprise at the sudden noise. "Just getting a bit of fresh air ma'am" she said nervously.

"Elke, I'm sorry if I seemed frosty earlier, I was being a *polho bicce*, worrying about what you and Bren might have been up to. Stupid really," explained Sirki. *She is stunning I wouldn't have been at all surprised if Bren had shown interest in her.*

"There is nothing between us I assure you. The Thegn was the perfect gentleman on the mission and he was always worried about you" answered Aesh, she was fascinated by Sirki's beauty and pondering on how she would like to kiss her full red lips.

Sirki, detecting the interest at the forefront of Aesh's mind, advised her. "You should be more guarded in your thoughts Elke, my mind reading is far in advance of most Psi" there followed an awkward silence until Sirki's curiosity finally got the better of her. "Your mekhanikal leg fascinates me, may I touch it?"

"It's an odd request but you're not the first to ask."

Sirki reached down to touch the mekhanikal limb. "Wow, it feels like real flesh, it's a bit cold though."

"It's covered with a metal foam that's soft but reacts like steel to sudden pressure and the titanium skeleton is bonded to my thigh bone." explained Elke.

"Can you feel anything in it?" Sirki asked curiously.

"There are sensors under the covering, it's not that sensitive but I can feel pressure which helps me to move about."

Sirki ran her hand to where skin and metal met, almost flowing into one another and found it hard to feel a seam... something was stirring within her.

"Fro Scartho, my mekhanikal limb ended a while back, that's the real me you're touching!" exclaimed Elke in surprise.

Sirki was now exploring the crease where thigh ended and pubis began, she halted the progress of her fingers. "Do you want me to stop?"

"No!" Aesh replied and aroused by her touch, kissed her. She knew it was wrong but this sensual woman with the heavy musky perfume was irresistible.

Sirki returned the kiss then moved her hand to the material of Elke's underwear pressing gently to discover a different crease. "Just say the word and I'll stop" she whispered into her ear.

"No, don't stop." Aesh took a deep breath, she wanted this to happen.

"We'd best be quiet." Sirki slipped her fingers inside the silk and brushed her lips lightly against Elke's to share a long lingering kiss while continuing to describe circles around her clitoris, after a while the *Huscarl* started to make soft mewling noises as Sirki brought her to climax. "Let's go down to the lawn, no one will see us there," she whispered as the woman caught her breath.

The moon seemed to be singing as she led Elke into the garden where they undressed and lay down together in the silvery light.

Bren was concerned for Sirki who was nowhere to be found and had seemed a little unsteady when he last saw her, after searching the rooms he went to the circular inner garden where Selene, who had joined Colm and Ife, mentioned seeing her totter unsteadily towards the pool. Wandering on to the terrace Bren heard an all too familiar giggle come from the darkness cloaking the lawn and switching to infra-red vision spotted the heat pattern of two figures in a passionate embrace, the right leg of one of them showed up a cold blue, *Aesh?*

As Bren walked towards the figures he heard Sirki exclaim in a stage whisper. "It's Bren!"

Aesh had managed to pull on some clothes and was holding her blouse in front of her ample bosom but Sirki, who lay there clad only in red stockings, appeared highly amused.

"Oh gods, Thegn, please forgive me!" begged Aesh, the spell now broken.

"Elke, I don't think this is entirely your fault, just make sure you're properly dressed before you go back inside" he said as calmly as possible.

Sirki propped herself up on her elbows. "Are we going to argue now?" she asked, ardently watching Aesh rush off carrying the rest of her clothes.

Bren was both angry and perplexed. "I thought you had spent the last six years pining for me yet first chance you get, you're into someone's knickers?"

"It just sort of happened?" Sirki found she couldn't explain her actions.

Bren sat on the lawn next to her. "Why did you do it, why drag poor Aesh into your games?" Sirki merely shrugged.

"She's my friend and you took advantage of her by using your *charisma* didn't you, just like you did with me all those years ago?"

"Fuck off Bren, I don't recall you complaining then because you wanted it as much as I did!" she snapped, her temper flaring. "She turned me on alright, her and those massive tits, can't a girl have a little fun?"

This wasn't like Sirki? He looked into her wide pupils. "You're stoned!"

"Nej Bren, just a little drunk."

"Curse it Sirk, you need to stop doing this!" *had one of her musician friends slipped her something?* "Did you do it because you felt you just had to beat me to it? Woden only knows how the woman's feeling."

"You knew what I was like when you made me your rightwife!" retorted Sirki. "And I have the body of a woman half my age, *you* told me last night that if I remember correctly."

"You promised me you would change!" he reminded her angrily.

"I have changed, nej pharma and I have cut down on my drinking and apart from my slip up with Effie and *you* started that business with Penni! There has been no-one else till now, well apart from Maz and that other one, whatshername? I have been the boring little loyal Fro, fucking Scartho." Sirki crawled across to Bren on her hands and knees and unzipped his fly to release a huge erection. "You find my being with women a turn on so if you tell me you don't, this is calling you a liar!" she slurred. *Sirki was right of course, the sight of her with Aesh had aroused him greatly.* Taking his manhood in her hand she pulled it back and forth then brought her tongue along the vein underneath before enveloping his glans with her lips to bring him to completion.

Sirki half-fell onto Bren's lap afterwards and despite her nudity her body temperature was very high. "I despair of you sometimes" he sighed. "Come on, we'd best return to the party before we're missed."

"I have got to have a drink dahling, help me get dressed." Sirki was coming down to earth very slowly.

Sari was checking on her children sleeping peacefully in their beds and glancing out of the window to look at the moon spotted movement out on the lawn. Switching on her night vision out of curiosity she saw a naked woman on her knees before a seated man and they were having some kind of argument then the woman put her head in the man's lap and Sari realised with horror that they were her parents. She quickly shut the curtains but knew that she would never be able to un-see that.

A noise on the landing caught her attention so opening the door a crack she peeked out to see one of the hired waitresses tiptoeing out of Aelfred's bedroom shoes in hand, he had already related to his sister how he had stumbled across Freya with her chap earlier on.

Bloody hell, they're all at it!

Going into the corridor she went to the door nearest the stairs to tap gently on it. "It's me, Saz," she whispered.

"You'd better come in" said Anya's voice.

Sirki, grabbing the first drink she could find, gargled with it then spying her latest conquest sitting alone holding a glass and looking lost, sat down next to her. "It was my fault all of it, please don't blame yourself."

"I should have said no!" started Aesh bitterly.

"Elke, I used my charm on you I just couldn't help myself. That's just how I am sometimes" insisted Sirki trying to make her feel better.

"Just how you are?" she retorted. "What were you thinking, what the hell was I thinking?" she spotted Trevelyan waving to her. "Kawaro and his wife are giving me a lift home. Please tell the Thegn how sorry I am."

Bren nodded to Elke as she left but she couldn't bring herself to look at him. Then spotting Sirki talking with the Queen, *another of her conquests,* he sat down to consider what had happened and scrutinise the partygoers milling about, *there are a lot of her old musician friends here, might one of them have thought it amusing to slip her something?*

It seemed unlikely but... *curse it, Sirki I can't take much more of this!*

"Dahling, have you thought about what I said?" Effie queried Sirki. "I have to leave now and I need to know if I can rely on you tomorrow, your contribution would be of great help."

"Jaa... tomorrow... better call me in the morning, I'm a bit fuzzy at the moment and I've just done something really stupid, again!" she replied.

"Care to tell me about it?"

"Nej, it'll keep."

"Check, you don't seem very with it sweetie, you should get some sleep then you can tell me all about it tomorrow" affirmed Effie, Sirki's pupils were like saucers. *Gods, I hope she's not doing pharma again?*

When everybody had finally gone home Sirki fell gratefully into bed, fully dressed, while the room spun wildly around her.

Heidi Glaser arrived home, sat on the couch, kicked off her shoes and mulled over the evening's events.

Playing the waitress had been tiring but rewarding. *Da N'tan's son had been quite fun even if he was a bit of a prat, the things she had to do for the cause! Shame he's a scunung, oh well can't have everything!* Peeling the communicator from her left hand she removed another from its hiding place between the pages of a book and pressing the golden lattice into her open palm waited for it to seat itself and power up.

The Gorgon's Head of the ACG rotated slowly over her open hand then a voice asked. "Glaser you have something to report?"

"I administered the psychotrope to the lilac-eyed *bicce* as instructed but it didn't cause the expected psychotic episode."

"That is a disappointment, if the *waelcyrie's* beloved Omega had a psionic meltdown it would have been a great victory for the cause, to say nothing of the damage she could have done" commented her controller.

"Are we continuing with the main operation?" she asked.

"Yes Glaser it is vital that we do, I can tell you nothing more."

"I understand but there is one other thing to report, something that involves the Da N'tan family, in particular one of their children and I think the Craeftwice will be very interested."

CHAPTER 13 – THAT MORNING AFTER FEELING

There are two large pictures of Freya on the wall of her music room; one of them shows her as the barefoot sangestre we all know and love. The other suggests a very different persona indeed.

Hardly recognisable as the same woman it dates from when she was lead singer with the moderately successful rock group Star Hammer, the singer is a vision in black leather and fishnets sitting on the floor in a most unladylike fashion with the two other band members standing behind her.

"I was eighteen when that was taken." said the singer on noticing my attention.

"It's certainly a striking picture, that's Tank and Gaz behind you isn't it?"

"Jaa, when I split they reformed as a duo called GazTank, it didn't last long."

"No as I recall Tank found religion and Gaz got married and works as a music producer."

"Jaa, we only had a couple of good songs in two albums."

"Freya, have you ever thought about getting married?"

"Nej, I'm having too much fun to settle down yet!"

"What about children?"

"You kidding me?" replied the singer in astonishment at my question.

(From the article "At home with Freya" by Evie Green in the Ratatoskr)

Sirki woke the next day with her makeup smudged, a splitting headache and a bitter taste in her mouth. Rolling on to her back she was relieved to find Bren there.

"How are we feeling?" he asked.

"Headachy, ashamed" she answered, the taste in her mouth was definitely chemickal. A vague memory drifted back. "Did we hump last night?"

"You were very insistent and very noisy. I said you wouldn't remember."

"I acted dreadfully didn't I?" the events of the previous evening came galloping back with an extra helping of self-loathing at the reins.

"Pretty much" admitted Bren.

"Have I said sorry?"

"About a hundred times" he replied

"Bren, I couldn't help myself, I must have been so drunk. Oh, that poor woman!" she clung to him, glad he was still there. "Not much good as an excuse is it? I'll have to apologise to her."

"Probably best you leave well alone, she'll doubtless be asking for a transfer."

Sirki began to sob and feeling her shaking Bren put his arm round her. "I hate to ask but you were as high as a kite, had you taken anything?"

"Nej, I've been clean for years!" sniffed Sirki.

"Then you must have been spiked, would one of your muso friends have slipped you something as a joke?"

"Nej, nej-one would never do anything like that!" she insisted tearfully.

"There's one way to find out, we do have a doctor in the house." suggested Bren. "Get up and when you're ready I'll get our son to do his stuff."

Aelf took blood, saliva and awkwardly requested a urine sample.

"Do you want a stool sample too?" asked his mother with an amused look.

"No mum, giving me your wee is embarrassing enough as it is. I'll get these to the New Winchester Haelinghus straight after breakfast."

The family sat around the dining table. Sirki had a ringing in her head that would not go away and Sari, who was helping Bern to use his spoon, couldn't look her parents in the eye.

"Do you know mummy came to see you both last night and you looked so peaceful but the moon was so bright that I had to close the curtains and do you know what? It was so light outside you could have seen people on the lawn without using night vision!" her mother and father exchanged sheepish glances. "And did you have a nice swim last night sus?" Sari smiled sweetly at Freya who pulled a face.

"You were swimming in the dark Auntie Freya?" Willa found this amusing.

Sari had to leave her brothur alone because Dame Hildegard had joined them

"Morning Grandma!" chorused Sirki's children.

"Yes, I see what you did there, very amusing. Good morning everyone" she was in a good mood for a change. "Bren, dear, do you think we could have the news on?"

Bren turned on the view-screen, Sirki usually disapproved of it while they were eating but today she would do anything to keep her mother-in-law happy.

"...*disappearance last night in Scartho. The young woman was a member of the Psi Wing and was last seen on Freeman Street only a short distance from her quarters. She had attended a concert with friends at the Bifrost Arena and after eating in the popular Canton area left on her own to make her way back. Blythe Te G'rath is twenty years old, a graduate from Havelok Academy and has recently been attached to the No. 6 Cohort of the 3rd Elites. As yet the Ward has no information regarding her whereabouts and Huscarls are assisting their officers to conduct a thorough search of the area. This is the third disappearance of a Psi in two weeks, if you have any information, no matter how unimportant you think it may be, please contact one of the numbers below.*"

The parents of the missing girl appeared and Bren cut the sound. "The grandkids don't need to hear any more of this" he said quietly.

"The third one" remarked Hilly. "And the Psi can't locate them. They're obviously being psionically suppressed and we all know there's only one group who could do that."

"The ACG no longer exist, they were disbanded years ago" pointed out Bren.

Effie wanted to discuss something important regarding the Psi, nej guessing what it was about, thought Sirki. *Were they plotting against her again?*

The newsfeed ran across the bottom of the screen.

"Yet another disappearance, the third this fortnight.

Ward say they have no clues to whereabouts of missing woman.

Rumours abound in New Winchester of a mysterious group abducting Psi.

Meanwhile in Slote, the Campward rescue Psi from attempted kidnap after a shootout on the C31.

In other news the RAF are confident that their newly designed steorraflota will..."

Sirki sat in the Morning Room wishing she had stayed at home, she had thrown up earlier and now Weyland the Smith was hammering his anvil in her head, worse still was the suspicion that something was going on that she was not party to. Mina, Bonnie and Elli were all sat with her waiting for the Queen's appearance. *All that's missing is the cauldron!*

The doors opened and a palace flunkey entered. "Her Majesty Queen Ethelflaeda the Third." Effie swept in with her usual aplomb and seated herself at the desk as all present stood and greeted her with required deference, Sirki swayed a bit.

"Good Morning ladies, please be seated" she regarded her friend. "Sirki you look like shit, how long did the party carry on after I left?"

"Ma'am I regret to say I am a little tired and cannot remember" she answered, *bit formal today aren't I?*

"Alright then, Mina could you please fill Fro Scartho in on the current situation?" requested the Queen, somewhat nonplussed.

The Highest sent a flash-thought to Sirki's muddled mind and she attempted to sort the information into order but found herself struggling. Some Psi' had disappeared and there had been an attempted abduction in Slote. Sirki remembered the township only too well, it was where she had met Bren and nearly had died there too. The memory of being strangled forced itself into her head causing panic to rise as she suddenly became aware of enemies nearby.

"Sirki are you alright? You're as white as a sheet." Bonnie's concerned thought came into her head and she held back an unnatural rage.

I could kill you conniving two-faced bicces so easily!

Aelf was still at the Winchester Haelinghus talking to an old colleague when his comm' shrilled, it was the pharma unit. "Doctor Da N'tan, these samples you asked us to test, you didn't say who they were from?"

"I insisted on discretion, why?"

"Doctor, we need to know it is very urgent!" was the Pharma-Suster's anxious response.

"My mother Fro Scartho, what's the problem?"

"Where is she?" there was panic in her voice.

"She's visiting the Queen," *this was worrying?*

"Ye Gods!" she cried in alarm.

A shocked expression came on Mina Srivastava's face and all three Psi' sprang out of their chairs to take up protective positions around the Queen then Sirki felt herself being telekinetically held in her seat, *they were locking her down, why?*

"What are you doing?" Sirki path'd to them. *She couldn't believe it, were these people her enemies after all?* She forced the thought down, they were her friends and the Queen was her best friend she must remember that and keep calm.

"Necessary precautions dahling, please relax" path'd Effie.

Sirki forced herself to a standing position despite their best efforts. "Don't mess me around!" she yelled angrily as the doors flew open and Palace Guards rushed in. They were all wearing torcs.

Sirki was physically forced back down and shackled to the chair. "You know none of this is of any use don't you? I could easily kill everybody in this room!" she yelled while struggling against her restraints. *Gods, why I am even considering this?* Her head was pounding, *enemies everywhere, must escape, stop it, kill them, stop it stop it!* Sirki took a deep breath. "I am in control for the moment, what is wrong with me?"

"You have been given a drug that causes psychological and psionic instability, it creates a severe psychosis coupled with paranoia causing a desire to strike out at anyone and everyone" the Highest informed her.

"Could it cause mood swings and flashbacks?" asked Sirki, the headache seemed to have lifted slightly.

"More than likely, but we can't say for certain, the survivors are unable to tell us anything" replied Mina

"What do you mean survivors?" asked Sirki in alarm.

"So far, four of our Psi' have attacked people for no apparent reason and without warning, one was shot dead by the Ward, a second died as the result of an explosion she had caused, another, shot by a *Huscarl,* is critically injured in the Jorvik Haelinghus and the fourth was captured by a Psi *saetere* in Oostende. All had the drug in their systems and the last, Neophyte Cara Pascoe, has no recollection of what happened. The psychotrope seems to have passed through her body but she is currently under close observation in the cacaern."

"Why hasn't this been in the news?" asked Sirki, the pounding in her head seemed to have subsided for now.

Effie continued. "This is being kept as quiet as possible, can you imagine the reaction if it went public that Psi' are going crazy and attacking people? You were to be informed of it at this meeting but we didn't get chance, when the drug has passed through your system you will be released but we will have to observe how you have been affected."

"I presume this drug has been synthesised by our old friends the ACG?" she had managed to start processing Mina's thought package and had discovered the likelihood of their re-emergence. "I began to feel strange last night but put it down to drinking too much, it must have been administered to me at the party?" *it explained everything.* "It seems to come and go in waves and I seem able to control it to a certain degree, how?"

"We don't know enough about this psychotrope to say but given your past experience with pharma and more importantly your link to the Helm, it would probably take a much larger dose to seriously affect you" expounded Mina.

A Psi was generally celibate, teetotal and only used pharma for haeling. Sirki would never make an archetypical *waelcyrie*. "How long will it take to pass through my system?" asked Sirki.

"Between twelve to sixteen hours after being administered, possibly longer?" replied Mina.

Sirki did a mental calculation. "In time for lunch, my daughters can keep an eye on me at home, they're more than competent." It was decided Bonnie would escort her back and Sari and Freya would keep her under house arrest until cleared by the Highest. "You are aware that what I said earlier was true, none of your precautions could have stopped me and that alone should be proof I am not dangerous."

"You know she's right, don't you?" remarked Elli after they had gone. "Much as I don't see eye to eye with my suster-in-law I have to say we're lucky she's on our side."

"I agree, the PRW will step up their efforts to find a way of counteracting this drug and the Psi Wing must assist them." stated the Queen.

"Certainly majesty but perhaps we should consider what should be done if Fro Scartho or any of her children were to actually become berserkers?" suggested the Highest. "I do have some ideas for containing them."

"You will assist the PRW to find an antidote for this drug and that is all!" replied Effie coldly.

"As you wish Ma'am!" replied Mina.

Sirki's children were suitably astonished when their mother was brought home under armed escort and when informed of the circumstances rather bemusedly took responsibility for their prisoner. Later that afternoon when her mind had finally cleared Sirki ran through the information Mina had path'd to her. The Psi' had disappeared in different locations. Psi Alicen Hogg had been rescued by the Ward in Slote. One of her abductors was dead, one badly injured and when the two that had been arrested were interrogated it was discovered they were not ACG but hired mercenaries. They had been given special equipment and instructions how to use it but had no idea why the Psi was required, just that they had to deliver their captive to a pre-arranged destination. The vigilance of the Ward in Slote had foiled the plan and it was suspected that a Dragonfly spotted fleeing the area was intended to carry the victim away.

"Not much to go on" she thought. *"Tog-Barr, the second victim, was based in Tolosa and the flyer from the failed attempt headed south-west which would have taken it in the same direction."* Sirki consulted an atellan, south of the area was the Pirren mountain range and beyond that, what remained of East Hispania now a scorched hostile wasteland and one of the largest flat zones on continental Europa, *a good place to hide from us,* it was only an idea and a fairly obvious come to that but she passed it on anyway.

Bren had flown to Scartho immediately after hearing the bad news and was presently walking along Freeman Street with Campaeldor Anderson. He still wanted to be in the middle of things but realised he was probably more hindrance than help, *after all, who wants the boss breathing over their shoulder?*

"Te G'rath walked to Pasture Street and spoke with the *Campward* before going over Elinor Road and out of their sight. The monitors show her stopping at Boot Street and the Helfled Barracks is just two blocks further on. "Penni pointed north past the marketplace to the barrack gates with the old Dock Tower visible in the misty background. "Te G'rath crossed the road here and entered Beggins Media, the place has been closed for months and this is where we lose her." They crossed the usually congested street past the Ward road block forcing traffic to take a detour. "Of course, at midnight this street is a lot quieter!" she shouted over the noise.

Upon entering the derelict store they were greeted by a dog-handler with a pair of neohounds and Bren stroked the head of one as it raised a piebald face to lick his hand.

"Good afternoon Thegn, ma'am" said the handler. They followed him up the stairs to look through the window to the corner where Te G'rath had stood.

"Someone stood here watching for her and there was a second person behind the door opposite, best guess is she was lured upstairs then jumped as she entered the room. The hounds tracked her downstairs to the back of the shop" he explained, leading them back to the ground floor.

At the rear of the building was a narrow lane that led down past the rear of the Dock Station to the waterfront, a great many tyre marks were visible here on the muddy road. "There are no monitors sited around here but we know they didn't cross the station yard as that would have been recorded, so we suspect they went straight down to the quayside" they walked back to the front of the building and journeyed in a Ward *waegn* to some quiet private moorings by a pier where the officer showed the pair an empty berth. The nameplate read *Wade's Steed*. "My dogs located her scent here and then it appears she was put aboard a *flota*. I'm afraid this is where we lose her."

Bren stared out across the estuary at the gulls soaring in great circles above the water. *She was only a young girl, what if it had been Sari?* "Penni, what's being done to find her?"

"We have flyers searching the estuary and Seaforce has jet-*flotae* scouring the coastline south, the Ward has her face on every news-screen and they are investigating every alleged sighting, they're doing all they can, Bren."

"Thanks Penni, I'm flying back to New Winchester to check on Sirki."

"Check Sir, send her my love."

As the flyer went supersonic Bren received further troubling news, another Psi had been abducted this morning in the Port of London. The Ward intercepted them and a firefight ensued but despite losing several men the kidnappers managed to board a lifter and escape with their captive to head southwest and the flyer had disappeared off the sensors almost immediately. *That made four now.*

CHAPTER 14 – SARI CENTRE-STAGE

Is it desperation to hope that you'll be mine?
I've wanted and I've wished for it for such a long, long time.
But will you ever notice that I'm more than just a friend?
My desperation, my desire, how is it all going to end?
(Excerpt from My Desperation – music and words by D.Guthric.)

Sitting in the green room at the *broadcasthus* Sari couldn't have been more nervous if she had been about to make a combat drop into heavy fire.

Her mother was sat with her. "You'll slay them dahling, don't worry"

"Aren't you supposed to say break a leg?" she asked anxiously.

"*Rikkoa jalka!*" joked Sirki in Soomilek.

The floor managers voice came over a speaker "Mz Jorvik to stage please."

After casting a nervous glance at her mother, Sari strode out to the performance area wearing a very short red dress and matching heels with her long blonde hair loose about her shoulders. Sirki dashed round to the side to get a good view.

The chat-show Vox Vulgaris was still being broadcast but it had a new host. "Ladies and gentlemen, I have the greatest pleasure in introducing a rising young star who is making her debut on this show tonight. Will you please give a warm welcome to Sari Jorvik!" announced Victor Frye.

The band struck up and Sari launched into My Desperation giving it everything she had, belting it out and dancing quite suggestively. When she had finished the audience broke into applause, some even cheered as Victor waved her to a chair.

Sirki was overjoyed, *another sangestre in the family!*

"Good evening young lady" he turned to the crowd. "Was that something or what?" more applause.

Sari was run through the typical barrage of questions Sirki had to endure as Freya, her service record in the Elites was brought up leading to a question about her injury and giving Victor the chance to draw attention to her shapely legs. The subject of her late husband was dealt with in a sympathetic manner and she talked about coping as a widowed mother. No mention was made of her lineage until the presenter finally dropped it. "And I believe you have a famous relative don't you?"

"Er, yeah" replied Sari. "My mother is the *sangestre* Freya."

"And I believe she's with us tonight!" stated Victor.

The audience applauded on cue as a camera drone sought out Sirki standing at the side of the set where she waved in mock sheepishness and blew a kiss.

Sari was flying high as they drove back.

"So my daughter how does it feel?" Sirki was driving her old Aurora, now considered a classic and worth far more than she had originally paid.

"I want to do it again, right now!" she answered excitedly. "Do you think I could make a career of it with the kids and everything?"

"I seem to recall I managed with three of you."

"Yeah, but you did have dad and my other mum *and* Mrs Jensen to help" replied Sari.

"Jaa that's true but I'm here for you *lapsi*" Sirki reassured her.

They arrived home to find Aelf and Bren watching the news. There had been another abduction, this time in Lutetia the old Frankish capital, considered one of the safest places outside of the Reignweald.

That makes five, thought Sirki.

CHAPTER 15 - SIRKI'S LITTLE BETRAYAL

"I used to busk down there in front of the entrance" remarked Sirki. "Hard to believe it now," she took a sip from her wine glass. Wodenshearg Station was a busy place, high speed vac-tubes departed to the Port of London and Tamworth while slower overland trains ran to other parts of the Reignweald from there too.

"Sirki, come away from the window someone might recognise you!" said a voice from the bed.

"Oh don't be silly, dahling, we're four floors up and besides I haven't been in the public eye for years, who'll remember me?" she replied then giggled as the news board over the station entrance displayed her picture with the caption. "AB Studios to produce Freya's daughter Sari Jorvik on new album!" it was followed by footage of her daughter on Vox Vulgaris.

"Sirki, you're naked, people will see!" the voice complained.

"It was so long ago, so much has happened since," remarked Sirki wistfully.

"Dahling, please I have to be back on duty soon."

She walked back to the bed and regarded Elke's statuesque body. "Why haven't you had this regrown?" asked Sirki running a hand along the metal limb to feel the runic script and knot-work patterns embossed on its shining surface. "They can do it now you know?"

"Because after all these years I've become rather attached to it" and they both grinned at the unintentional joke. "Besides it'll take a year to regrow *and* then I'll have to learn to walk again. It doesn't bother me and the Thegn pays for regular upgrades..." she stopped upon remembering who her lover was. "Sorry Sirki."

"Don't worry dahling." She replied. "Bren understands my needs and he has been very understanding in the past, I usually tell him when I, you know?" Her last extra-marital relationship had been before Bren went missing. She had briefly rekindled an old passion with Maz, a socialite who was married to a politician. Sirki revelled in the fact that she was bedding someone from the exalted circle who hung around the Queen and considered themselves above the *jumped up Soomilek.*

"Does he know about us then?" asked Elke in surprise.

"I think he suspects, he has asked some pointed questions recently. I'd better tell him when I get home."

"Are you sure that's wise?" following the incident at the party Sirki had contacted Elke to apologise but it had led to an afternoon of passion in a room at the Arkadia. Several weeks had passed and they had become regular visitors to the hotel by the station.

"Jaa of course it will be alright, do you have to go back so soon?" asked Sirki kneeling beside her on the bed.

"I'm due at the airdock in an hour."

"That gives us plenty of time." she dipped her finger into the wine to draw circles around her nipples, Elke licked the sweet liquid from them then sitting back on the bed Sirki dipped her finger again to trace a moist line from navel to pubis which her lover followed eagerly with her tongue...

Sirki decided to come clean about her little betrayal as soon as she returned home. They were dividing their time between her beloved house outside New Winchester and Scartho once more, Bren wanted them to move to the Hall permanently but she was reluctant to leave the place where she had so many happy memories and Sirki also found the burh ugly when compared to New Winchester. She would be honest about her fling with Elke and tell her husband she still loved him, *he would be alright with it, he understood her desires.*

Sirki drove through the gates at her home and the Elites on guard duty snapped smartly to attention, this was something she'd learned to put up with since her husband succeeded his father as Thegn but on approaching the house Sirki noticed Bren's leaf-pattern Tiger wasn't there.

"Anya!" she called as she entered her home.

"Yes ma'am?" her young housekeeper emerged from the kitchen.

"How many times have I told you? You don't call me ma'am it's Sirki, where is the Thegn?"

"He's gone to Scartho *ma'am*" Anya emphasised the word.

Have I upset her somehow? Aloud she asked "When did he leave?"

"About an hour ago, he came straight in, packed some bags then left telling me he was going to Scartho and not to expect him back any time soon" her voice wavered slightly.

"Just like that, with *nej* explanation?" asked Sirki.

"Yes, but he did say he'd left something for you in the sitting room." answered Anya, clearly upset. "He was in a very bad mood!"

Sirki curiously entered the room to see a small drone sat on one of the low tables. It was a new model like a golden discus and readily available in the shops, at her approach it hovered into the air to begin a playback on the large wall screen. The picture showed a rather familiar window and a woman with wavy chestnut hair standing in it, the focus was not clear but it was quite obvious she was naked.

It was the Arkadia Hotel opposite the station in New Winchester and the woman was her!

CHAPTER 16 –
SARI IN THEIR SIGHTS

A few weeks later saw Sari back at the AB studios in Cambrycge, she had just finished recording "Soomi Queen" a song Dag had written for her mother but never recorded, Sari had, of course, performed it in her raunchy style.

Adrian was ebullient. "That was brilliant my dear, your mum couldn't have done better and speaking of Sirki, how is the old tart, has she sorted things out with your dad yet?"

"No Adie, he's still in Scartho, I think she's really done it this time." replied Sari with sad resignation.

"Ooh that's not good news, send her my love anyway" he replied.

Sari said her goodbyes and rushed off to pick up her brother, who had been spending time with old friends from Adenbrock Haelinghus and was a little worse for drink. Sari warned him not to be sick in their mother's *scrid* but needn't have worried as he fell asleep almost immediately.

Aelf was shortly woken by Sari shaking him, "Hei brothur, wake up I think we have company."

"Wha?" he mumbled, *what was his suster playing at?*

"A vehicle has been following us since we left Cambrycge." she informed him.

"It's probably just going the same way, s'nothing." he settled back in the passenger seat but she poked him in the ribs. "Ow!"

"We're past the Port of London on the S3 you'd think they might have turned off by now?" she slowed down and the following lights slowed down. "There did you see that?"

"No, I'm asleep."

"They're being so obvious they probably want us to speed up so they can to try and run us off the road."

"You're being paranoid Saz." he sat up and looked in the wing mirror, there were some lights there and they were quite close. "This is a busy road, seems like a daft place to try something, anyway who would do that?"

"The ACG maybe, someone drugged mummy after all and it's been weeks since the last abduction, perhaps it's our turn?"

"Why would the ACG single us out?" he enquired.

"Duh, do you not remember how they went after mummy when she was carrying Fri? They would love to get their sticky mitts on one of us," replied Sari. "Because of the unique DNA we carry to say nothing of the threat we represent to their unpleasant cause?"

"So why don't we just drive to the nearest *Wardhus* and tell them?" he thought that was the simplest solution.

"Because then we won't find out what they're up to" responded Sari.

"Why do I feel I'm not going to like this?" protested Aelfred on seeing that his sister was actually excited at the prospect. They left the main road at junction five and as expected the mysterious vehicle followed. Her plan was to drive parallel to the main road and re-join at six, *after she had discovered what their pursuers wanted, of course.* Sari pulled the Aurora into a layby on the heavily wooded road and the pursuing vehicle went straight past, it was a dark panel-sided Pony.

"See they didn't stop, looks like you were wrong" remarked Aelf triumphantly.

Sari cast him a glance. "Do you not know anything about ambuscade? They will be lying in wait around the corner!" reaching under the hem of her skirt she produced a small pistol and pushed it into his hand. "Here Alfie, take this… What?" she asked upon noticing the look of disgust on his face. "Does handling a weapon go against your principles or did they not teach you to shoot at the Academy?"

"No, it's just that it's been warmed by your body heat."

"Oh for fuck's sake Alfie and you a doctor, don't worry it was in a leg holster!" she reached back and flipped up the small rear seat to expose a compartment containing an assault rifle. "I can only guess what mummy kept in here but it does come in useful" she remarked while strapping a short *seax* to her left leg. "I'm glad I put on flat heels for driving. Come on. bro', let's see what the night brings us."

Aelf reluctantly got out of the *scrid* and the siblings quietly advanced through the darkness using their infra-red vision. Sure enough, just around the bend was the *waegn* parked in the middle of the road. Crouching down they observed two figures either side of it, their faces hidden behind night-vision masks.

"There are two more, one either side of the road hidden in the scrub and at least one more in the wood" path'd Sari to her brother.

"Who are they?" he asked.

"ACG!" she path'd with loathing. *"And they're operating some kind of suppression field to stop us calling for help."*

"What do we do now?" Aelfred, unlike his sister, had never seen action.

"You stay here and when the shooting starts fire at those two with my popgun to draw their attention, don't worry I'm not expecting you to hit anyone, check?"

"Check" he answered reluctantly then watched as she disappeared into the trees to his left. Sari like her genetic mother was every inch a *cempestre*.

"Don't get killed" he path'd the *Huscarl*s luck charm to her.

"Don't intend to, don't you get killed!" she responded while picking her way carefully through the undergrowth, the enemy would be able to see her with their night-visors but her genetically enhanced vision outclassed anything the ACG could invent. The first of the black-clad soldiers was

taken down by a left handed blow from her *seax* but as she wiped the blade clean on his jacket another appeared and managed to get a round off before she dropped him with a one-handed shot from her Sterlinger. A volley of shots followed from the direction of the roadside to tell her Alfie was doing his bit so she moved quickly back to the kerb to pick them off. The man stationed to the right of the *waegn* began firing wildly into the trees so Sari rolled out of the undergrowth and shot him before vaulting over the vehicle to land on the sixth and knock them senseless.

She hauled her unconscious captive up by the collar and wrenched off their night-visor to exclaim in surprise. "Well look who it is!"

There was a noise behind her but before she could turn a single shot rang out and another dark-uniformed figure sank to the floor, *there had been seven of them!*

Aelf walked towards her lowering the pistol. "I took an oath, I swore to preserve life not take it away and thanks to you suster, that oath is broken."

"But by doing so you saved my life brothur!" exclaimed Sari then said. "Look what I've got!" and he stared at the unconscious woman in surprise.

It was the waitress from the party.

In the back of the *waegn* they found a large metal cabinet with an illuminated control panel and a trefoil of toroidal coils fixed to the top, each with a glowing blue dot at the centre.

Sari tried pressing several buttons to no avail until finally her brother leaned in to flick a switch on the side, the lights went out and the background noise of the psionic world returned. Glaring at Aelf she contacted Sirki who knowing it was best not to involve the Ward, arranged for the Palace Guard to clear things up. Effie's household troops could be relied on to deal with the job competently and discretely.

Sari carried the comatose ACG operative to the Aurora and after throwing her into the back seat waited for the Guard to arrive. New Winchester was only twenty miles away so it wasn't long before a pair of maroon Tigers turned up. "Keep a beady eye on her bro' I'll be back shortly" instructed Sari as she got out.

He was watching her remonstrate with the Guard Undercempa when a noise came from the back seat. It was the waitress waking up. "Who are you?" he asked but she remained silent. "The other night we, I thought…"

"Just doing my job *scunung*," she nodded towards his sister outside. "She's a born killer that one, not you though, you are quite different."

Sari got back in. "Oh so you're awake are you?" she observed before knocking Glaser out again.

"Saz, why did you do that?" Aelf was aghast.

"So she can't sweet talk you, brothur, strap her in" she started the vehicle.

"Where are we going, aren't the Guard taking her to New Winchester?" he asked.

"We're taking her home, mummy wants a word" replied Sari.

Glaser woke up bound to a chair by her wrists and ankles with a throbbing head and a *Huscarl* standing guard over her. Glaser recognised her as the one with the metal leg from the party.

"So what now abomination, beatings, questions, more beatings?" she asked. The soldier remained silent, *this was a strange interrogation chanber it had a piano and pictures of the lilac-eyed scunung on the wall?* Glaser realised that this was the *hore's* house and she was in the music room! As if on cue the double doors opened and the creature walked in flanked by two of her spawn, she was dressed strikingly in a long bottle green dress split high on the right thigh and a short *seax* dangled at her left hip from a gold chain belt.

"Did you drug me the other night?" asked Sirki.

Glaser did not reply.

"She's has an implant up her nose that stops us reading her mind, I can cut it out if you want." suggested Sari.

"You will do nej such thing!" snapped her mother. "Alfie, can you remove it without harming her?"

"Yes, but I don't have the equipment to hand. I would need to fetch it from the city."

"I haven't the time for that." Sirki closed her eyes and tentatively probed at Glaser's mind. "Your device generates pain at a Psionic level to prevent us from fiddling with it" she stared into the *saetere's* face. "But know this ACG girl, I have had three children and pain is no stranger to me."

Glaser felt a tugging at the back of her nose then a sharp sting as the implant wrenched itself free to be dragged down and out of her left nostril by an unseen force. It flew across the room to be caught in the fine linen handkerchief that Sirki had produced from her belt purse.

She regarded it with distaste. "Nasty little thing, Aesh, take it into the kitchen and give it a wash, someone from the Palace will pick it up tomorrow. Alfie, tend to her please" she ordered.

Glaser's eyes were streaming, her nose was bleeding and she made an angry show of not wanting his help but Aelf persevered and she allowed him to tend to her.

"Right young lady, what's your name." asked Sirki then smiled. By refusing to tell her it had sprung to the forefront of her mind to be easily read.

"So Heidi Glaser, why did you drug me?"

"Go and fuck yourself abomination!" she retorted.

"If that's how you want it?" she sighed and turned to her children. "Skedaddle the pair of you, Heidi and I need to have a little chat in private."

They both protested at this but Sirki insisted on being left alone. When they had gone she picked up a chair and turning its back to face Glaser, straddled it. The split of her dress allowed her green stockinged right leg to be fully exposed and display the tattoo of Thor's hammer above the garter.

"Naughty girl!" purred Sirki on noticing her attention.

Glaser's eyes were drawn to a face surmounted by a crown of wavy chestnut hair pinned into place at the sides, her lilac eyes seemed to sparkle and below the pretty perky nose were red Cupid's bow lips which were slightly parted. Heidi could see the tip of a pink tongue resting on her bottom teeth, Fro Scartho was so beautiful and an intoxicating musky scent threatened to overwhelm her.

She dragged herself out of her reverie to snarl. "*Scunung*, I will not succumb to your wiccan trickery. I have been trained to resist!"

"Oh that's such a shame I so did not to want hurt you, is this more like what you expected?" Sirki launched a blast of nerve fire at her and Glaser yelped.

"I know how painful this is, my dear, I had to suffer it myself during training" continued Sirki in her melodic voice.

"If I wasn't tied up I would ring your scrawny neck." spat Glaser.

"I'm afraid that has been tried before" Sirki indicated her scarred throat then drew her *seax and* catching the light on its *glaem* blade she played it across Heidi's face. "My youngest daughter would use this on you quite happily I'm sure, but I have very different ideas to her" the voice sank to almost a whisper and Glaser found herself straining to hear it. "I really think you should tell me everything I want to know, it would be so nice if you did" Sirki quietly slid the blade back into its sheath leaving the *saetere* looking attentively to where it had been.

She leaned forward and gently turned Heidi's face to her's.

Fro Scartho was so beautiful, how could she withhold anything from this goddess?

"Who do you work for?" asked Sirki pressing *record* on her wristband.

"The Andgiete Craeftgemot" replied her prisoner.

"But were they not forced to disband thirty years ago?"

"A group of them escaped and set up elsewhere" answered Glaser.

"Now that's interesting, I really would like to know where they are."

"I can't tell you that because I don't know."

"Why not, don't they trust you? I trust you" the voice felt like velvet to her ears.

"It's like being part of a chain, you only see the link on either side and I was but one part of a cell based in New Winchester" she admitted. "The rest of my comrades died at the hands of your imps this night."

"You must know where they are though, how do you receive instructions?"

"I have a communicator which connects directly to them but only within a specific timeframe." replied Glaser.

"Do you have it with you?" *This could be advantageous.*

"No it is hidden at my home."

Sirki sent a telepathic message to Effie to dispatch a Guard unit to search her apartment. "And how did you become part of this group?" she continued.

"During a protest against allowing *scunung* to stand for the Witangemot I was rather vocal and afterwards some people suggested I could be useful to a certain group. I met with them several times and carried out some nuisance *actions* on their behalf before being asked to join. I then received training at a location in Frisha and was fitted with an implant."

"Where is this location?"

"I don't know, we travelled in a flier with blacked out windows" replied Glaser. "But it was in the middle of a forest."

"Why did you join the ACG?" Sirki was curious.

"I believe that you are attempting to supplant the human race and a world controlled by abominations is something that cannot be contemplated, you must be stopped at any cost!" she replied in all honesty.

"But Heidi, we were created by humans to protect them, to be their obedient servants and be willing to die without question. Some of your *craeftwitan* remembered what humanity meant and interfered with the programme to make sure we retained individuality and free will. You norms created us and like it or not we are here to stay!"

Glaser did not reply.

"Would you be willing to die for your cause?" asked Sirki.

"If it came to it I believe I would" she answered.

"You are brave Heidi, I wonder if I could be in your position?" Sirki felt it was time to get back to the matter in question. "Why did you drug me the other night?"

"To create the same psychosis that we did in the others, it was thought if you were to become unbalanced you might hurt or kill people around you and this could take the Reignweald's attention from our operation." answered Glaser willingly.

"Your operation, oh of course, so why are the ACG kidnapping Psi?"

"I really don't know, I am told as little as possible in case I am captured and interrogated." she laughed sardonically. "All I know is that is of vital importance to the cause."

"You obviously intended to kill or kidnap two of my children this night and I believe it to be the latter because of the shackles and tranquilisers found in your *waegn*." stated Sirki.

"Our orders were to acquire only your daughter, not your son. We didn't even know he was there."

"Why were you told to kidnap Sari, why did you want her in particular?" Sirki felt herself getting angry.

"I overheard what was being said at the party and stayed despite the risk of you becoming dangerous. After overhearing various comments I deduced that she is somehow the child of three people, you, the Thegn and that Huscarl *bicce* Anderson. I informed my controller of this and we were told to acquire her at all costs." she informed Sirki.

Sirki was barely able to control her anger. "You are responsible for this?" She stood, clenching her fists at her sides. "I should kill you, you are *nej* more human than you imagine us to be!" she released her hold on Glaser, who realising what had been done to her, glared sullenly. Sirki summoned the others who had been listening in via her wristband. "What do we do with you now Heidi?" wondered Sirki aloud.

Sari strode up to the girl to grab her hair and pull her head back while half drawing her *seax*. "I'm going to cut your throat you cunt!" she snarled.

"*NEJ*" ordered Sirki. "We are better than that! The ACG will work out we have their *saetere* and they know we will break her" she turned to Glaser. "You're as good as dead and you know it. The Palace Guard are busy taking your home apart at this moment and it is bound to be noticed, if we were to shove you out of the front gate you might last a couple of days before your ACG friends found you and as I recall they do not reward failure."

Heidi looked uneasy at this.

"We could drive to her the centre of New Winchester and drop her off near one of the monitor cameras so it would be recorded?" suggested Sari. "That ought to do it."

"Perhaps, not tonight though?" mused Sirki. "Aesh, escort our guest to the smallest bedroom and lock her in. Heidi, you are to stay here for the time being."

"What?" Sari was incandescent. "You're turning your home into a fucking hotel for the ACG?"

Aesh untied the agent and escorted her from the room.

"Mum, I have to agree with my suster, this traitor should be handed over to the Palace or at least the Ward" added Aelf.

"She could be of further use, she knows how these people work" explained Sirki. "Her's was not the only *saetere* nest in the Reignweald and she knows that if she escapes her former masters will kill her."

"Unbelievable!" exclaimed Aelf before leaving the room.

"Mummy, I can't let the kids stay here with *that* thing under the roof, I am packing their things and tomorrow we are going to Scartho to join dad." Sari had had enough.

"I understand *lapsi* even though it makes me very sad, Aesh will escort you back safely in the morning."

"Are you sure you can spare your *bicce*, hasn't she got her work cut out servicing you or have you intentions on the spy now?" she spat. "No wonder dad left you!"

When Bren left upon discovering her latest affair Sirki had suggested another triangular relationship including Elke but this time he emphatically refused and she had brazenly moved the infatuated *Huscarl* into her home. "Dahling I'm just worried for your safety." Sirki assured her. "I still love your dad we're just having a few problems at the moment."

"Loge, and my genetic mother, do you still love her?"

"*Juu*, if I'm honest I love her more" confessed Sirki, she missed Penni so much.

"Yet you have that *Huscarl bicce* living with you?"

"She is just a fling, a passion that's all."

"Gods, you astound me! I'll take my own flyer in the morning, I don't need your girlfriend to escort us, good night mother!" Sari stormed out.

Aesh returned to the room as her daughter left. "I have locked the prisoner away for the night." she paused. "You do realise this room is only soundproof if the door is closed don't you? I heard just about everything that was said, Sirki, I know this is just a fling but it hurts to hear you say so. I do have feelings you know, if I'm in the way just tell me?"

"*Nej*, I still want you with me." Sirki felt dreadful, *how many people could she upset in just a few minutes?*

"I'm going up, do you want me in your bed when you come up?" asked the *Huscarl*.

"*Jaa*, Elke, please, I need some company tonight."

Sirki sat tinkering aimlessly at the piano, Penni had found someone else, Bren had finally given up on her, Aelfred was pissed off, she had upset Elke and to top it off her daughter was taking the grandchildren away tomorrow.

Sari said nothing at breakfast but eventually gave a brief farewell to her mother, the grandchildren made a big fuss of their *mummo* before they went.

Sari hugged Anya tightly and after giving her mother a disgruntled look climbed into the flyer. They watched until it disappeared from sight then the housekeeper glared at Sirki before flouncing into the house as Aelf came to stand beside her.

"I suppose you're going too?" inquired Sirki.

"No mum, I'm staying to help Aesh watch over Glaser, you do know that Heidi can't stay here indefinitely?"

"I know but I think she has more to tell us."

"She would slit your throat the first chance she got, ma'am, I say we hand her over to the Palace" Aesh had joined them.

"Is she locked in tight?" asked Aelfred.

"Yes, but I haven't taken her breakfast up yet" replied Aesh.

"I'll do it" he volunteered. "Don't worry I'll be careful."

"He's soft on her" observed Elke as he went inside. "Are all you Da N'tans bloody stupid or what?"

"He's inherited his dad's introspective nature and my humanity and I'm proud of him for that!" answered Sirki. "But I think we may be about to lose the option on keeping Glaser."

A black dot on the horizon was growing into the shape of a Flying Beetle.

CHAPTER 17 - DEVELOPMENTS

The armoured airship landed on the rear lawn to disgorge a tithe of soldiers flanking a figure in a black cowl. They were Alphas in Palace dress uniform with cornflower blue collars, Psi Wing Guards!

"I've come to meet your guest" path'd the hooded figure.

"You had better come in" answered Sirki.

Aesh escorted Glaser into the lounge and sat her down to face the two women on the couch.

"What now?" Heidi had lost none of her sullen demeanour.

"She is not restrained?" exclaimed the hooded figure.

"She cannot escape from me and has nowhere to go if she could" returned Sirki.

Glaser scowled as Mina Srivastava lifted her hood to regard her, the Highest's hair was white as snow and her face lined, she was ninety two years old but still in perfect health and as sharp as a pin. "*Galdrea,* Fro Scartho believes you have some value still, do you?"

"The *dryicge* already made me tell her everything I know!" she replied insolently.

"Interesting... you mentioned you contact your superiors at specific times?" remarked the Highest and Glaser nodded. "Would that be midday by any chance?"

"Midday or midnight when possible, how can you know that?" asked Glaser.

"That's my secret," replied Mina. "This communicator you were given has only the one channel I take it?"

"Yes it was set on one channel when I received it" Glaser was being open without any form of coercion. *If keeping the abominations happy could guarantee her safety then so be it.*

"We need you to send a message to your controller today, at noon. You will tell them that the mission has failed, that you are on the run and need help." ordered Mina.

"While you, of course, track the signal, how fucking stupid do you think I am?" spat Heidi.

"Remember what we discussed last night?" Sirki reminded her. "Shall we just drop you off in New Winchester in front of the Palace?" Glaser blenched and Sirki continued. "Now will you do it for me? I'm not using any *wiccary* this time, just appealing to your better nature *and* your desire for self-preservation."

The main dish at Winchester Airdock and the receiver at the new *Huscarl* garrison in Kernow were detailed to triangulate the signal when Glaser sent her midday distress call...

Later that evening, thirty *Huscarls* of the 3rd Elite encircled a *ciethehus* on the London dockside. The building was home to the Tamesis Worthy Marchant Company which allegedly shipped agro-botanical chemickals to Europa, Oostende in particular. The address had been given to Glaser as a safe place of refuge and the surrounding area had been sealed off by the Ward to avoid unnecessary casualties as an assault force, under the command of Bydel Banerjee entered the building from the street and waterfront. The only real opposition was encountered on the dockside where Banerjee's men had to fight their way through a maze of crates and when calm was restored they took stock, one *Huscarl* had been badly injured by a grenade while three others were slightly wounded, the ACG had lost eight men with five taken prisoner including their officer and a wide range psionic suppressor along with a new mark of torc headsets was discovered in a *waegn* parked inside.

More importantly, the officer was captured with an *atellan* containing some interesting looking codes. After a PRW *rihtleech* removed the implant from the nasal cavity of the ACG Undercempa he was personally *interviewed* by Mina Srivastava and as suspected, the codes held the key for the scrambled radio signals. The device also revealed the location of the ACG Europan training base and orders regarding Glaser were discovered in the atellan's memory too, if the *saetere* managed to reach the safe-house she was to be summarily executed for endangering operations.

The 2nd *Cohort* of the South Essex *Here* was on manoeuvres in Northern Frisha when their Cempa received orders to capture the facility with as little collateral damage as possible. Since the base was not large its small garrison put up only a token resistance before surrendering to the Reignweald forces, they attempted to wipe the memories of their *atellans* but a PRW *craeftwitan* assigned to the task force was hopeful something useful could be retrieved.

The reply to Glaser's distress call had been traced to Oostende, specifically to a hostelry in the old harbour quarter and a watch was set on the Blue Dolphin alehouse. If Glaser reported here it was likely that other ACG agents did so once again Jocasta Blane found herself in the old fishing port but this time in an official capacity. She was sitting on the harbour-side sipping a cocktail, non-alcoholic of course, when her *Huscarl* contact joined her at the table. It was none other than Cempa Minto, the officer who oversaw the incident at the forum, despite wearing colourful clothes and dark glasses to conceal his bright blue eyes his large frame and mien marked him out as a *Huscarl*.

"Care to buy a thirsty fellow a drink?" he asked.

"*Well Minto, what do you know?*" path'd Blane in greeting.

He glanced across the harbour to the Blue Dolphin, "*We have two detector waegns on the headland to track the signal and my scotae are all over the dock raring to go when you give the word, so Psi Blane, what now?*"

"*We sit tight and wait, I'll get you that drink.*" she stood and walked to the counter. Minto still found it hard to believe a

Psi could look like Blane, her red hair positively glowed in the sunlight and her shorts displayed shapely legs.

With her complexion it's a wonder she doesn't burn in this sun, he thought her very attractive, *if she's atypical I wonder if she's ever...* he suppressed the thought quickly as Blane was returning.

"Mister Minto, you need to learn to control your thoughts" she remarked handing him an ice-cold bottle of Thor. "Have you never heard of sun block? *Oh and that thing you suppressed just too late, yes I have but only in the line of duty.*"

Minto gave a grin of embarrassment. "Sorry 'bout that, I don't normally have much truck with you lot outside of battle did you well er... like it?" he knew Psi did not normally indulge in carnal pleasure.

"I found it quite acceptable and wouldn't rule out doing it again" she answered. "How are you fixed for this afternoon?"

"Huh" he exclaimed.

"I'm just jesting, my handsome!" she informed him with a smile, *he's quite good-looking.*

They sat for half an hour then walked past the Blue Dolphin arm-in-arm like a proper couple, the sign outside boasted "The best food in Old Oostende" *it seemed quite a nice place* she thought, shame it was heading for a big fall.

"*Madam Hierophant*" the call came from one of her sister Psi stationed in a tracking *waegn* "*We're picking up a transmission and they're talking about the raid in London. We have triangulation on a point twenty miles out to sea.*"

"*Out to sea?*" queried Jocasta.

"*Yes ma'am, Seaforce has a syndigbat on patrol quite near to Oostende and orders will be issued to redirect it, check?*" replied the Psi.

"*Check, we'll move on the hotel.*" affirmed Blane before giving the word to Minto.

*Campscrid*s screeched to a halt in front of the Blue Dolphin and armoured *Huscarl*s rushed in to disturb the diners. Minto and Blane who were following, rushed upstairs to burst into the office where a man sat poised to send a message on a desktop communicator, Minto raised his Draca pistol but the man was frozen in situ as if playing at *statues*.

The Cempa looked at Blane. "You?" he asked

"No need to say ta cock, just doing a proper job." replied Blane, mimicking his Kernowek accent again.

Two of the *kitchen staff* dashed out of the back door in an attempt to escape only to run into the arms of waiting *Huscarl*s. "Not bad Ma'am, we got the whole bleddy cell without firing a shot" observed Minto.

"Not bad at all Cempa and by the way my friends call me Cassie or Casta" she smiled.

A short time later, out at sea, *Aeglaedere* Beck looked up from the tracker screen. "Sensors confirm a small object one half mile south of our position, sir!" the Royal Seaforce Flota Sif had travelled to a point twenty miles out from Oostende. "Position corresponds with Beacon 1957."

"Full power, hard a larboard!" ordered the Capitan and the submarine picked up speed to head towards its target, once there it surfaced before slowing to stop at a distance of 100 yards allowing Captain Paulinus to examine the object from the conning tower with his binocle. It was a red warning buoy anchored there to warn of a hidden reef, it checked out as a genuine marker but several parabolic dishes fixed to it spoke of an unofficial modification.

Paulinus forwarded his observations to Oostende and was then ordered to hold station and await further instruction. Shortly afterwards the order came that special attention was to be given to the angle of the antennae but they were not to be tampered with in any way so the sub's drone, a disc-like flyer three feet in diameter with stereo vision and a pair of multipurpose claws, was sent skimming across the waves.

Upon closer inspection the dishes were found to be attached to a large square enclosure painted the same colour as the buoy and secured to the beacon tower by sturdy bolts while a thick cable ran from it to disappear into the hull, no doubt connected to the same power cells that drove the official warning lamp and signal radio. The angle and position of the antennae were duly noted and when the drone returned to the submarine Paulinus received a new set of orders, they were to sail to Oostende and meet with a Psi there.

The *syndigbal* remained on the surface for its journey to the harbour so Paulinus stood with *Frumlida* Delaney in the conning tower observing the port as they drew closer.

"What do you think they want sir?" asked the chief petty officer.

"Who knows with Psi? From what I've seen they're a strange lot."

"Never met any myself, sir" replied Delaney.

"Seen a couple at Pompey, they're pale thin creatures who look like a good breeze would blow them away. It's hard to believe they're related to those herculean sods the Alphas" continued Paulinus. The vessel was now heading for the large modern dock adjacent to the picturesque old harbour.

"Looks like we're expected" observed Delaney pointing to a group of figures on the dockside. As the sub manoeuvred into its berth the two sailors took stock, eleven *Huscarls* stood at attention wearing battledress with maroon berets, they were toting enough weaponry to start a small war and had the swords they venerated so much sheathed at their sides. The soldiers all had a similar look with corn blonde hair and deep blue eyes regardless of ethnicity, Paulinus thought he had never seen so many lantern jaws before, and some were women!

"Like a pack of bloody werewolves" muttered Delaney as he went below to supervise docking.

Two figures came forward as the submarine moored up. The first was a tall man who resembled the others, *obviously the officer*, the other was a sturdy but shapely redheaded woman with pale blue eyes. She was wearing leaf-pattern drabs and a black cowl, her only weaponry being a short *seax* at her side.

Sif tied up, the gangplank was lowered and Paulinus walked down to meet the reception committee. The *Huscarls* all clicked their heels smartly while the woman merely nodded. "*Wassael*, I'm Capitan Paulinus of the RSF Sif," he noticed a blue badge with a golden trident and a IV on the woman's right cuff.

She saw his look. "Yes I'm a Psi, are you surprised, Capitan?"

"Aye ma'am" she was fourth level, a high ranker. "It's just that you look nothing like one… I mean… nay offence meant."

"None taken" she continued. "I am Hierophant Blane and this is Cempa Minto of the 5th Elites" she gestured to the officer.

"The Fifth, you're fairly a new outfit aren't you?" asked Paulinus.

"That's right, Capitan, the Legion celebrates its fifth anniversary this year aptly enough!" answered Minto swelling with pride. The 5th Elite Guards had been personally commissioned by the queen in recognition for years of loyalty and were based in Kernow, the smallest nation of the Reignweald. The entire country was smaller than the Thegnweald of Jorvik yet nevertheless managed supply a large amount of recruits for the *Huscarl*s. With over fifty percent of the Kernowek population *novae*, and growing, the Reeve had petitioned the Palace for its instatement as a Thegnweald even requesting the queen herself act as Thegn but they had settled for her son, the Atheling Sigebert known as Jack. His older (by two minutes) twin sister Gil would accede to the throne after Ethelflaeda.

"So what do you want with me?" enquired the Capitan after he had been driven to the *Huscarl* base next to the airdock. He was sat in Minto's office with the odd couple facing him.

"So Ianus, how much do you know about this mission?" asked the redhead.

"Not much" he replied in all honesty.

"Check, now this is off the record so I'm not telling you this. The Andgiete Craeftgemot, ever hear of them?" she asked.

"I was only a baby when they tried to depose the queen but I did learn about them at school, they don't exist now do they?" Paulinus was puzzled as to why this mattered.

Blane remembered her involvement in the run up to the coup and the danger she had faced. "Capitan Paulinus, they are still very much in existence and are spreading like a stain, we are trying to find their latest hiding place to eradicate them once and for all."

"And the buoy is important to this?" this was scary stuff, he had no real axe to grind with the *novae* but he knew people in Aengland who would welcome this revelation, and sadly some were in Seaforce.

"The buoy is transmitting a signal to a satellite operated by the ACG." Blane informed him.

"The ACG can launch satellites?" he was surprised at this.

"Not in their current incarnation, but before the coup they were at their peak and worked alongside the RAF on the Ket anti-missile system, it would have been simple enough to launch a satellite to a higher orbit. They probably had some sinister use in mind for it but thirty years later it's still up there nice and convenient for their secret communications."

"Can't the RAF track it?"

"Space is somewhat large Capitan, and we don't have the facilities that were available before the Q-war but we now know where to look by using the angles of the topmost dishes. We need to wait until the correct time of day for them to transmit and then you may disconnect the device and remove it, if this proves impossible you will have to destroy the buoy" she answered.

"I could have done that already!" Paulinus interjected.

"We would prefer to have it in one piece if possible, Ianus can you trust your crew?" asked Blane.

"Of course I can and I feel insulted by that question, you may as well ask if you can trust me!" retorted Paulinus.

"I know I can trust you Capitan, I read you moment I met you" replied Blane.

"What? This is an outrage, you didn't ask my permission and I'm pretty fucking certain I wouldn't give it if you had. By Mithras, there's little wonder some people distrust you!" he was fuming.

"Which people are they?" asked Blane with interest.

"Curse you, *bicce!*" he snapped.

"At least you didn't call me a *dryicge* or *scunung*. I'm sorry Capitan but we have a deep heartfelt hatred for the

ACG. I was once in danger of being tortured by them and they are not nice people, they represent the worst that is possible of *your* humanity so we have to take these precautions and I apologise." she explained.

Minto who had been silent up to now, grunted and nodded in affirmation.

"I can see your reasoning but it doesn't make me feel any better" replied Paulinus reluctantly.

"Hmm, well this isn't going to make you very happy either, I need to meet your crew, all of them. We can do this easily or Minto's *ferdrinc* can board your vessel and make it very hard!" she hated doing this but orders were orders and this came from the Highest herself.

"What if I refuse, if you arrest us who will disconnect the bloody device for you?" he asked.

"Then it's Plan B, we blow it out of the water, which of course will leave an unmarked danger to shipping but there you go. If I was to say please would it help?" she asked, *curse it, if I was Fro Scartho he'd be eating out of my hand by now but you can't teach what she has.*

Paulinus grudgingly allowed Blane and Minto onboard his vessel informing the crew it was a goodwill visit from the local commander and his rightwife. They were escorted around the sub while Jocasta, wearing a figure hugging dress, scanned for ACG agents. The crew were very courteous to their guests, especially to the psi who they took to be a norm.

Minto shook Ianus' hand as they left the submarine. "Thank you Capitan, you have been most accommodating."

"Oh thank you so much, it's been so interesting." gushed Blane and pretending to kiss Paulinus on the cheek said. "Watch your *Frumlida*, he's not with the ACG but he harbours anti-nova sentiments."

"Thanks for that, but I knew that already and didn't need to read his mind!" he retorted. *Paulinus trusted Delaney and hoped his judgement was correct.*

As Blane and Minto drove back to base he ventured. "So if you're pretending to be my rightwife in the line of duty, how far does that pretence extend?"

Jocasta found her new colleague amusing, *what the hell it wouldn't hurt would it? "Alright, I don't have to go off duty just yet so get me back to base before I change my mind,"* she pathed.

At midnight Blane was woken by her Psi contact in the monitor *waegn*. A transmission had been intercepted originating from Port Dubris in Kenta, the shire had been a bastion of support for the ACG and anti-*nova* feeling still ran deep there. If anywhere in Aengland was hiding an ACG cell, it would be Kenta.

Poking Minto in the ribs she announced. "Oy Cad, get up, it's show-time!" she swung her legs out of bed to stand up and the *Huscarl* took note of the Ansuz tattoo on her right thigh, *only Psi' wear the rune of Loge the trickster and communicator*. He sported a line around his right wrist to show allegiance to Lludd Llaw Eraint who lost his right hand and had it replaced by a metal one, rather like the Aenglish Tiw. His eyes wandered to her ample bosom.

"Stop ogling my tits and get dressed, soldier!" ordered Jocasta.

After receiving word from Blane the sub manoeuvred as close as safely possible to the hidden reef and the drone was sent out for the second time in as many days. The retaining bolts of the antenna housing were carefully unscrewed and after thoroughly checking for booby traps a line was attached then the drone withdrew to a safe distance and taking up the slack in its claws, reversed quickly away The whole thing scraped along the top of the buoy and off to end hanging by its thick power cord, there was no explosion so the drone cut the cable and returned to the Sif with its prize.

Blane thanked Paulinus at the quayside. "Well done Capitan, sorry if we ruffled your feathers earlier you did a great job."

"Thank you ma'am, have you found what you were looking for?" he asked watching the transmitter being loaded into an olive green *waegn*.

"We have Capitan and appropriate action will be taken." answered the Psi.

On returning to the submarine he found Delaney waiting in the conning tower. "Did the werewolves get what they wanted sir?"

"They did *Frumlida* and they're human beings not werewolves."

"If you say so sir, did they tell you what it was all about, the buoy and everything?"

"Sorry, Chief, it's classified" he replied before adding. "Delaney, I know you're a bit mistrustful of our *novae* cousins but we are all on the same side."

"I know that sir but they're just not *us* if you know what I mean?"

Oh I know exactly what you mean and I'm going to be watching you closely from now on, Frumlida. Curse you Blane for putting doubt in my mind!

Two figures stood on the quayside watching the submarine pulling away.

"It's out of our hands now I take it?" asked Minto.

"The RAF will deal with the satellite and then the 3rd Elites will finish the job" answered Blane.

CHAPTER 18 – SATELLITE

Gugnir, so named for Woden's magical spear, was not a single weapon but a ring of satellites, six powerful *liegswaepn* platforms orbiting equidistantly 500 miles above the ground and maintaining position with gyroscopes and thrusters. The Ring completed an entire cross-polar orbit in one and a half hours always vigilant for a Ket missile launch, further out in geostationary orbit were the four communications satellites Arke, Hermod, Mercure, and Thoth but orbiting somewhere between them and completing an orbit once every twelve hours was an unknown object now located by following the signal from the buoy. The little satellite, nicknamed Sigin, after Loge the trickster's loyal wife, had redirected the signal to a point roughly 130 miles south of Tolosa. The precise location of the receiver could not be traced but now they had a starting point and the Reignweald also knew exactly where the satellite would be at any given point. But the problem was, what to do about it?

The answer came from a RAF craeftwitan at the Steorra dock. The Gugnir Ring had an effective range of about 600-900 miles maximum, more than enough to hit a missile before it reached apogee if launched from the Ket territories or continental Europa but it fell short of Sigin's orbit by over eleven and a half thousand miles. They couldn't increase the range of the *liegswaepn* platforms but perhaps one could be moved closer to the target.

"This craeftwitan fellow is actually suggesting we move one of the Gugnirs out of the defence ring, what if the Ket should decide to launch?" demanded the somewhat vexed *Wigfruma*. "Admittedly they've been quiet for a long time but they could be plotting anything, how do we know they're not in league with the resurgent ACG?"

The Foreign Secretary replied patiently. "Sir, as far as our intelligence can tell the Ket continue to direct their attention eastwards and apart from the odd minor incident it has been nearly five years since any serious border incursion. The last missile launches were twenty seven years ago and I seem to recall Gugnir destroyed only one of those, combined fire from ground based liegswaepn batteries and a lot of luck brought down the other! It's hardly a high success rate and yet we replace them every ten years at great expense," she reminded him and several *witan* nodded in agreement.

The Home Secretary launched into his argument. "Ladies, gentlemen, if we were to divert one of these weapons and carefully reposition the remaining five, the delay in traverse of a single platform across Ket territory would be but three minutes more and I believe we could live with that until a replacement can be launched. Might I remind you that while the Ket are theoretically capable of launching an attack upon the Reignweald the resurgent ACG are actually carrying out a campaign against us, firstly by using mind altering drugs to turn our Psi' into paranoid psychotics even managing to administer this drug to the Omega herself. And when you consider her potential it was fortuitous she was not greatly affected, especially given the fact she is often in the company of the Royal Family. Secondly and more sinister is the kidnapping of Psi' and given the ACG's past record of experimentation and torture I dread to think what these poor girls, most of whom have yet to reach their second decade, have suffered since their abduction. With this in mind I beg you, my fellow *witan*, to agree to this motion. We have a unique opportunity to cut the ACG off from their *saeteres*, their agents in the field!" a brief ripple of applause followed and he carried on. "The satellite's signal was tracked to southwest Frankia, the Pirren Mountains to be precise. The 3rd Elite *cohort* based in Tolosa has been mobilised and their Campaeldor will be joining them shortly with several thousand troops to assist in conducting the search."

The Foreladtwa stood to address them. "So, my fellow *Witan*, will you give your assent to the proposed motion that we deviate one of the defence satellites from its orbit in an attempt to destroy the relay station?"

After vigorous discussion the entire *Witangemot* found itself split down the middle meaning they had no choice but to approach Queen *Interferer* who had held back until now, her decision came as no great surprise to anyone.

"They want what?" asked Bryce Campbell, as Head Controller of the Nevis radio antenna the defence system was his responsibility. "We have managed the Gugnir Ring since it was established and now the bloody Aenglish just want to take control?"

"It's only for a short while Bryce," the Foreladtwa of Caledonia assured him. "They want to re-purpose Gugnir 1 for a special mission."

"And what might that be, may I ask?"

"Nay Bryce, you may not, this order comes from the Witangemot of the Reignweald and with the sanction of the Palace!" he signed off and removed the brown lenses from his eyes. Caledonia had been covertly run by *novae* for thirty years now but still they dared not reveal themselves, the population, while not openly hostile were uncomfortable with the idea of *novae* running the country. Caledonia was held to be a rational neutral country and considered a safe pair of hands so governance of the powerful weapon had been handed to them. The knowledge that such a powerful weapon was under the control of their fellows suited both Queen and *novae* alike.

Bryce Campbell threw up his hands in disbelief then made a call to RAF New Winchester.

As Gugnir 1 crossed the North Pole its attitude thrusters fired and the satellite slowly began to gain the speed required to break orbit. It would take the small vehicle a week to reach the same altitude as its target and as it was the oldest member of the Ring, due to be replaced the next year, its sacrifice was deemed acceptable.

With Anderson's permission Connor took an armoured convoy out to search for the signal's destination. They were keeping air activity to a minimum to avoid arousing the ACG's suspicion but when the Campaeldor arrived in two days with the larger force it would be impossible to hide the operation, meaning Connor had just a small window of opportunity to catch the enemy unawares.

The only stipulation imposed on him was that a high ranking Psi *saetere* be attached to the mission. She was a fourth level atypical who was something of a legend in the Psi Wing, having been involved in the downfall of the original ACG she had recently captured a psychotic Psi and taken part in the operation that uncovered the relay station at Oostende.

Minto had become close to Blane and was sorry to see her leave but she promised to return as soon as possible realising she would miss him too. Bizarrely, Jocasta had found her deviation from accepted behaviour had been accompanied by an increase in psionic power.

Connor's squadron was comprised of a Fox *campscrid* scouting ahead of a mighty Einherjar RCW with three Spearman troop carriers bringing up the rear. While riding with Blane in the first carrier he noted that she somewhat resembled Fro Scartho in profile and also had a similar resonation. *Did she come from the same genetic strain? It seemed unlikely but...* Connor decided it prudent to ask at a more convenient time.

The expedition pushed forward into the forest and as the vegetation began to thicken the tracked RCW was brought forward to force a path through the dense undergrowth that slowed their progress but soon they would have to stop and make a decision as to their next move.

The party made camp on what little level ground could be found then Connor and Blane, forced to share a tent, fell into conversation. A question was gnawing at her. "So this Campaeldor Anderson, I haven't met her before, what's she's like?"

"She's from Kernow" he replied. "She was so warm and friendly when I first met her but recently she's become hardened and sour. I suppose it's the responsibility, I remember how the Thegn changed when he was promoted."

"We all change" replied Blane, considering what was happening to her then asked. "Those rumours about the Campaeldor and Fro Scartho, are they true?"

"What rumours?" this was none of her business as far as he was concerned. "I thought you Psi knew everything about everyone."

"No, I'm not part of the coven, *they* don't tell me anything." Jocasta was referring to the tight group formed by Mina, Bonnie and Elswyth Da N'tan. "Nor do I move in such exulted circles to have met the Thegn or Fro Scartho."

"And you a fourth level Psi?" he queried.

"If your face doesn't fit you're not in and look at my face, it definitely doesn't fit" she answered.

"It looks fine to me but I have to admit you don't look like a Psi," he could see the resemblance to Sirki again. "Look, the Campaeldor and Fro Scartho are close friends and they were once *extremely* close friends and that's all I'll say, check?"

"Yes, check," she said knowingly.

"You don't come from Soomi do you?" he asked curiously.

"No, Wessex, New Winchester why do you ask?"

"It's just that you look like someone I know from Soomi." replied Connor.

"Well I do have Soomi blood, my grandma came from Purri. Her parents ran a coffee plantationary there."

"Were they *novae?*" he asked.

"My *suuri-mummo* was but her husband was norm, that's where I get my red hair from." she smiled. "Who's this person you know?"

"Oh just a girl from years ago, we'd better get some sleep, ma'am, we need an early start if we're to find anything before the circus arrives, check?"

"Check, good night Connor" she could feel he was being evasive *why?*

Connor's attempt at sleep was ruined when the Tithengealdor in charge of fire-watch spoke urgently outside the *feldhus*. "Sir, the picket's spotted unusual activity up ahead."

"What?"

"Looks like the enemy," he replied.

"Coming this way?"

"No sir, the picket thinks they have no idea we're here."

"Check, we'll come and have a look."

Blane had managed to fall asleep and it gave him great pleasure to wake her. *"WHAT?"* her thought echoed in his head.

"Come on ma'am, we need you."

The picket, having heard noise upslope from their position had cautiously investigated to discover a group of men in dark uniforms dismantling a large parabolic dish antenna. Connor and the Tithengealdor joined them with Blane in tow to act as their telepathic relay and waited for the rest of the group to catch up.

"They appear to be dismantling it sir!" observed the picket's Undergealdor. *"Looks like a bloody big satellite dish, is that what we're looking for?"*

"I'd bet a thousand marks it is and we've camped right next to the bloody thing" replied Connor.

"I would hazard a guess that they've been spooked into taking the installation down by our increased activity in Tolosa." path'd Blane as reinforcements arrived.

A low flat vehicle hovered into sight. *"There's a lift-waegn coming collect it but why put it here?"* Connor wondered.

"It's right on the edge of a massive flat zone, I can feel it like a wall in front of me, if we were any further forward I wouldn't be able to relay your thoughts." replied Blane.

"Then how does it communicate to their base?" he mused. *"A landline, maybe a light relay…"* they began to unbolt a lensed device fixed to a tall mast sat on a tripod next to the dish and Connor realised it was a light amplification relay. It would point directly to another in a chain leading right to the ACG base. *"Fuck! It's the best lead we've got, Tithengealdor get those bahstards before they take the bloody thing down!"*

As the *Huscarls* moved in the *waegn* attempted to flee only to be downed by a grenade round sending it crashing into the installation. At this the ACG squad leader callously launched a grenade into the wreckage to destroy it completely and killing many of his men in the process. The rest fought if they were invincible, without concern for their own safety, which of course they were not.

Connor had seen this behaviour on the eastern border fighting Ket clone troops and after checking the bodies a shiver ran down his spine, the dead soldiers were virtually identical to one another.

The Tithengealdor, another veteran from the East Frisha campaigns, examined the dead soldiers to exclaim. "Fucking hell, not here?"

Some of the younger *Huscarls* looked puzzled. "They have done it my fellow *ferdrinc!*" explained Connor. "The bahstards have finally managed to breed their own clones!" *This could get very bad if we don't stop them quickly.*

Their officer had been killed, so Blane tried probing two prisoners but on attempting to enter their minds found herself blocked by their implants. "I won't find anything out until they're removed, we'll have to return to town and get a *rihtleech* to do it."

"If they have many more clones we may be in for a bloody conflict..." warned Connor, the light relay had been destroyed making it impossible to deduce the location of the next station. *The ACG had won the first round.*

Gugnir 1 was far from Nerth and slowly gaining on its prey which was now at the furthest range of its liegswaepn and the weapons platform was travelling so fast it would get at best two shots as it hurtled past the target. The vessel used the last of its fuel to turn the energy weapon towards the enemy satellite and the on-board camera, set to maximum zoom, revealed a tiny X shaped object shining in Sol's light. The image was all that could be resolved of Sigin at this distance, the satellite itself was a large silver cylinder with disc antennae and wing-like solar panels, rather like Gugnir 1.

A great many people were in the *steorhus* at New Winchester Airdock watching events unfold on the long-range tracking system. Several dignitaries were present including Freya Da N'tan as the representative for Scartho with Dexter Sartorius, who she had dragged in on her arm as consort, and all were watching intently as the main view-screen displayed Sigin's tiny image against the blackness of space.

"Gugnir 1 is 750 miles from target and closing" announced the monitor operator.

"Passing furthest range now, coming to optimum in 5, 4, 3, 2, 1, fire!" ordered the Aeldor Controller.

There was a flash and the picture was lost, where there had been two blips on the tracker screen now just one could be seen heading rapidly away. A cheer went up, *they had done it!*

Gugnir 1 travelled on alone in the darkness oblivious to its achievement, as it had passed within 300 miles of the target its liegswaepn activated and a glowing blue line briefly linked the two small spacecraft before Sigin exploded silently into a rapidly expanding cloud of sparkling fragments. One had struck and damaged Gugnir 1 which was now spinning end over end on its journey further into the void to begin a long elliptical orbit of its home planet. Gravity would one day capture the small vehicle to pull it back for a fiery homecoming.

Campaeldor Anderson was aboard the newly commissioned King-class *entaflota* Athelstan, it was twice the size of its fellows Henghist and Horsa II at its flanks while a pair of Raven *hereflota* followed closely. Two and half thousand fighting men and women were travelling to an area south of Tolosa to join Cempa Connor. It would take several more hours to reach the landing zone but it was large enough to land the entire fleet only twenty miles from the base of the Pirren.

Scartho had lost two of its Psi' while ACG *saeteres* had attempted to abduct the Thegns daughter and Fro Scartho herself had been drugged.

The Thegnweald was seeking a reckoning.

CHAPTER 19 – CONFESSION AND RECONCILIATION

It seems I always hurt you, the last thing I mean to do.
Please forgive me.
I'm sorry I that strayed again, I wish I could stay true.
Please forgive me.
I know it's why you left me but I can't believe we're through.
Please forgive me.
(Excerpt from Sometimes I can't help myself – music and words by
A.S.Vigsdottir.)

Sirki cried out Penni's name at a very inappropriate moment, for Elke, who was feeling increasingly inadequate, it was the final straw and following a shouting match she had moved out of the house.

Sirki was currently sprawled in the lounge feeling dejected, she had managed to alienate everyone close to her with the exception of Freya, who she hardly ever saw and Alfie. *And she didn't know how he really felt.*

"Wow you look miserable, anyone would think you were the prisoner?" Glaser was now allowed free run of the house but had been put under compulsion by Sirki making her unable to leave the property of her own volition. "Penny for your thoughts?" she asked.

"Penni is partly the problem" answered Sirki disconsolately.

Glaser mulled over what she'd said. "Sorry I was genuinely curious, didn't intend to be sarcastic."

"Ever been in love Heidi?" asked Sirki.

"Once, it didn't last, since becoming a *saetere* I can't afford the distraction."

"I love two people and have lost both of them, what would you do?"

"How did you lose them?" asked Heidi.

"One left to find a new life, the other because I was stupid and hurt him."

"Have you tried saying sorry?"

"I have lost count of how often."

"Look it's not really my business but why don't you go and see him, say how you feel." *this was absurd she was trying to help with her captor's love life?* Against her better judgment Glaser was warming to the family in spite of the fact they were the enemy. Words like *dryicge* and *scunung* no longer seemed appropriate to describe them, they led normal lives, they loved and grieved, *was she being entranced by their presence?*

Sirki had already considered this solution and now Heidi had confirmed it was the right thing to do. "Alfie is still here, if I left you alone with him do you promise not to try and escape?"

"You know I can't leave without your permission, Fro?" answered Glaser truthfully. "And besides, only death awaits me out there. If the ACG find me it'll be a bullet to the head if I'm lucky."

Sirki instructed Aelfred to watch Heidi, a task he didn't seem at all reluctant to take on. She didn't bother mentioning the *Huscarl*s camped in the grounds *it would be a good test of her compulsion*. Sirki considered driving there then remembered she was still Fro Scartho, no matter the state of her marriage, and commanded one of the Elites to take her in their flyer. The Midge landed at the Hall an hour later and after taking a deep breath, Sirki strode purposefully in waving aside the attendant and making straight towards the door leading to the private quarters.

She had almost reached her goal when a familiar voice made her jump. "Well good morning to you daughter-in-law, I trust you are well?" it was Hildegard, sitting in a high backed chair and reading a newspaper, Sirki was so worked up she hadn't detected her presence.

Sirki bowed her head formally. "I am well thank you Dame Scartho and yourself?"

"My, we are correct today Sirkku or would you prefer Fro Scartho? Do you know I am actually glad to see you, have you come to your senses at last?"

Sirki was a little taken aback. "*You're* glad to see me?"

"My son has been melancholy for weeks and despite my disdain for your dubious lifestyle you make him happy" then she asked with characteristic bluntness. "Is the *Huscarl* mare still sharing your bed?" Sirki shook her head. "Good I'm glad to hear that, sit down a moment dear I'd like to talk to you."

Oh, here we go, she's going to tear me off a strip.

"It is definitely finished with this Aesh isn't it?" she continued.

"She has gone, I came to apologise to Bren," affirmed Sirki.

"Sirki, I have always liked you despite your mercurial temperament but you are a Thegn's rightwife and you must settle down as I once had to." insisted Hilly.

Sirki gave her a quizzical look. "You, Hilly, I can't believe you had to toe the line for anything?"

"I was quite the girl in my twenties and enjoyed life to the full, even on a tour of duty I always found time for horizontal pleasure, as it were. Then I met Bren's father, he was handsome charming and the heir to Scartho, I'm afraid it all rather turned my head and I became his rightwife. Now, he always had a twinkle in his eye and even after our betrothal had several lovers as I am sure you can imagine?" related Dame Scartho.

Sirki remembered Bren's father Aelfred with his mischievous grin and knew where her husband's good looks came from, she smiled and nodded.

Hilly continued. "Well I was still in my prime so I sought solace in the company of other men, quite a few in fact. This carried on for some years until I fell pregnant with our third child then the reality of my wayward behaviour caught up with me. Sirkku, I have never spoken of this before so please do not tell anyone, not even my son!" she paused and took a deep breath. "My daughter Elli is the half suster of Bonnie Ashby, you see I'd been having an affair with her father and knew when I fell pregnant it could not be Aelfred's as he was out of the country. I lied about her conception date and everyone believed Elli was born premature but I confessed all to Bren's father and to his credit he forgave me. I never cheated on him again after that and he didn't me. Then of course there was that awful business with Bonnie when her parents were killed and she was raped, Aelfred insisted we took her in and treat her as our own. So when people mockingly refer to her as the Da N'tans other daughter they are not that wide of the mark."

Sirki was moved to tears. "Why have you never shared this before, it would tear me apart if I held back something like this?"

"I am getting old Sirki and I need to get it off my chest before I die, I shared this with you this to show that I too have a past and understand more than you think."

"Hilly you mustn't keep this a secret any longer, now I know this how can I not tell Bren the truth?"

"You're right of course, I *should* get them together and tell them, but first you must make it right with my son, he loves you and has his father's forgiving nature. Just don't let him down again.

"Thank you Hilly, I do love him you know," admitted Sirki.

"Good, you'll find him in the morning room doing his paperwork, your daughter's here with her children too. I don't know what you did to upset Sari but you could kill two birds with one stone, as it were."

Thanking her mother-in-law, Sirki entered the inner quarters. "Mummo!" shouted Willa who was playing a ball game in the long hall with her brother, Sirki made a big fuss of them both then saw Sari standing in the open door of the drawing room.

"I'm going to talk to mummy now" Sirki told them and went into the room.

Sari, keeping the door open to watch her children, sat down next to her mother and started a telepathic conversation. *"So mummy, is the bicce still at the house?"*

"Elke has gone" replied Sirki.

"Not that sow, the enemy bicce!"

"Jaa, she is my guest, Sari, and I think she is starting to accept us."

Her daughter was not impressed. *"Accept us? She would kill you the first chance she got and as good as said so."*

"It's just tough talk, she's just misguided not a killer, I can tell!" affirmed Sirki.

"She drugged you, it could have caused chaos! I should have killed her out on the road." Sari path'd angrily.

"Yet she has never killed anyone in her entire life, just carried out a few acts of sabotage and spied on people. You killed five people that night Sari and poor Alfie had to shoot another to save you, what makes you better than her?" Sirki asked.

"I am ferdrinc and they were the enemy, it's my duty!" Sari was bristling.

"You are no longer a Huscarl you are a member of the public! The Ward could have arrested you for what you did, why do you think I asked the Palace Guard to clear everything up?" Sari had nothing to say in response, so leaving her daughter Sirki went into the morning room to find Bren. *"Moi,* husband." she said in greeting.

"Hei Sirki, it's good to see you?" he replied cautiously.

"I think you should know Elke has gone, I'm alone again."

"Of course you are!" he exclaimed sarcastically. "And you expect me to welcome you back with open arms?"

"Nej, I suppose not, I just wanted to say how much I miss you, you left me Bren I didn't ask you to go."

"I couldn't share you with someone else, not again!" he affirmed.

"You didn't mind with Penni?" she reminded him.

"That was different, things have changed. You need to decide what you want from our marriage."

"Bren I want you back nothing else" declared Sirki honestly.

"I can't trust you anymore Sirk, you hurt the people closest to you, it kills me to say it but it's the truth!" he answered.

"If I hadn't been drugged none of this would have happened."

"Always making excuses for your behaviour, the drug was well out of your system when you sought out Aesh. Sorry Sirki, it doesn't wash with me any longer, if I take you back how long before you're off again with someone else who takes your fancy?"

"I've never wanted any other man since I met you *rakas* but you know I have needs and you don't usually mind."

"Well things have changed!" he reiterated.

"Please Bren, don't make me beg." Tears welled in her eyes.

"I don't want you to do that" he had missed her greatly despite her infidelity.

"*Anteeksi, anteeksi rakastan sinua!*" pleaded Sirki in Soomilek, she fell to her knees openly sobbing. "Please forgive me dahling!"

Bren felt dreadful. "I have to go to a dinner with the Burgher and a parcel of bigwigs tonight, both mother and Sari have accompanied me recently but people are starting to speculate on your absence, will you come with me?"

Sirki considered it, *Alfie would be alright with Glaser for one night.* "Bren I'd love too but I'll have to fly back home to change first, check?"

"Check, we'll treat it like a first date and see how it goes from there."

Sirki would have liked to have seen Penni but she was leading the expeditionary force to Frankia and Sari actually managed an awkward goodbye before she left for New Winchester.

Freya arrived at her mother's home curious to see the ACG prisoner and smiled as Glaser did a double take before realising who she was, greeting her meekly she asked. "Fro, I hope you are well?"

"As well as can be expected with an enemy in my mother's house. She believes you to be redeemable and I respect her judgement far more than my suster does, can you be trusted?" Freya carefully scanned her while waiting for a reply.

"Your mother's generosity in guaranteeing my safety is beyond comparison and I am grateful for her leniency, I know you are trying to catch me out but I have come to the conclusion you are not so very different to us. It's hard to admit how mistaken I have been" answered Glaser tactfully.

Freya could feel Glaser's caution but did not detect any deceit in her statement. "My mother has the most forgiving nature of anyone I know and is an example that sadly, few of us can hope to imitate, my brothur is most like her in temperament"

"You seem kind, like him" Glaser pointed out.

"I try my best, sometimes I even succeed" Freya smiled. "However my younger suster has a sharper edge, you would do well to keep out of her way."

Sirki returned to greet her daughter warmly and after explaining the situation to Aelf, quickly packed some things then prevailed upon the *Huscarl* pilot once again to fly her back to Scartho.

Freya had returned to her quarters at the Airdock leaving her brothur alone with their *guest* who presently lay floating in the pool wearing a costume borrowed from Sirki, who hardly ever wore one. The glass panel wall had been slid right back allowing Heidi an unobstructed view of the clouds scudding across the sky, she climbed out to walk to the edge of the patio and take a deep breath of fresh air. *A cage was still a cage even if it was a gilded one*, she looked at the lawn stretching away, *all she had to do was step onto it and she would be outside the house.* But it was impossible, the Fro had placed an obligation on her and she was trapped just as much as if behind iron bars. Glaser returned to lay down on one of the beds by the poolside while at the far end of the garden the watching *Huscarl* relaxed.

"Hej Heidi" a voice started her from her catnap, it was the son.

"Hei Al, we're all alone, well apart from all the soldiers keeping an eye on me" she couldn't see them but wasn't naïve enough to believe the Fro would trust just her son to watch over her.

"Yeah mum just wanted to make you sure you're safe. Well actually, that's bollocks they're here in case you manage to break her charm."

"One has to admire your honesty."

"Always the best policy in my line of work." he admitted.

"You're a rihtleech aren't you?" asked the girl.

"An operating surgeon actually, so Heidi, tell me, the night of the party when we er… was that for real or just part of your act."

"I needed to see if the psychotrope worked on your mother and thought the safest thing to do would to be with one of the family, you obviously liked me so it seemed the best path to take."

"Loge, you hate us so much yet you can do that?"

"Call it a perk of the job" she informed him. "I enjoyed it, don't get me wrong!" He had the Alpha physique, golden blonde hair and his father's good looks, if he were a norm she could have fallen for him.

"Well thanks for that" he retorted scornfully, Heidi had an attractive snub nosed face, smooth dark skin and a long limbed body, Aelf felt perturbed by her callous nature but still found himself wishing they had met under different circumstances.

The dinner would go on till late so Sirki opted to stay overnight at the Hall. Bren was waiting outside her room when she emerged wearing a long yellow dress split almost to the point of decency on the right side, as was the current fashion, to display her Mjolnir tattoo above a black stocking top as she walked. Her lips were painted ruby red, her eyes were black lined and flicked out at the side in the old Egyptian style.

"You wore those colours the first night we were together." Bren recalled.

"I'm glad you remember that, I did it especially for you" she replied coyly.

"It was a night I'm unlikely to forget in a hurry" he confessed.

The evening went well, Sirki was the embodiment of politeness, using her charisma to charm everyone in their company and she did not get drunk. However, at one point during a particularly boring speech she did pull her husband's hand under the table to thrust it into the split of her dress allowing him to discover her complete lack of underwear.

"Oops, I knew I'd forgotten something?" Sirki path'd as he ran his fingers through the curls. Bren smiled, *Sirki was back.*

"Aren't you going to invite me in?" he asked as they stood outside her bedroom door upon returning.

"A lady does not invite a gentleman into her chambers on a first date!" replied Sirki. "But then again I'm no lady so are we going inside or will you just pleasure me in the doorway like the first time?"

Needing no further encouragement Bren picked her up and carried her into the bedroom.

Aelfred woke as his bedroom door opened and upon hearing the soft footfalls on the carpet, knew it could be only one person. Switching to night vision he sat up saying. "My, my, Heidi you appear to have forgotten your clothes?"

"Loge, I forgot you lot can see in the dark!" she recollected. "Well, I'm here and I'm naked?"

He pulled back the covers. "You'd better get in I wouldn't want you to get cold."

Bren and Sirki lay together in the warmth of their bed. "So Sirk, Aesh left you. Dare I ask why?"

"I shouted Penni's name out when I came and she was not impressed. Poor Elke, she felt so guilty about you leaving me and hearing *her* name at that point was the final push that tipped her over. We had a blazing row and she was packed and gone next day."

"You shouted Penni's name not mine? I'm a bit put out about that."

"Oh come on *rakas*, I'm hardly likely to have confused you for Penni, you possess something she definitely does not have."

"So if it had been a man, you would have shouted my name?" he enquired.

"Nej I would have bit my lip and let him carry on" she teased.

"*Bicce*, so you fell out because of a slip of the tongue while she slipped you the tongue?"

"You bahstard" laughed Sirki, straddling him.

"I love you too dahling" he replied.

It was breakfast time in both Da N'tan households. Aelf and Heidi were in high spirits at the kitchen bar despite Anya's obvious disapproval, while at Scartho Hall, the Thegn and Fro Sirkku were smiling at each other, a lot. Dame Hildegarde cast a knowing glance at the pair and ate her cereal quietly while the children threw food at each other until told to stop by their mother, who was glowering at Sirki.

As they finished Sari had a request. "Grandmother, could you look after Will and Bern until this evening? I have to go to the studio because Adrian wants me to record a new song."

Hilly, seeing a chance to heal the rift between her daughter in law and youngest child, answered. "I'm so sorry dahling, I have an important appointment in the Burh today but I'm sure your mother could stay a bit longer and look after them or even take them back home with her."

Sari looked pained. "Dad, what about you?" she asked.

"Sari stop this, you know your mother is more than capable." He replied.

"Please dahling I'd love to look after them?" asked Sirki, then path'd to her daughter. *"Sari I'm your mum, let me back in, your dad and I are together again and I've learned my lesson."*

"I want to stay with mummo per-leeze!" started Willa.

"Mummo, mummo" chirped in Bern.

"Very well mummo can look after you." replied Sari while pathing to Sirki. *"Look after them mummy, do not take them out of Scartho and I do not want that ACG bicce anywhere near them."*

"What's a, ay-see-gee *bicce*?" asked Willa.

"Don't listen in when mummy speaks without words Wil." Sari admonished her daughter.

"*Dottir*, I will take the greatest care of them." affirmed Sirki.

After breakfast she walked to the main doors with her daughter to see Sari's black roadster standing on the drive. "You're driving not flying?" asked Sirki.

"Yes I like to drive to Cambrycge, it takes longer but it's a nice fast road and it's a good stressbuster." she answered.

"You are taking an escort of course?" she had expected to see a *Huscarl scrid* ready to follow her daughter.

"Mummy I am quite capable of looking after myself" she remarked sharply. "I am, as you reminded me, a cold-blooded killer and I have my Sterlinger just in case!"

"I didn't quite say that dahling and I do worry about you."

"The kidnappings seem to have stopped since I dealt with those ACG bahstards, as it is the only one left is living comfortably in our house."

"I only ever mean well but sometimes I screw things up a bit."

Sari softened her attitude. "Look mummy, I'm like my genetic mother I can't help it, I'm a *cempestre* and nothing will change that. We will work things out I'm sure," she kissed her mother on the cheek then climbing into the Sigurd Leopard, smiled and waved briefly before driving away.

CHAPTER 20 – MISSING

Sirki, accompanied by several obvious *Huscarl* minders in civilian clothes, took the children to Elfenland, a fairground east of Scartho. They had a wonderful time and she spoiled her grandchildren terribly.

Bren meanwhile flew to New Winchester Airdock where Sleipnir was being readied for its next mission. This time it was going to Dimension 95, their next door neighbour, so time dilation would be minimal but at Sirki's insistence he had declined joining reluctantly handing command to Ficteregealdor Hogg. Flytgealdor Petronius was chief pilot replacing Singh, who had joined an expedition led by Da N'tan's old superior officer Gurdeep Mistry to the jumble of islands that had once been Bharatavarsha, all the other members of Sleipnir's first mission were there including Aesh who glanced guiltily at him before making herself scarce.

"*Bore da* Bren, shame you're not coming with us" Geraint Llewelyn was animated. "We'll miss you on the trip."

"Wilf is a good man, you can rely on him to make the right decisions," affirmed Bren, who would dearly loved to have been accompanying them.

"Look at this!" the Craeftwitan showed him a picture on his A-pad. "These pictures were taken by a Skuld probe yesterday." It showed a fixed wing aircraft high in the sky with a pair of tube-like engines on each wing.

"That's a pre-antigravity lifter that had to keep moving to stay up." remarked Bren. The next showed a yellow brown vehicle of an unusual design. "It's a rather ugly *scrid*," he remarked.

"Ya but if I zoom in on it, look on the back see it's an Austin, doesn't your wife own one of those?" he pointed at the picture.

"Sirki's Aurora is a classic, that looks like someone filed the corners off a small camp*scrid*" retorted Bren, her old Austin was a swan compared to that squab.

"It is a funny looking thing right enough but Allegro is the old Romano word for cheerful, what do you think it says about the vehicle?" Llewelyn pondered.

"Comical scrid?" suggested Da N'tan.

"Ha-ha very funny, but don't you see? It's an *Austin* and that hunter chap Tockway worshipped Nodens, it's as though all dimensions have some similar aspects. We could be looking at a series of almost identical parallel universes."

"Well it's an interesting concept, Geraint, you will be careful won't you?" asked Da N'tan.

"Don't worry Bren, we don't intend to antagonise the locals we're just going to observe and record, *then* we will decide if it's worth setting up an observation base there." the *craeftwitan* reassured him before going off to check the jump controls. Bren briefly spoke with Hogg before casting a glance at Petronius who walked off quickly.

As they finished their preparations Bren noticed Aesh had returned. "Good Morning Elke, are you well?"

"I am fine, Thegn." she felt uncomfortable. "Thank you for not dismissing me from the project sir."

"Why, should I have done?"

"Sir, it's just with what happened and all that."

"Aesh, what goes in our private lives has nothing to with this. I trust in your ability to look after mission security and will not let what happened get in the way."

"Thank you sir, I'm so sorry about how I behaved at the party, it just sort of escalated!" she was contrite.

"Aesh I'm not blaming you, I know it was Sirki's doing, we had a sort of understanding and she broke the rules. My wife can be something of an irresistible force when it suits her."

"Sir, are you and Fro Scartho together again?"

"Yes, thank you for asking, Aesh."

"I'm glad of that sir. I felt awful about you two splitting up in spite of… you know?"

"I understand, Aesh, I hope she didn't hurt your feelings too much?"

"No, thank you sir… sir, what Sirki suggested the three of us do, I would have… if you'd wanted it?" replied Elke, a little sheepishly.

"I know, but it was my decision not hers." he looked at the crew as they began boarding. "Take care of them, especially Llewelyn he's not what you call worldly."

"Sir, I remember that and don't forget I still have Kawaro for back up."

Freya had come over from the nearby Stardock to join her father and together they watched Sleipnir disappear off on its new mission. "You don't fancy a trip to another dimension then daughter?"

"Dad, I'm more than happy to fly into orbit but to vanish into Woden knows where? No thank you!"

"But I did Fri and I didn't come to any harm."

"No, you just disappeared for nearly six years and we all thought you were dead!" she reminded him.

Sirki was on their way back to the Hall with the grandchildren when her communicator chirped, it was Adrian Barnet. "Hei Sirki you old tart what's going on with your daughter?"

"Moi Adie, is Sari being a diva?"

"Well quite possibly dear as she hasn't turned up and these session musicians don't come cheap you know? I may have to send them home soon," he explained.

"She set off after breakfast and should have been there hours ago?" Sirki had a sudden feeling of foreboding.

"Well she's not here my dahling," replied Adie. "If she turns up I'll let you know."

Sirki signed off then closing her eyes reached out with her mind to locate her family and loved ones. Bren and Freya were to the south of her at New Winchester Airdock,

Aelfred was close to them, probably at the house. She searched further, to the south-west there was a warm presence that she instantly recognised as Penni but of Sari there was no sign. Panicking slightly she linked telepathically to Bren, who told her not to worry too much yet and that he would alert the Ward to search the road to Cambrycge and join them himself.

The drive back to the Hall seemed to take forever and upon arriving she explained the situation to Hilly then leaving the children with her, shut herself in the morning room to sit at Bren's desk, it was time to call for help. *"Mina?"*

"Sirkku you don't contact me unless it's trouble, what can I do for you?" responded the Highest.

"It's Sari, I can't locate her and I'm worried."

"Krishna preserve her, she has been abducted?" asked Mina.

"I don't know. I can feel nothing, it's as though she has disappeared off the face of the nerth."

"How did it happen, was she not escorted?"

"She's a headstrong experienced warrior and doesn't consider her own safety." answered Sirki.

"All of the Psi' will be put on alert, we will find her." the Highest replied reassuringly.

"Gods, if the ACG have her, Mina, I don't want to think about what they might do!"

"Be strong my friend, I know your daughter is very powerful, you believe you have hidden it from me but I am more perceptive than you realise."

After Sirki had broken contact Mina reached out into the Helm and waited for the entity to notice her. She didn't have to wait too long.

"Mina, it is most unusual for you to want to make contact?" the thought felt like velvet.

"A daughter of the one has gone missing and I do not believe her to be dead."

"You want my help in finding her?" SHE asked.

"Even the one herself cannot locate her, surely you can?"

"Which daughter?"

"The one she bore for the Beta, the one with all the abilities."

"My curiosity is aroused. I will join you, please do not be shocked by what you are about to see!" a figure stepped out of nowhere and Mina *was* taken aback.

"You look just like..!" she gasped.

"What did you expect, have I not already shared the truth with you?" asked the entity in a voice that was as pleasant as her thought pattern, she had an entrancing musky scent.

"But the resemblance is…" Mina continued.

"*Hist*, I can spare you but little time." The being closed her lilac eyes and concentrated. "This is indeed odd? This daughter is alive and physically intact but her mind is in much torment and disturbingly her whereabouts are masked even to me by some clever diversion, thine enemy is indeed most resourceful!" she opened her eyes. "I am sorry Mina but even I cannot precisely locate her."

"What hope is there if she is beyond even your powers?" asked Mina. "You once told me the daughter has the capacity be as powerful as *the one* and if our enemy has her it could go very ill for us."

"You must look to the south-west, that is all I can say for certain. You must find her Mina or she may find you first, be on your guard at all times."

"I will my Lady."

"Also, there is no longer any need to refer to Sirkku as *the one*."

"As you wish" agreed Mina.

A thoughtful look crossed the entity's face. "There is another in this world, one who may eventually be equal to Sirkku in power. I can feel it now I am on your dimensional plane."

"That would be her other daughter Freya."

"Nay that is not so, she is powerful but it is neither her nor the daughter who has vanished." she stated enigmatically.

"Who?" asked the Highest in surprise?

"It is as it was with Sirkku and the woman has only recently been awakened to her future potential" she paused. "I have much to do and my presence here can be of no further benefit, forgive me for not being of more use" and with that she vanished.

The *scrid* was found over halfway to Cambrycge near Stonyford and when Da N'tan landed the Ward had already sealed off the area.

The Cempa in charge showed him the scene of the incident. "A farmer reported finding the vehicle and thought it was an accident until he saw all the spent ammo." He took the Thegn to Sari's Leopard which was on the verge with its rear end smashed in, bullet casings lay scattered everywhere and Bren recognised them as coming from a Sterlinger's ammunition.

"It looks like she put up a hell of a fight, it started over here" continued the Ward Cempa. "Then she crossed the road" there was another scattering of shell cases. "We've found blood everywhere, looks like she offed at least four of them before she was hit."

"Hit, what with?" Bren feared the worst.

The Cempa held up a clear bag which held a collection of dart shaped projectiles.

"Tranks and judging by the amount fired she didn't present an easy target. Best guess is they shoved her off the road with something big and heavy, there are skid marks immediately in front of the crash site, someone in front slammed to a halt and a big boy at the back drove into her as she braked." He indicated several places. "She was caught in a cross-fire and pinned down immediately."

"My poor Sari!" thought Bren, aloud he asked. "There were no bodies?"

"Just the one Sir, we found her over here." The officer led Da N'tan to a spot in the undergrowth where the bloodstained foliage was flattened down and marked with a small numbered card. "The body was dressed in black ACG drabs but it was a young *nova* girl. We checked out her ID and you're not going to like this, her name was Blythe Te G'rath, she was one of your missing Psi from Scartho. They took their own dead away but left her for us, she had been shot by a Sterlinger."

A further search discovered the imprints of a Dragonfly's landing gear in the soft earth of a nearby field.

Sirki was devastated on hearing the news, *I should have insisted there was an escort... she looked just like Penni when she smiled... we hadn't made up properly*. Melancholy was dragging her down as the cold horror of what might befall her youngest daughter ran through her thoughts. The walls seemed to be closing in on her and a dark shadow crawled like a spider into her mind. *"Hello it's me again"* said a voice from the past.

Sirki left the drawing room and went quickly to her chambers, scarcely noticing the bed had been remade since last night's fun and games, finding her night case she flipped it open and pulled the lining from the lid to retrieve the one-shot syringe hidden there. Holding it to the light she regarded the clear liquid with nervous anticipation, all she had to do was plunge the needle into her arm and her troubles would vanish for a while.

"Go on, I'm waiting" coaxed the voice of her addiction. *"It's been such a long time."*

But even as Sirki craved the wonderful floating nothingness of demetol a memory bubbled up from her mind. She always kept a hit hidden away but had never taken it, the very knowledge of its existence was reassuring and bizarrely helped keep the urge at bay.

The last time she had come this close was when Bren was missing and the blackness had become too much to bear, she had been on the verge of injecting when Sari blurred into the room to snatch the syringe from her hand. "I knew you had a stash mummy, why do you want to take this shit?" she'd raged.

"Give that back to me now!" Sirki had shouted. "I need it!"

"Why, so you can be high for a while and then what, you'll need a bit more and then some more?"

"I can beat it Sari, please let me have it back" she had pleaded.

Sari grabbed her mother's left arm and checked it, then her right. She pursed her lips. "Alright there are no marks, you've taken nothing yet."

"Do you want to check my legs, stomach I can inject in a lot of places you know?"

"Promise me you will never take demetol again." Sari had demanded.

"I will try" she wanted to mean it.

"Can you make an oath like a true *nova*, like a *Huscarl?*"

"I think so" Sirki had asserted.

"Then promise me that you will never take demetol again!" her daughter had insisted and Sirki had half reluctantly sworn an oath on Thor's Hammer.

She looked at the syringe, *she had made a promise and this would solve nothing.* Taking a deep breath, Sirki went into the bathroom, squirted the one-shot into the sink then after running the taps to wash the drug away snapped the needle off against the porcelain before throwing the syringe into the bin. If the chance should arise to help her daughter she would need a clear head.

Having stiffened her resolve Sirki retreated back to her home in Wessex taking the grandchildren with her in spite of Sari's entreaty to not let them near Glaser.

Freya accompanied her and together they told Sari's children that their mummy had to go away for a while. Sirki hated lying to them but they were too young to be burdened with the truth then she broke the news to Anya, telling her to take some time off but she refused tearfully stating she owed it to Sari to help look after the children.

Glaser approached nervously. "Fro, I cannot apologise enough for the actions of my former compatriots and I am ashamed to have been involved with these people. If you wish to read my mind further I will not resist." Sirki politely declined, Heidi had told all her she knew and it seemed pointless to invade her privacy again.

A development came when paint flecks on the crashed Leopard were found to have come from a black Pony Super, the ACG *waegn* of choice. Traffic monitors had recorded two such vehicles at a nearby road junction earlier that day and later, one of them, its front end badly damaged, was found burnt out outside the city. The Cambrycge Ward were chagrined at the ease at which the ACG were operating inside their jurisdiction and upon receiving information that the other vehicle had been sighted, parked outside a house, moved quickly to surround the property. After armoured officers smashed down the front door there followed a ferocious exchange of fire and only one of the occupants, a certain Walder Aecermann, was taken alive to be arrested and interrogated. After proving very uncooperative he was locked in a cell to mull over his situation with the promise of a more vigorous *interview* come morning.

As he slept a woman dressed in white approached him in his dreams, she was beautiful and barefoot with bright blue eyes and flowers in her long blonde hair.

The woman smiled at him baring fanged teeth like those of a predatory feline as two striped blue cats the size of tigers appeared at her side to eye him hungrily. The terrified prisoner found he was unable to move as the cats came stealthily towards him.

"Did you take my daughter?" the woman hissed.

"I don't know you or your daughter!" replied Aecermann, *he had to wake up!*

One of the cats put its teeth around his leg and he could feel its hot breath on his skin.

"One more time, did you take my daughter?" The voice cut like a knife.

"You're nothing but a dream, I will wake up now!" he shouted.

"Wrong answer!" she spat, the cat closed its jaws and he heard the crunch of bone, the pain was excruciating. The second creature came closer, it's jaws were over his face and he could see its long teeth as rank breath washed over him. "Try again, she's a blonde girl with a very bad attitude and was driving a black *scrid*," her eyes blazed with lilac flame as her hair darkened to chestnut.

"Oh gods, you're the Dryi... yes, yes we used a suppression field to stop her calling for help then we used these controlled *waelcyrie* girls to suppress her Psionic power and she fought like a lion!" he was in agony. "Please make it stop!" the cat released its grip.

"Where is she now?" the voice had anger in it and the face was now positively demonic.

"I don't know, she was taken in a flyer to somewhere in Frankia I think, I don't know anything else, I swear it, I don't know anything!"

The awful countenance regarded at him for a while then hissed. "Good enough."

The cat grabbed his head in its jaws and bit down hard.

The duty officer heard the scream and ran to Aecermann's cell to find him in a contorted position on the bed his dead eyes staring at the ceiling. There was not a mark upon him but the look on his face would haunt the officer for years to come.

A couple of streets away, a classic white Austin Aurora pulled away and drove into the night. Bizarrely the city's traffic monitors blacked out as the vehicle approached and came back on only after it had passed undetected.

CHAPTER 21 –
THE SEARCH
BEGINS

Cempa Connor picked his way through the encampment to find the Campaeldor sitting on the bunk in her tent staring at the floor, almost half of the 3rd Elite Legion was camped at the foot of the Pirren Range and the local militia had turned out in force out to assist

"Ma'am, Psi Blane has sent a report on the captured clones."

"Sorry, what?" she turned to face him with eyes that were red-rimmed as if she had been crying.

"Are you alright Campaeldor?" asked Connor.

"Ya Cempa, I have just had some bad news from Scartho, my dau… my best friend's daughter has been abducted by the ACG," she replied shakily.

Guessing who she meant he exclaimed, "Fro Jorvik?"

"Ya, since all the information we have points to this mountain range as being where the abductees have been taken it's imperative we find their base and capture it, it's the only hope she… they have."

"It's a big area ma'am over 300 miles long, 11,000 feet at its highest point. We're looking at an area of about 2000 square miles and it slopes rapidly upward on this side, telepathy won't work up there and our radio signals are absorbed after a short distance.

"Your plan?" she asked.

"We start where the antenna was found and work upwards and outwards but it's not going to be an easy task even with three thousand *Huscarls,* and the local militia helping us."

"Then you had better fucking get on with it!" she snarled.

"Ma'am the report from Blane?" he asked cautiously.

"Does it reveal the location of the ACG headquarters?" she seemed animated at this.

"No Campaeldor, removing their implants left them without any memory of its location. It appears they obey orders without question but are more self-aware than the Ket clones."

"What use is that to me Cempa? Take your men and start searching now!" Anderson dismissed him tersely.

Sirki had path'd Penni to tell her the bad news, she had wanted to return to Aengland immediately but realised the best chance of finding their daughter lay here in West Frankia. The pain of the loss was tearing her apart inside but she had promised the distraught Sirki she would not give up until they had found the base.

As Connor left, Cempa Rika, who had been waiting outside entered, upon seeing him Anderson's composure broke and he held her tightly as she tearfully informed him of the news. "Penni, I realise you and Fro Scartho are close and it must hurt that your friend's daughter is missing but you have to stay strong, you mustn't let the troops see you like this!" he knew of their past relationship but was unaware of the truth behind Sari's parentage.

"*Merasta* Hal, was I too hard on Connor?" *should she tell him that Sari was her biological daughter?*

"A bit perhaps, shape up dahling and go shout at the other Cempae to make it an even field."

Jocasta Blane was sat in Connor's office staring at the picture of Sirki on the wall, Walder Aecermann, a suspect in the kidnapping of her daughter had been found dead in his cell with a look of abject horror on his face. *Probably down to Fro Scartho, I wouldn't blame her.* Blane's participation in the operation had officially ended with the interrogation of the clones and now she felt like a spare part. Through a window she could see a Flying Beetle being loaded with materiel for transport to the Pirren base camp so, making a decision, Jocasta snatched up her armoured jacket and dashed outside.

Connor was perusing the Pirren Mountains about to board a Brock *randscrid* when a thought came into his head. *"Hei Connor?"* he turned to see Blane standing there.

"Are you planning on coming up the mountain Ma'am? I thought you Psi didn't like flat zones."

"I'm of no use in Tolosa and it won't be any different to wearing a flat hood, besides I feel for my suster Psi and want to help" she answered.

Connor shrugged. "Fair enough, get on board."

The long convoy set off for the Pirrens with its escort of Flying Beetles and upon reaching the edge of the flat zone split into several smaller groups. Connor and Blane transferred to a smaller Brock *randscrid* with two *Huscarl*s, the nimble lightly armoured vehicle would enable him to move easily among his troops and communicate with the cohort when long-range radio became impossible. The sloping landscape would soon prevent passage of even the heavy tracked vehicles and after that they would be on foot with limited communication while the enemy would occupy the high ground.

"We're about to cross into the flat-zone, Hierophant, you still feel alright with it?" asked Connor.

"Let's just do this, check?" she said by way of an answer.

"Check, let's go Undergealdor." he ordered and the Brock started climbing.

To Jocasta it felt as if the sun had gone out of her life as the background noise of thousands of minds was cut off sharply, she had half-expected it to be like finding peace and stillness in her cowl but there was a dead feeling to everything and the whole world seemed to have turned grey. *She would get used to it.*

CHAPTER 22 – ESCAPE

The base had been on a high state of alert ever since the Elite force had established itself at the foot of the mountains and North, demoted to supervising the cloning bays for her perceived lack of commitment, was checking the second stage growth tanks in Bay 1 when she spotted Roke standing at the entrance.

He motioned her over. "Ma'am I hear the Psi captives have been returned."

"Have you seen Madel?" she asked quickly.

"No, ma'am, that I have not but something important has happened there's a huge amount of excitement among Merton and his cronies, it's the talk of the *aethus*."

"I used to be one of the cronies" she thought, then. "Could you find out?"

He sighed. "I will try ma'am, but with Reignweald war machine on our doorstep, security has been tightened up considerably."

Next morning Roke was summoned to see Milby. "Craeftwitan North seems to confide in you a lot."

This was worrying! "We have spoken the odd time, sir. I find her a very pleasant person."

"Oh come on Roke, you told Burns that North has a thing for the Tog-Barr *dryicge*, she obviously shared that much with you?" Milby asked.

"The craeftwitan did indicate she had a soft spot for the girl that is true sir and did suggest I warned *Saetere* Burns off." he replied.

"Very well, you may go," as he left he heard Milby speak into his communicator. "Please tell Craeftwitan North that I would like to see her immediately."

"Oh fuck, I've dropped her in it" thought Roke as he exited Milby's office.

North was astonished after nervously reporting to her new appointed superior, Craeftwice Merton had informed Milby he was so pleased with Tog-Barr's performance he was willing to allow North limited access to her. Avril remembered when the Craeftwice used to tell her things in person, *had she had fallen so far?* After hearing this the scientist sat late into the night writing a new programme on her atellan.

Roke brought Madel to North's lab next day. "They want you to check her programming." he informed her. "And if you wish I am to *ahem,* leave you two alone for half an hour."

"Roke, you know this whole thing is a charade, you invented it for Woden's sake?"

"Yeah ma'am but we need to them to believe it if we are going to go through with this?" replied the soldier. Over the weeks North and Roke had concocted an outlandish plan for releasing the psi which could get all of them shot if discovered.

"Check, Tithengealdor but you have no need to leave," she looked at Madel sitting blank eyed in the chair. "Poor girl, what have I done to you?" the psi seemed quite healthy and her blonde hair had grown into a short mop giving her an elfin look, North attached the electrodes to her head once again.

"Well Tithengealdor let's see if I can undo the damage?" North had subtly altered the original programming to suppress Madel's personality rather than wipe it and had finally worked out a way to reverse the process but there had been no way to test it. She altered the settings on the console and pressed the send button, *if this works it may be possible to bring them all back!*

Madel felt the whiteness receding, *had she beaten them?* The fat man wasn't there now but the sympathetic woman and the soldier were, so she kept quiet.

"Madel, are you there?" asked the woman, North was sure there was life in her eyes now but

Tog-Barr, pretending to be subdued, said nothing.

"Madel, I'm not trying to trick you. I have brought you back at great risk to us all!" North informed her.

"Back, where have I been?" she blurted out.

"You have been away for some time, do you remember anything?" asked North.

"No, I thought it hadn't worked," she reached up gingerly to feel her scalp. "My hair's grown, oh gods I don't remember a thing!"

"Listen Madel, we're going to get you out of here but you must act as though you are still under control, if they suspect anything they will kill you, me and even the Tithengealdor, do you understand?" North explained.

"Yes" Tog-Barr replied. She looked at North then at Roke. "You, I understand, Avril, your crisis of conscience made you feel guilty about what you do but what about you, *heremann?*"

North was amazed how quickly Madel had recovered her composure.

"I used to have a daughter about your age, I couldn't save her so perhaps I can save you?" he answered.

"Roke I didn't know, what happened to her?" North asked.

"My wife and daughter both died when your lot attacked our township" he looked at Tog-Barr. "One of your flying bugs burned out an air raid shelter with its energy weapon."

"You were a Wight?" asked Madel in surprise. "Small wonder you hate us, both sides did bad things back then… I'm sorry you lost your family."

"I don't hate you young lady, it was a long time ago and you're far too young to have been part of that" he informed her.

"How on Nerth did you end up in the ACG, we were once on the same side as the *novae?*" asked North.

"You'd be surprised how many old Wights there are in this base. Most joined up because of our mutual hatred of the *nova* but I don't like the things I've seen here and this business with you, mizz, has rattled me, I want out!" he explained.

"Yes, it doesn't pay to have a conscience" agreed Avril.

"North, can you remove this thing from my head?"

"Yes but I haven't got the equipment here. I'll need to take it from the *bonecraeft* lab when there is no one is about," she replied.

"And we need to make plans to leave," stated Roke.

The Tithengealdor escorted her back to her cell but as they passed some of the doors she could feel resonation behind them.

"There are Psi' in there," she said quietly

"Aye and you helped obtain them while you were under their control."

"I helped to take them?" she asked in horror, this was something new to her.

"Yeah sorry about that young mizz, it was out of my hands I'm afraid."

"Your people are bahstards."

"Not my people anymore!" he re-locked Madel in her cell, oblivious to the fact a newly installed camera had been monitoring them.

"How was she?" asked Milby when North came to make her report.

"The programming is holding up well, I checked it with an algorithm written specifically for the task."

"Did the Tithengealdor leave her alone with you?" he asked with a slight smirk.

"There was no reason for him to, why?" she retorted.

"Oh, I thought since you were sweet on the *dryicge* you might like some alone time with her."

"I feel pity for Tog-Barr and I would never take advantage of a helpless girl like that, how dare you insinuate such a thing?" she shouldn't have snapped but she disliked Milby, *had she given herself away?*

"Well fine then, you may go!" galled by her attitude and now a little suspicious he went to seek out Merton, finding him outside Lab 3.

"Wassael Milby, our project has reaped a greater reward than we could ever have imagined."

"Quite a prize indeed sir, is she installed now?" asked Milby.

"Safe and sound behind this door, was Craeftwitan North happy to have been reunited with her little toy?"

"I think North is slipping further from the path, she told me she felt pity for the *scunung*" he replied.

"That's a shame, her work in the project has been exemplary until recently. A watch had better be set on her" advised Merton.

"And that Tithengealdor she confides in, Roke, he may not be entirely trustworthy either. We ought to have him put under observation too." suggested Milby.

"I quite agree. North would be a great loss to us but the Tithengealdor could be disposed of readily enough if he's stepped out of line" stated Merton but unbeknown to them, a little further down the corridor and out of their sight, a pair of ACG soldiers had been listening to the conversation with great interest.

Roke was in his room when he heard a noise outside and a piece of folded paper was pushed under the door. Opening it, he read the message inside. *"Erwyn I don't know what you and that North woman are up to but Merton and Milby are suspicious, be bloody careful!"* there was a small skull drawn underneath and he instinctively touched his right arm, below his sleeve was a very similar tattoo, *one of his fellow Wights had sent him this warning.* The situation had changed, they would have to move sooner rather than later *and it might already be too late!* Roke went *to a nearby storeroom to remove two large holdalls then risked using his communicator to tell Avril it was time.

"We'll use the way out by the cacaern block, we need to wait till early morning then make our escape picking up the young mizz along the way" he informed her upon arriving at her accommodation.

"Will Madel be safe?"

"As long as they think she is still under control" he reassured her and they settled down in anticipation of an uncomfortable night, the Tithengealdor bunked down on the couch with his assault weapon close to hand while North lay on her bed in the drabs Roke had provided. She slept fitfully only to be woken by a noise in the other room and upon entering saw Roke crouched over a prone body with a large knife in his hand. Another was slumped against the wall near her door and each looked the same as the other.

"Clones!" she gasped in horror.

"Sent to fetch you but they didn't reckon on my being here, our time has run out and we need to go!" he wiped his knife on the clone's uniform then after sheathing it shouldered his gun and picked up one of the heavy bags. "You grab the other then we get Madel."

Tog-Barr heard unfamiliar footsteps outside her cell door and feigned sleep as the light was turned on from the outside and when it opened she sat up placing her feet on the floor.

Two grim faced figures in uniform, shaven-headed and virtually identical, entered the cell.

"You are to come with us now!" said one tersely while holding forward ward-cuffs.

Realising the ACG was on to their deception Madel acted first. Blurring into quickspeed she pushed the nearest clone's chin up sharply to hear a crack and as he dropped she kicked the other in the groin before bringing her knee sharply into the clone's face as it folded. She slowed down only to see a third in the doorway raising a pistol but before Madel could move it slumped lifeless to the floor and there stood Roke, knife in hand.

"I hate these bloody things!" he muttered then noticing the two bodies on the cell floor remarked. "You are full of surprises, little mizz." He wiped his blade clean then taking a small flat box from a shelf outside the door handed it to Madel. "Take this and keep it close to you at all times, your survival depends on it!"

She took the box without question, tucking it into the breast pocket of her prison coveralls then stated. "My suster Psi', we must rescue them too."

"There isn't time, come on!" urged Roke.

Sadly she acceded and followed him noticing along the way the guard post was bizarrely unmanned and a monitor camera hung loosely from the ceiling, further along the corridor they squeezed down a tight passage where they found Craeftwitan North waiting for them in a dark rectangular chamber.

Madel spotted carvings on the walls representing the Seven Degrees of Initiation and realised this was a disused Mithraeum. The Hispanic lands had clung to the old Romano religion with a fervour that North Europa had not and this had been a place of worship before the ACG reclaimed the base.

"They sent clones to take Madel from her cell." Roke explained to North as he removed the grilling from the far wall above the plinth where Mithras statue would have stood. "I took one out but the little mizz had already dealt with two others."

North looked at her in surprise, Tog-Barr seemed frail and willowy.

Madel smiled wryly. "I have the speed and resilience of my Alpha-Beta cousins but lack their size and strength"

Roke opened one of the large bags. "This pipe is one of the breathers for the base and it leads straight to the outside world" he explained handing thermal gear to the two women. "We'll come out below the snow line but it's going to be cold until we descend some distance." They climbed into the tube which was large enough to allow them to walk in a crouch and Madel could feel dampness in the air along with a fresh welcoming breeze.

"Here, these are for you" said Craeftwitan North holding out a pair of night vision goggles.

"Thanks Avril but I can see quite well in the dark." she informed her.

They moved back down the pipe as Roke fastened the hatch in place from inside. "We need to get as far away as we can before daybreak" he handed Madel a package wrapped in cloth, inside was her short *seax* in its scabbard. "Took it from the armoury, I know how much these blades mean to you people."

Madel smiled and buckled it to her waist then with Roke in the lead they began their journey along the air-duct. After what seemed like an eternity to North, they reached a large metal grid and beyond it could be seen the stars.

Roke connected wires around the frame then set to work with a power wrench. "The grid has a closed circuit alarum but I've short-circuited it," he pushed at the grid to swing it upwards and outwards then began fastening a climbing rope to one of the sturdy hinges at the top.

North glanced out into the freezing night to see a sheer drop into darkness. "You didn't tell me we would have to climb!" she exclaimed in alarm.

"We'll abseil down to more level ground," he explained. "I grew up in the Alpen regions and used to do this sort of thing as a child."

"I have never done this before, I grew up on the coast miles from any mountains!" she wailed.

"I've never done this before either, Avril, I'll go first!" said Tog-Barr with excitement in her voice. "What do I do?"

Roke showed her how to use the descender and handed her a pair of gloves from one of the holdalls then Madel strapped on a harness and stepped out onto the mountainside.

"Whatever you do don't drop that little box I gave you!" Roke called after her.

"Check" she replied before rapidly abseiling down the steep rock face as if it were second nature.

"I don't believe it, she's down already" announced Roke shortly.

"Tithengealdor I can't do this!" North was terrified at the prospect of dangling on a rope in the cold and dark.

"All you have to do is put on this harness, clip yourself to this rope and I'll belay you down slowly" he assured her. "You can't stay here, they'll kill you!"

North nervously agreed to be lowered down, it was a lot higher than Roke had suggested and she kept her eyes screwed tightly shut for most of the descent but when she reached the ground Madel grabbed her with surprising strength.

"I knew you'd be alright" she said with a smile.

Roke descended with practised ease to join them then reaching into the second holdall held out weapons to the pair.

Avril reluctantly took a pistol but Tog-Barr waved the proffered gun away.

He shrugged. "Let's get moving while we still have darkness on our side" they began climbing down the steep hillside as fast as they could but as the sun rose they could hear distant voices. "We have a head start but they'll soon catch up" observed Roke.

"What is this box for?" Tog-Barr asked, holding it up.

"It's your control unit, it generates a signal that stops the anti-tamper circuit activating but it doesn't have much range in the flat zone so keep it close to you" answered North.

"Anti-tamper circuit, I don't much like the sound of that?"

"There is a tiny charge in the implant which will explode if it is removed incorrectly or you stray too far from the unit's range and because of its location at the top of the nasal cavity it will effectively fire fragments of bone into your brain" she confessed.

"You people disgust me, get this thing out of my head now!" demanded Madel.

Against Roke's advice they stopped while North retrieved her case from the holdall, she had brought all of her equipment plus some inactive implants which she planned to hand over to the Reignweald as proof of her good intentions.

"Madel, I didn't have time to get any analgesics from the pharmacy, it's not going to be pleasant."

"I don't care, get it out!" she snapped.

"Check, lay down and Roke, hold her head firmly. Madel you must stay very still!" ordered North then she produced a long tube with a complicated handle from the case before setting up her small atellan.

Tog-Barr winced as the flexible silver tube was inserted into her left nostril and as it worked its way in she felt panic rising. "Stay calm Madel, try not to struggle, I'm guiding it as carefully as possible." North informed her while watching the rhinoscope's progress on the screen.

"Steady little mizz, I won't let you go," said Roke calmly.

Tog-Barr felt a sharp pain at the top of her nose then, North, watching the screen intently, manipulated the rhinoscope to release and extract the implant. It was really hurting and her eyes began streaming.

"There all done" North announced holding aloft the gleaming tube, a four legged implant, pink and insect-like was held in the small claw on the end looking far too big to have come down Madel's nose. North flicked the implant into the undergrowth where it landed out of the range of the control box to detonate with a sharp crack.

After Madel wiped her watering eyes she pushed some gauze into her bleeding nostrils and they continued quickly downwards in the cold morning air. With the removal of the device her Psionic powers had returned and although they were severely diminished in the flat, dead, land yet she felt nearly normal for the first time in weeks.

They descended until a fast flowing torrent crossed their path effectively blocking their progress and leaving them with no choice but to work their way along the bank as it wound its way downhill. They saw a small furry creature with a long nose, disturbed at their approach, jump into the water to swim rapidly away.

"A desman, it's very rare to see one and it's supposed to be a sign of good luck." remarked Roke. By way of an answer a series of shots rang out from above, ricocheting off the rocks. "Now that's just grand isn't it?" he said sagging to his knees, he had been hit in the stomach. "Go, I'll hold them off."

Blood was pouring from the wound and Madel dragged him to the cover of some rocks "Roke?"

"Just go little mizz, now!" he hissed through the pain.

"I don't know your name." she replied.

"It's Erwin, now please go or this will have all been for nothing." he sighted along his assault weapon as best he could. "Go now!"

The two women followed the watercourse downhill but as it widened they heard gunfire upslope. "Have a safe journey over Bifrost, Erwin Roke," said Madel as it was quickly cut short.

After descending further she paused to let Avril catch her breath while the psi strained to listen over the roaring water but even with her acute hearing it was hard to tell if their pursuers were gaining on them. Madel regarded the water flowing by, the torrent was fast and there were very few rocks.

She spotted movement uphill. "Is your box of tricks waterproof?" she asked.

"Yes why, oh no, we're not surely?" North looked at the fast flowing water in dismay.

"Hang on to it tightly." Madel grabbed hold of her and pitched them both in as bullets sang around.

The stream was run-off from the mountain snow and unbelievably cold but it was taking them in the right direction. North found that their journey was smoother than she had anticipated and realised this was due to Madel using her restored telekinetic powers to keep them from hitting anything.

Eventuall they flew off a small cataract to splash into the deep pool below and upon breaking the surface Madel towed the exhausted craeftwitan to the edge of the water and dragged her out.

North was astonished at the resilience and stamina of the girl. "We could never hope to beat you, could we?" she was spent, cold and wet but the Psi was hardly out of breath.

Madel was feeling the bridge of her nose where a bruise was blossoming. "Why do you wish to beat us?" she asked. "We are only trying to make the world a better place."

"Because some people like things to stay the way they are, they don't want them better." she replied.

"Then they are fools! Come on Avril we cannot delay, I will carry your box." insisted Madel before striding off downhill and the Craeftwitan followed with some effort, *there were trees ahead perhaps they could hide there for a while and recover.*

"They're coming, we must move, it's not much farther to the woods!" Madel began pulling her along as figures could now be seen moving down the hillside.

A shell whistled over their heads to explode behind them scattering their pursuers as a huge armoured vehicle crashed out of the treeline firing the heavy machine gun atop its turret. A soldier waved them forward from the open cupola and they rushed to the side of the now stationary Einherjar as more armoured vehicles burst from the woods. *Huscarls* began disembarking from them and for the first time North actually felt pleased to see enemy soldiers. Her reverie was short lived however as she became aware of bright blue eyes regarding her with suspicion then remembered she was wearing ACG uniform.

As a *Huscarl* approached with his weapon raised Madel stepped forward. "I am Neophyte Tog-Barr and this woman is my friend."

He lowered his firearm. "You are Tog-Barr, one of our missing Psi? Welcome back Mz, you must wait here for the Cempa" and he pointed to a small armoured vehicle that was tearing along the treeline.

The women were given self-heating blankets to put over their wet clothes and as the Brock halted Connor climbed out followed by Blane. "Wassael Psi, you are alright?"

"Yes Cempa, thanks to this woman, she is an ACG craeftwitan and has put herself at great risk to help me escape."

"*Galdrea!*" one of the *ferdrinc* muttered under his breath making North feel as uneasy as Madel must have done in the ACG's hands.

The Cempa narrowed his eyes. "Hierophant Blane, you'd better have a look at this woman."

North looked at the female officer and at first thought she was a norm. Then she saw the Psi badge above her right cuff, *she's an atypical!* North hadn't believed they existed and now this one, a level four, was regarding her intently. She was reminded of how easily Madel had read the guard's mind and she was a Neophyte, a mere novice. She shuddered, feeling as though "someone was walking on her grave".

"You seem honest in your intentions Craeftwitan North, now I need to know the layout of your base so please concentrate on it" the Psi had a pleasant voice but her pale blue eyes seemed to see right into North's head, she thought about the base and everywhere she had been inside it.

"Don't you want to know the way in through the air duct?" she asked.

"There is no need, Madel took notice of its position and I already know where it is" answered Blane. "Anyway your colleagues will have sealed it off by now."

"That's it?" North asked.

"Just one other thing, do you know the whereabouts of Fro Sari Jorvik?"

"Who is she?"

"The Thegn of Scartho's daughter, she disappeared four days ago and it was doubtless something to do with your people." Blane informed her.

Craeftwitan North recounted the important event that Roke had spoken of and Blane nodded. "You're coming downhill with me, North, there are people in Aengland who will want to meet you."

They bundled her into the Brock then Blane and Tog-Barr joined her and it was driven quickly down to the encampment. As they crossed from the flat zone Madel felt a lightening in her mind and the familiar wonderful feeling of being connected with the psionic world returned, she was truly herself once more.

"I'm coming to ensure your safety" explained Blane to Craeftwitan North. "I'm the only one here of equal rank to the Campaeldor and she's behaving very erratically at the moment."

"Now I feel really uncomfortable."

"Don't worry, I can handle her" said Blane reassuringly.

As the *randscrid* pulled into the base camp a welcoming committee of a female officer and four Elite Guards was waiting for them.

"Blane, hand over your prisoner, I want to interrogate her personally" declared Anderson, North could see that the officer was beautiful but her face wore a mask of anger making her more afraid than ever.

"No, she is to be transferred to the PRW. I contacted the Palace on the way down here and it has also been cleared with the Wigfruma's office," countered Blane. "You will supply me with a flyer and I will escort her personally!" she added before pathing to Anderson. *"You will find out nothing more from this woman than I have already and you are letting your feelings cloud your judgement, I can see the truth of Sari Jorvik's parentage in your thoughts for your anguish is making you transparent."*

"*I am in Hell!*" confessed Penni.

"Join your ferdrinc in the attack on the mountain, she may yet be found there. The information this prisoner can provide could prevent anything like this happening again."

"I will detail a Midge for your journey and I hope you are not wrong in what you say!" Penni said aloud. As the Midge flew off north Anderson boarded the Athelstan and it lifted from the ground to head south flanked by its sister ships, Henghist and Horsa II.

CHAPTER 23 - THE BASE.

The air-duct had indeed been sealed so Connor's *cohort* could not have gained access even if it were at ground level. They were coming under heavy fire from ACG emplacements and suffering casualties, several Beetles had been lost to *liegswaepn* or triple-case missiles but worse still hundreds of clone soldiers were now moving in to attack. The other *Huscarls* would be rapidly making their way to the sound of battle but they were in trouble, the Cempa could see a liegswaepn emplacement further ahead. It would be a way in but the position was heavily defended.

"Hei, need some help down there?" a pilot in a Wasp fighter was close enough to achieve radio contact in the flat zone.

"Yeah, if you could mallet that emplacement above us and suppress its support group" answered Connor.

"On our way!" replied the pilot, three Wasps buzzed over at supersonic speed and the mountainside above the beleaguered soldiers erupted in blue flame as they fired their energy weapons simultaneously.

"Move in, take the position!" ordered Connor and the *ferdrinc* blurred uphill fighting their way into the wrecked emplacement to secure a foothold before advancing further into the base. As a perimeter was being established they could feel explosions rocking the mountain as the newly arrived *entaflotae* made their presence known by bombarding the ACG defences, as reinforcements began streaming in behind them Connor ordered his troops down the tunnel and deeper into the stronghold.

The corridor came to a wide junction where on the wall letters in peeling paint read, "← *Tienda de municiones del Este*" and "*Residencia Oeste*→" the invading force now split into two groups while aboard Athelstan the Campaeldor Anderson watched anxiously from above. She would have given anything to be down there in the thick of the battle.

"Reignweald *heremenn* have gained access to the perimeter tunnels and are making significant progress against our forces, the enemy have deployed three *Entaflotae* including one of the new King class type, they are destroying our heavy weapon emplacements and every clone has been mobilised including those held in stasis" reported the ACG Cempa to the Craeftwice.

"Curse them all, curse that treacherous *bicce* North, curse Roke and the little *scunung dryicge!* This is all their doing, Milby, nearly thirty years of careful planning is slipping away!" a wild eyed Merton snarled.

"Sir, the other plan, do we enact it?" asked Milby worried for his leader's sanity.

He nodded. "It is more vital than ever. Ensure that everything is safely loaded aboard the flyer and remember to take as many incubation units as will fit. Supervise it personally Milby then leave for the other facility, you will be safe enough there, the bahstards know nothing of its existence!"

"Sir you are not coming?"

"No Craeftwitan, there will not be room for many onboard, you are in charge now, my dreams are ruined and it is your turn to be *glaem*. *Farvel* Milby, they will not take me alive."

"*Farvel* sir, have a safe crossing" the craeftwitan left the office feeling numb inside. His leader was taking a path he doubted he could.

Milby heard a single shot as he ran down the corridor to Lab 3 and shortly afterwards a black stippled Beetle flew out of a hidden exit on the south of the mountain far away from the battle raging to the north. Turning slowly the vessel flew across the sea towards the Western Isles, hidden from detection inside a stealth bubble.

Anderson joined Connor in the cell block where two blank faced and passive Psi' had been discovered and led out with their control units safely strapped to them, they would be flown to Aengland where North would hopefully restore their personalities and remove their implants as she had with Tog-Barr.

Merton's body had been found sat at his desk, pistol still in hand but of the one called Milby they found no trace. Over a thousand prisoners, mostly craeftwitan, staff or ACG soldiers had been taken with about three hundred clones adding to the number.

Of Sari Jorvik they had found no trace whatsoever leaving Penni in utter torment, now she would have to tell Sirki she had failed.

Connor showed the Campaeldor a dark chamber they had forced their way into. A twisted metal door labelled Laboratory 3 lay upon the corridor floor and inside was a row of ovoid glass containers set upon a long bench with several larger tubes mounted against a wall. The room was a smaller version of several demolished cloning facilities discovered in the lower levels.

"They obviously didn't have time to destroy this one" explained Connor. "What's interesting is that the others were wide open but this one was sealed like a fortress. It took a lot of explosives to get in and I was half afraid we were going to bring the roof down but we did manage to cut the power off doing it."

"But you found no-one?" asked Anderson.

"No ma'am but the interesting thing is three wambs have been removed along with four of the larger tubes. If you could follow me to this service lift, we've rigged it to a power cell to make it work." Connor showed her to an elevating platform which raised them to a long chamber with a single opening to the outside world at the far end. "This would appear to be a hangar for a single lifter, probably a Beetle."

She looked around to see one of the larger tubes lying broken on the floor. "They dropped this one and had to fetch another."

"My thoughts exactly ma'am, three small wambs to grow the foetii and three larger for the final product, Campaeldor, I don't want to speculate wildly but…"

"Connor, don't say anything more I don't even want to contemplate it!" she interrupted, then. "Cempa Rika is coming to take control, give him all the assistance he needs! I shall have to go to Scartho to personally tell the Thegn his daughter was not here."

"Check ma'am… I'm sorry!" he could feel her suffering.

Anderson quickly made her way down from the hangar and out of the room. She needed to be away from this awful place, finding a quiet corridor she sat against the wall to bury her face in her hands and sob. *Gods, please not Sari!*

At another location Milby supervised the unloading of the package and installation of the equipment, he had already made his plan.

CHAPTER 24 - AFTERNOON TEA.

The *Psihearg* was both nerve centre of the Psi Wing and the official residence of the Highest, the most powerful Psi in the Reignweald. The building, an imposing five stories tall with high sloping roofs, had been built less than a hundred years ago on the south side of the river facing London House, home to the Witangemot of Aengland and the Reignweald. Audrey Ashby, aka Bonnie, had been summoned here for a private audience with her leader and was dressed in Psi official Number 1 dress, dark blue with a cornflower blue trim, her multi-coloured hair now bleached purest white. She was even wearing a uniform skirt with her legs clad in cornflower hose.

She found Mina sitting by the large ornamental fountain in the atrium. "Good afternoon Ashby, will you join me?"

Bonnie did as requested. "You asked to see me my Highest?"

"I am getting old Ashby and I think it is perhaps time to nominate my successor before it is too late. I have given great consideration to this and of all my Mystagogues I believe there is only one suitable candidate and that is you, Ashby. Your Psionic power is at least equal to mine and appears to be growing, this coupled with the aptitude you display in its use it has left me with but little choice... Audrey Ashby, I hereby nominate you as successor to the position of Highest, will you accept?"

Bonnie was taken aback, she was eccentric in both manner and dress and her habit of frequently following her own path rather than correct procedure had earned Mina's wrath on more than one occasion. Now she was being offered the most powerful position in her order. "Ma'am this is a great honour but are you sure I'm the right choice, what about Fro Scartho or Fro Elswyth?"

"Sirkku would not want the position and her suster-in-law is too withdrawn and would not be right for it. Despite your previous disregard for the rules you are by far the most suitable candidate, do you accept?" returned Mina.

"Yes, my Highest I accept." *I hope I don't have to take the position too soon!* There were very few reasons for Mina to relinquish her role, death being the most obvious.

"Then it is settled but there is one thing I must share with you and you alone. It must go no further so do you swear to your god to never reveal it?" Ashby affirmed to Loge and Mina Srivastava revealed a secret that no-one else in the world knew.

Blane and Tog-Barr had also received a summons to the *Psihearg* and arriving an hour later were shown to Mina's private quarters to find the Queen and the immediately recognisable Omega there, also present were two Psi' who Blane did not know.

"Jocasta, Madel, let me introduce you to my other guests." began Mina. "You will doubtless recognise her royal majesty Queen Ethelflaeda and Fro Sirkku, Thegnestre of Scartho, these others are Mystagogues Audrey Ashby and Fro Elswyth Da N'tan." there followed the usual round of inclined nods.

Effie took a seat and they followed suit as was proper then a silver tray holding a large teapot and crockery was brought in followed by sandwiches and a cake-stand.

Jocasta and Madel both felt ill at ease as neither had been in such exalted company before. Blane noticed the five women were regarding her intently, *do they find it difficult to believe I'm a Psi too?* She would have to be very careful here as even the queen, who had only ascended to Psionic ability through bearing *novae* twins, was reckoned to be at least level three.

Fro Scartho was smiling at her, could she read Blane's mind despite her safeguards? The woman was reckoned to be the most powerful telepath on the planet but she rarely used her abilities and never got involved with politics *or so it was said*.

"Sirki, can you be mother?" Effie broke into Jocasta's reverie.

Fro Scartho obligingly poured tea and handed round the cups, it felt bizarre to Madel that a Thegnestre was serving her but the afternoon began well with polite conversation and congratulations for Blane's participation in discovering the ACG base then Madel was questioned about her experience.

She recounted the story of her abduction, how she had been in the market in Tolosa when she lost all Psi communication before feeling an injection and waking up a prisoner of the ACG. She recalled the pain of having to wear a torc, the numb feeling from the implant controlling her actions and the fading to nothingness of her conscious mind. Her audience had read the reports but to hear it at first hand brought the experience home to them.

Fro Scartho then astonished Madel by throwing her arms around her. "You poor thing, how you must have suffered" said Sirki, thinking of her missing daughter. "Did you see or hear or even feel anything of any other *novae* while you were a prisoner?"

"Only the two that were rescued by the *Huscarls*" her fellow captives, implants removed and identities restored by Craeftwitan North had been reunited with their families. "I'm sorry, ma'am, I know nothing that will help you."

"It may be possible for me to recover the lost memories of what happened while you were under their control" Sirki informed her. "It may be traumatic for you but it could help us to find Fro Sari. You are under no obligation to do this but will you give me permission to enter your mind?"

Madel gave her consent and then suddenly felt Fro Scartho inside her mind as if she was wearing it like a glove, it was very different to any training exercise she'd had. She remembered enticing the unfortunate Te G'rath to her fate then another Psi in the Port of London had been lured in the same way. She was a Brythonic girl called Ceri ferch Rees who put up a struggle but Madel had held her tightly while *Saetere* Burns injected her with the knockout drug. Sirki felt the girl's shame at this recollection.

Of the abduction in Lutetia she had no knowledge as another group had carried it out then came the memory of hiding in undergrowth by a roadside, the crunching noise of vehicles colliding and a figure firing a weapon as the four controlled Psi' concentrated on suppressing her powers. The figure ran across the road towards Madel giving her a clear look at her face, it was Sari Jorvik! She loosed off several more bursts then fell as the tranquiliser darts took effect. All contact with Sirki was suddenly broken.

"I'm sorry, I didn't know, I didn't remember!" cried Madel as Fro Scartho, clearly upset, rushed from the room followed by the Queen.

"Madel are you alright?" asked Jocasta.

"Can I go home please?" she croaked.

"Well time is getting on I suppose?" suggested Mina. "Elli could you make sure Mz Tog-Barr is flown safely back to Scartho. Blane, stay here a moment we would like to talk with you further?"

Shortly after they had gone Effie and a red eyed Sirki returned then the Queen said goodbye and left them to it. Sirki drew herself up and taking a deep breath nodded to the Arch Psi.

"Jocasta Blane." asked Mina "You were born in New Winchester but your grandmother came from Soomi did she not?"

"Yes?" she was baffled by the question.

"Apart from myself, no-one here has personally met you before yet we all recognised you immediately." Mina informed her.

"I'm not following you" *where was this going?*

Bonnie produced a picture viewer. "You should look at this but you may want to sit down first."

Blane looked at the viewer which showed four women stood in a line, one was clearly Fro Scartho, another looked like...

"That's my grandmother when she was young, where was this taken?" demanded Blane.

"Actually it's your great-grandmother or should we say G3V11b." stated Mina.

"What?"

Bonnie changed the picture to show the same woman in close up. The image was accompanied by the text.

Proteus developed from Zygote Batch - #3
Vat – 11
Classification – b (Beta)
Sex – Female
Successful birth, no recorded anomalies
Note; known as Elvene to the others.

She adjusted the view again to bring up a picture of what appeared to be Fro Scartho with the accompanying description.

Proteus developed from Zygote Batch - #3
Vat – 14
Classification – b (Beta)
Sex – Female
Successful birth, anomalies as follows; hair colour, eye colour, weaker physique
Note; she has been given the nickname Isolde but is known as Threevie to her own kind.

Seen together there were striking similarities between the two faces, Jocasta felt slightly uneasy. "Are you saying my great grandmother and Fro Scartho are related?"

"In a way, but that's not Sirkku Da N'tan that is *her* great grandmother and they were both test prototypes of the *Novae* Breeding Programme. Jocasta, you are the direct descendant of an experimental clone just as is Fro Sirkku." Mina informed her.

Blane looked at Fro Scartho and could see a slight resemblance apart from, of course, eye and hair colour.

Sirki smiled. "Don't look so concerned Jocasta, it's not so bad."

"We're clone susters?"

"Nej but our great grandmothers may have been!" answered Sirki.

"We have known that the descendants of Group 3 are among us for thirty years now but Sirki is the only one positively identified so far, may we take a saliva sample from you?" asked Bonnie.

"I suppose, what happens after that?" Blane asked.

"We would like you to stay until the test results come back then you can carry on with your life as normal, just let us know if you change in any way." answered Mina.

As Blane left for her allocated quarters Sirki caught her up. "Jocasta, you have changed recently haven't you?"

"No." Blane lied.

"Oh, but you have my dear, firstly you are in a sexual relationship and that is not normal Psi behaviour, secondly you are pregnant, only a few weeks but that is seriously non-Psi behaviour' stated Sirki.

"How can you know all that?" she asked.

"I can feel it in you Jocasta, the Psi' are detached from matters carnal whereas I revel in them. I think you need to tell the father don't you? Best to do it face to face when you return to Frisha, I didn't have that option the first time" advised Sirki.

"Thank you, I think?"

"My door will always be open to you, Jocasta, remember that if you have problems in the future," and with that she went to re-join Mina and Bonnie.

"So Sirki what do you make of Blane?" asked the Highest.

"She is the same as me but has not fully woken yet" she replied.

"She's in her late forties, isn't that a little late to become like you?" asked Mina.

"I was only twenty five but it took my near death for it to emerge, who knows how long it would have taken otherwise and remember I wasn't really a Psi before that."

"Based on the pair of you is it possible that descendants of the two other surviving #3 Betas are the same?" asked Bonnie.

"More than likely" Sirki smiled. "It would be nice to find all of us."

"It will be interesting if she has children as you did." remarked Mina.

"Oh, she will have a child, of that I am certain" added Sirki with a smile.

Having given a sample to an offestre from the London Haelinghall, Blane relaxed in a bath and contacted a certain Elite Guard officer in Oostende.

"Hei Cad."

"Hou Cassie, how did your meeting with the Highest go, have you been promoted yet?"

"No I haven't been promoted, the afternoon went rather strangely and I found out something astonishing!"

"What was that then?" he asked.

"I'll tell you when I get back."

Oh and are you coming back any time soon?" asked Minto.

"Cad, I will return as soon as I can, hopefully the day after tomorrow and I need to talk to you about something rather important..."

Jocasta spent a restless two days in the capital taking the opportunity to visit some of the sights. She was presently in the *Psihearg* gardens staring over the Tamesis where she could see London House, as a young Psi *saetere* she had infiltrated the ACG offices there.

Feeling Sirki's resonation she turned to face her. "Well, what is the result?

She handed Blane a written report. "Both our great grandmothers were cloned from the same genetic material which makes us sort of third cousins" Sirki informed her. "And like me, you will become what the Psi' choose to call an Omega, it's your *wyrd*."

One night later Cadoc Minto woke from his slumber as Jocasta slipped into bed beside him.

"Hold me dahling I have some incredible news ..."

CHAPTER 25 — WHO GOES THERE?

Sirki woke in a cold sweat and pulled back the covers to expose Bren's chest then ran her fingers over his ribs. "What's the matter *rakas*?" he had woken immediately.

"I felt Sari's presence, she was in such pain and there was blood and you were dying."

"It was just a dream Sirk" he enfolded her in his arms and she hooked a leg over him in her manner.

"It seemed so real Bren. I can't feel her anywhere, even when you were lost in the Helm I knew you were alive but Sari has vanished. What have they done to her?"

Bren could feel her tears moist on his chest. "We'll find her somehow my dahling" he said reassuringly. But he had no idea where to start.

Dame Hildegard finally plucked up the courage to summon the unknowing half-sisters then confessed all.

There was a long silence until finally Elli finally spoke. "And dad knew this?"

"Yes Elli dahling, I'm glad to say he had a very forgiving nature" answered Hilly.

"Small wonder you took me in after... you know?" remarked Bonnie not caring to remember too much of her past.

They embraced Hilly warmly and stayed to talk until late into the evening confirming they felt no animosity for her or what their *fathers* had done then after saying goodnight, the half-siblings walked together to the main door.

"Well sus, I have to return to the Port this night. The bloody Highest wants to see me, I don't think she ever sleeps?" announced Bonnie.

"Good night sus, you know it seems strange saying that even though we have been like susters for years" Elli embraced Bonnie, holding her tightly for a moment.

"I think I've always known you were my suster" said Bonnie a little surprised at her uncharacteristic display of warmth.

So Bren's only my half-brothur, I'm almost glad about that! Elli thought while waving as Bonnie's flyer lifted off.

Madel Tog-Barr was making her way to her parent's house on Lacetown Road in Scartho when she was briefly illuminated by the headlamps of a black *waegn*. Feeling a chill down her spine she watched curiously as the vehicle disappeared in the direction of the town centre. *It's probably just some workman coming home late, was she becoming paranoid, it wouldn't hurt to tell someone though would it?* After all, she had some powerful new friends.

Dame Hildegarde had retired to her quarters to sit in her favourite chair with a glass of aquavit. *Sirki had been right, a huge weight had been lifted from her mind and not only she did she feel happier but the girls had taken it rather well.* Switching on the view-screen she almost laughed to see footage of her daughter-in-law in her Freya days singing "My Love is the Moon" but after listening to half of the song she turned to the news channel. *My son may love her but her singing still grates on me,* she fell into a doze to dream about her missing granddaughter but woke with a start after a few minutes. The room was now in complete darkness and on discovering the power was off she felt a chill down her spine. Switching to night vision Hilly drew her *seax* and called the guard post. "The bloody lights have gone out in the family quarters" she informed them.

"Ma'am we will look into it immediately, are you alright?" came the reply.

"Of course I'm alright you arse, just get the bloody lights back on!" she snapped then noticed the bright golden glow coming from under the door.

Tithengealdor Webb was walking the rounds in the family quarters, he had been in the 3rd Elites for forty years and was now a member of the Hall Watch whose duty was to patrol the old building and keep alert for intruders. As jobs went it was pretty easy, the Hall stood in a garrison burh right next to 3rd Elite headquarters and was surrounded by a high wall with a well manned guard house but nevertheless, it was considered a prestigious position and Webb took great pride in it. When the lights had suddenly gone out he reported it to the wardhus and they instructed him to call on Dame Hildegarde to reassure her of their diligence.

"She can bite his head off as well" thought the Duty Officer who had suffered her wrath.

Webb knew that only the formidable old dame and the reserved daughter were here at the moment but as he made his way towards the family rooms he could see a strange golden glow around the corner.

"Who is it?" he asked quickening his pace but there was no reply. "Who goes there?" he demanded in his old parade ground voice but as he turned the corner, pistol drawn, the light winked out leaving only the after image of a glowing figure.

Webb, who was standing opposite Dame Hildegard's room, jumped as the lights came back followed by the door opening. "Well that was bloody odd!" remarked Hilly upon sticking her head out.

Elli Da N'tan stalked through the Hall checking for suspicious activity, Tog-Barr had path'd her concern but it might be nothing more than a touch of paranoia, *who could blame the girl after what she had been through?*

Then she felt the icy chill and instantly recognised it for what it was, a Psi of great power scanning the building, and upon hearing the lights had gone out in the family quarters she called the Guard into action, *this was no accidental outage.* After checking that her mother was safe Elli climbed the High Tower, one of the oldest parts of the building, to stand on the parapet. The Hall had been built on the loftiest point in Scartho and the burh sprawled away in all directions except to the north where steep cliffs faced the mouth of the estuary. The cormorant flag flapped overhead in the stiff breeze as she stood trying to feel the source of the intrusion but there was nothing. On a whim she went to the main gate and ventured outside accompanied by several soldiers and following her intuition she led them along the west wall almost to the cliff edge where a trace of *something* could be felt before moving down the embankment and pushing through the light scrub to a small parking area for the viewpoint, a popular spot for nocturnal trysts.

Several vehicles with steamed up windows were parked here and the occupants found their courting disturbed by the sudden appearance of armed troops. Some did attempt to drive away but were halted in the narrow lane by the appearance of an armoured vehicle.

"Over here, ma'am!" a *Huscarl* was pointing at the road surface where, by using her night-vision, Da N'tan could see the warm outline of a recently departed vehicle.

"Interview this lot and find out if anyone saw a black Pony Super parked here!" she ordered before contacting Mina Srivastava in London. *"Only the breakers for the family quarters had been tripped and both my mother and a trusted watchman saw a strange light. I traced some slight psionic remanence down to the Cormorant's Rock viewpoint where some of its nocturnal visitors recalled seeing a black waegn similar to the one reported by Tog-Barr."*

"Interesting, could it be that one of our own susters was responsible for this?" she path'd.

"It is possible but one would have to ask why, Highest?" was Da N'tans reply.

"And you, a Mystagogue, could not identify this Psi?

"No ma'am there was only the slightest trace."

"Apart from yourself, Ashby and I there are only three others I know of who can conceal their presence, your suster in law and your two nieces, one of whom is missing, presumed abducted. This is a matter of the utmost concern for it is not inconceivable that Sari Jorvik may now be under the control of the ACG, we must be on our guard!"

Elli realised whatever rancour she felt for her brothur and his rightwife they must be told of this terrible possibility...

The Da N'tans had taken their grandchildren to New Winchester to show them the Gardens of the Gods on their way to visit Effie at the Kingshall. The royal couple greeted them warmly then Effie turned to her husband. "Fredi sweetie, can you and Bren take the children and show them the horses. When you come back we'll have tea" suggested Effie. "I want to talk to my dahling Sirki."

"One can't say one doesn't know one's place old man" related King Fredi as he led Bren and the grandchildren out to the stables. After the attempted coup, the royal couple had settled their differences and were as happy as Bren and Sirki attempted to be.

"So my love, Mina believes Sari may be under the control of those bahstards?" asked the queen when they had left.

"I don't want to believe it Effie, not my little girl!"

In the Palace grounds the children were with a stable hand giving an apple to Valor, the queen's favourite horse while the King regarded them fondly. "They remind one of the twins when they were young" he remarked. "But then old chap, they do have your family bloodline."

"Yes sir" Bren had been the queen's lover before and after her forced marriage but had baulked at providing her with the offspring her husband could not. She had approached his reckless younger brother however and he had eagerly stepped in to fill the breach as it were. "Speaking of which, how are they doing?"

"Jack is doing very well as Thegn of Kernow, Gil was at the palace earlier but she's gone off to Beormingham to open a new manufactory, doubtless warming up to take the crown when the dear rightwife packs it in."

"Is Effie planning on abdicating then?" Bren hardly ever saw his *unofficial* niece and nephew.

"I seriously doubt it" he replied then asked quietly. "Bren, are there any developments regarding your daughter?"

"No sir, the Highest believes the ACG have her somewhere out there" he felt a lump in his throat.

"They are absolute bahstards!" spat the King. "It must be terrible for the both of you."

Bren was choked. "We thought we'd got rid of them thirty years ago then they turn up in the Pirren so we take them out again, yet they still survive and my baby girl is in their hands."

"Why is grandad crying" asked Wil, returning with her brother.

"Oh he's just got some dust in his eyes my pet, let's go and see if your mummy and Auntie Effie have got that tea sorted out. Don't worry about grandad he'll catch us up when he's ready," replied the King.

That night after making love Bren had fallen asleep but Sirki lay awake looking at him, the premonition of a few nights ago had returned to haunt her. *Whatever was coming she would protect her family, all of them, including Sari if she could.*

Over in Scartho another pair of lovers lay in post-coital wakefulness. "You're not yourself tonight Pen?" remarked Rika, a dark cloud had hung over her for some time now.

"Sorry Hal, this business with Sari is draining me" she replied. "I feel so helpless and there's nothing I can do."

"It must be awful for Bren and Sirki, it would tear me apart if it was one of mine," Hal had two grown up children with his late wife. "Hei what's up?" he asked, Penni had begun to cry.

"It's just that... Poor Sirki, I wish I could do something, anything, it's just..." her voice tailed off.

"You still love her don't you?"

"I've never met anyone else like her, she's unique."

"Then what am I doing here?" he asked a little testily.

"Hal, I like you a lot and I feel we do have a future together but I can't just forget, particularly at the moment." confessed Penni.

"So you want me to stay around until she reels you back in?" he asked. "How do you think that makes me feel?"

"Hal, I would never let that happen!" she assured him.

It wasn't much by way of reassurance, he would take it but something still niggled at him. "And if someone else catches your eye?"

"Sirki is the only woman I've had a relationship with" she replied. "And the only man I want is you Hal, I swear to it."

"I'm sorry Penni, but you're still hiding something, be honest, tell me, I don't care what it is, or how bad?"

"Time for the truth again I suppose?" she had wanted to tell him so often but hadn't dared. "You remember when I got myself shot?"

"How can I forget, we all thought you were going to die?"

"Well, you know how I couldn't have children after that? Sirki bore a child for me using one of my eggs and Sari is that child. Sirki is only her surrogate mother, she's my biological daughter."

"Oh Gods, Pen I'm so sorry, this must be killing you?"

"So now you know why I'm not at my best."

Hal held her tightly while she clung to him and sobbed.

CHAPTER 26 - A NEW HIGHEST

Freya finished checking the field control circuits in the Sparrow, *wherever Sari was she still had a job to do.* She climbed out of the cabin closing the hatch and descended the steps but on reaching the pad Freya had the distinct feeling of being watched so scanned around using her prescience, another gift from her mother but was unable to detect anyone who should not be there. After passing a moment with the pad crew Freya drove to the residential block but she wasn't feeling particularly tired so decided to walk to the airdock's official alehouse, the *Landing Pad.*

Sleipnir had returned yesterday and a couple of the crew were there celebrating. Marcus Petronius was busily boasting of his experiences in Dimension 2, as the neighbouring dimension was now being called and it amused Freya to see Aesh standing behind him miming putting her fingers down her throat and puking. She listened in briefly, hearing that in this new world the Reignweald did not exist and its inhabitants were considerably behind them technologically, Aengland was called England and only four nations were joined together in a United Kingdom. Worse still, proud little Kernow was just a shire in this alternate version of their home.

"Auntie Penni won't like that." thought Freya as she sat at a low table with a glass of mead.

"That Petronius is a cock!" Aesh was stood before her. "Would you object to me joining you?"

"No, you are most welcome" replied Freya. "And you are right, he is a cock."

"Is there any news of your suster?"

Freya shook her head.

"How's your mum taking it?"

"Badly, Elke, why don't you go and see her?" asked Freya. "I'm sure she would make you welcome."

"Best that I didn't" she replied taking a sip from her drink.

"So what's it like in this other world?" Freya was curious, there would be an official report out soon but Aesh would put a more personal slant on it.

"Odd, they are very like us but so different at the same time. They are very intolerant of other nations while believing they are so much better, altruism isn't very widespread and do you know, they spend a disproportionate amount of time watching and talking about football?"

"What! That's just kicking a ball around, don't they play rugby?" Freya was astonished at this.

"Yeah, but football seems to dominate sports broadcasting on their *television* sets."

Freya thought about the word, "Far-off-see? It's a combination of Hellenic and Romano words, they must have a similar history to us?"

"Yes, but they don't honour the old gods, in their world the Romans didn't follow Mithras very much and instead worshipped a god called Iesus, it's a bit like Mithraism without the bulls yet it beat all our gods into submission and something else very different is that William the Bahstard beat King Hrald and the country was ruled by Northmen for years *and* there are no Thegnwealds just a load of nobodies claiming things they don't deserve, most of them couldn't even lift a sword let alone use one!"

"Yuck! I don't much like the sound of this place" stated Freya.

"It has a rough charm even though the beer is shit and the food dreadful." Elke took another drink. "It is very boisterous and somewhat hostile but weapons are prohibited almost everywhere, even their Ward, which they call Police, do not openly carry guns."

"Do they have *novae* there?"

"We could not find any, there are some who claim to have telepathy and such but the only Psionic emanation Fordyce could find was from us. There was a man on the television who claimed to bend metal with his mind and Bella was very interested in that but he was clearly a stage conjuror fooling the gullible," she attested.

"It all seems very interesting but I prefer going into the real firmament over disappearing into nowhere and coming out somewhere else" admitted Freya.

"Well if isn't Freya Da N'tan and another of her mother's ex-girlfriends?" butted in Marcus, slightly the worse for drink.

Elke leaned forward, grabbed his crotch and squeezed. "Now be a good little man-child and fuck off before I tell everyone how I had to beat up those *skinheads* who were going to *kick your head in!*" they watched him stagger away. "If your dad still has any influence on this project please ask him to get that twat off it!"

Freya went back her quarters alone, Dexter was visiting his parents in the Port of London, they were nice people and devout Mithrans, it was strange to think of a world without its diversity of deities. *It would be quite dull.*

Bonnie was strolling across Westhearg Bridge in the warm evening air and paused halfway to look at the dark water of the Tamesis flowing underneath. North of her stood the collection of buildings known somewhat incorrectly by the singular title of London House, it was the meeting place of both Reignweald and Aenglish Witangemot. The ancient clock on the Queen's Tower rang out eight as she crossed the river towards the south bank and her destination, the *Psihearg*. The Psi headquarters was also misnamed for although it had the appearance of an overgrown temple it was not a place of devotion but the administrative centre of the Psi Wing where Mina sat like a spider in a web of thought.

Bonnie had formally accepted the offer and one day would have to take on the mantle of Highest, a job for life that she was in no great hurry to inherit but there were plenty of eager young Psi' working in the *Hearg* and she planned on delegating responsibility to make the running of the group easier, in her opinion Mina had fingers in too many pies.

As she reached the building there was a thickening in the hum of the Psionic landscape. *Yes that was the best way to describe it,* the normal hum of thousands of minds was slurring and slowing. Someone was operating a massive suppression field nearby!

Was this a prelude to an attack on the Psihearg?

Going into quickspeed she blurred to the gatehouse. "Get a patrol out, search the area for any unauthorised vehicles, take a third level Psi with you and contact the Ward" she ordered to the Guard Cempa. "Put the *Psihearg* on full alert but no alarums, I want complete discretion."

Running into the main building she spotted a group of Acolytes sat in the atrium deep in telepathic conversation, they had not noticed the diminishing background noise because they were closely linked. "You three follow me, I may need backup" she shouted as she raced up the stairs. *"I wish I could levitate like the Da N'tans, why don't we have any lifts in this place?"*

Mina felt the suppression field envelop the building cutting her off from the Psionic world but the *Psihearg* going *flat* would be a signal for the backup Psi Guard force based across the river to move in. Then the lights on the entire top floor went out and a bright glow illuminated the office behind her. Mina turned her chair to face the light but did not switch to infra-red and saw a beautiful naked figure floating there, the hair was being blown about as if by a gentle breeze and its skin emanated a golden light which was so brilliant Mina was glad she was using normal vision. The shining figure regarding her with malevolence was obviously a Psi avatar, *but whose?*

"Who are you?" demanded Mina standing to face it, the being began to float towards her and she backed away as it advanced, its pointed teeth were bared and the golden light burned as it approached.

"This is being projected from somewhere outside the building!" Mina called up her avatar, Kali Ma, who charged the glowing figure knocking it end over end.

The figure flew forward bathing Mina's avatar in its radiance and she could feel its flesh burn as if it were her own. Kali grabbed the figure's head in its clawed hands and twisted the head but it turned as though the neck was boneless before raising a hand to blast Mina's projection backwards, draining her strength.

"Is that the best you can do you old haeg?" it roared.

Mina recognised the attacker's voice. "You!" she cried.

"Who did you expect?" the figure answered pouring its golden light onto her avatar, Mina felt its pain and screamed.

Kali Ma now aflame flailed at the figure scoring several hits but the avatar continued the assault undiminished. Mina, no longer able to keep up her defence, fell exhausted to the floor and her avatar dissipated as the figure continued menacingly forward.

Every Psi in the world felt Mina's death as Bonnie finally reached the Highest's door to throw it open and spot the glowing being hovering over her prostrate form.

A white figure flew from nowhere to bowl into the golden creature and both rolled away from the Highest's body. The new combatant resembled a human sized porcelain doll, talon-fingered, fang mouthed and wearing an old fashioned dress and bonnet, the golden woman floated to her feet and enveloped Bonnie's avatar in its brilliance burning away dress and hair as it fell into a crouch.

The white figure now devoid of all features turned its head up to the figure and opened freshly painted eyes as a snub nose popped out while a fanged slash like mouth opened below.

"Bad choice of attack Goldie, don't you know that ceramic isn't bothered by fire?" the doll remarked then stood and stepped forward to slice down with a taloned right hand, leaving four long slashes from breast to pelvis. Golden light poured from the wounds and the avatar let out an ear-splitting howl before dissipating.

"Oh Gods that thing, whose was it?" asked one of the Psi.

"I don't know, but I do have a horrible suspicion" answered Bonnie before going over to examine Mina's corpse. Apart from the look of horror on her face she had not a mark upon her.

In a street nearby a black Pony Super screeched off on hearing sirens only to crash headlong into a Spearman RHW coming the other way, the armoured vehicle was hardly scratched but the *waegn* was wrecked and the suppression field died away instantly. Three mangled bodies were pulled from the vehicle, all were clones wearing unmarked black drabs but of the rogue Psi there was no sign.

Bonnie contacted Elli to warn her of the powerful avatar and informed her of her suspicions.

"But you defeated her easily enough?" remarked Elli.

"That is true. I damaged her avatar so badly it will take a while before she can regenerate it but I had the element of surprise on my side" replied Bonnie. *"She will be hiding somewhere recovering her Psionic power."*

"You are Highest now Bonnie." Elli reminded her.

"I didn't want it to be this way suster" she replied.

"I know but Mina was never going to retire."

"You do realise who it was, don't you?" asked Bonnie.

"Yes ma'am, my brothur and his family, have they been informed?"

"Sirki is distraught but is confident she can restrain her if attacked." replied the new Highest sadly.

Mina couldn't remember how she got here, the avatar had closed on her and she had felt the heat, then nothing.

"Open your eyes Mina" said an all too familiar voice.

She did and was astonished by her surroundings. "How I am still alive?" she looked around. "Is this *the meadow*, are you really her?"

"To answer your questions, you are not alive your physical body is quite dead. I simply rescued your consciousness and carried it here, it was the very least I could do after your years of loyalty. You are now but a manifestation of your own mind, as if you were in a Helm construct but with no chance of return" the being stood before Mina, feet bare on the lush grass. "And this is indeed *Fólkvangr* but I am no goddess, merely a different lifeform. If this was your afterlife would it not conform to your Hindu belief system?"

Mina gathered her thoughts, *thoughts, was that all she was now?* Then remembering why she was here asked. "You could have destroyed her or at least stopped her?"

"Could I?" answered the being. "Your successor did an excellent job of incapacitating the avatar without any assistance."

"I knew Ashby was the right choice" agreed Mina.

"As for destroying her, she may yet be useful to us alive."

"Us?" this was the first time the entity had referred to anyone else. "What use could this destructive creature be?"

"If she destroys Sirkku's physical body then she will have no choice but to join us here, she has been fruitful during her time in your world but this is her rightful place and she is long overdue."

"Destroy Sirkku! I thought you were on her side, our side?" gasped Mina.

"We are working to save many worlds from the Jotunn, not just yours, and in all honesty there is but the one side, mine!" answered the entity. "Now go enjoy your new existence for this is a most pleasant place."

Sirki was curled up on the couch hands clasped over her head. "It couldn't be her, Bren, she wouldn't attack Mina."

"Do you doubt what Bonnie told us? You said yourself the description matched that of her avatar."

"Don't say it!" cried Sirki.

"What, that our daughter is now under the control of the ACG?"

"I don't want to believe it!"

"Are we safe, is she so powerful?" asked Bren.

"There are very few who could possibly stand up to her alone, Bonnie and I are two of them."

"And the others are?" he asked.

"Your suster maybe and perhaps Freya but our new Highest has a plan, high level Psi' are being organised into teams of five with armed back up and since it took only four acolytes to capture Sari the first time they hope it will be sufficient" then Sirki cried. "Oh Bren this can't be happening, I just want to shut my eyes and it all go away!"

CHAPTER 27 - SARI

Sirki normally swam naked but since the grandchildren were now living with her she had chosen to wear a swimming costume, much to the relief of Heidi Glaser who found Fro Scartho's poolside nudity as disconcerting as Anya did.

The ex-*saetere* had been a *guest* here for several months now and had become quite attached to Sirki's son, Sirki had removed the compulsion but she was happy to live as part of the family, free to come and go as she chose. She never left the house alone however, partly because she imagined her every move would shadowed by the Palace Covert Unit and partly out of fear that, despite their decimation, the ACG would be looking to settle the score.

Heidi was right on the first count but on the second, who knew?

She lay on a recliner enjoying the afternoon sun with Bern on the bed next to her sleeping in the shade.

Freya was in the pool with her mother and Willa, who swam like a silkie, while Bren and his son were in the gym trying to outdo one another, she reflected on how idyllic it must seem to an outside observer but could feel the turmoil inside her mother who was putting on a brave face for the grandchildren. A mask she had worn ever since Sari disappeared.

Sirki swam to the edge and climbed out, her green swimsuit cut to the point of decency and clinging to every curve.

"Mummo what is that drawing on your leg?" Willa pointed to the Mjolnir tattoo displayed on her thigh.

"It's my display of faith to the god of thunder." she replied.

"Can I have one too?" Willa continued.

"When you're sixteen you can choose to honour one of the gods and then you can have a tattoo showing it. You can see Auntie Freya has one on her leg too, Uncle Alfie has one on his arm and grandad has a tattoo round his wrist to show his allegiance to the brave god Tiw." Sirki informed her.

"Does mummy have one?" she asked.

"Of course *lapsi*, she has a tattoo like *mummo's*." Sirki tried to avoid mentioning Sari if possible.

"Will mummy come back like grandad did?"

"I do hope so dahling, shall we see if Ani has made that lemonade." answered Sirki desperate to change the subject, they had told the children that *mami* had to go away for a while and would be back soon. It wasn't a good excuse and had caused some distress, they seemed to be coping with it now but Willa still asked awkward questions.

"It's alright mummo" replied her granddaughter, who seemed to understand despite her tender years.

After dinner, Freya, returned to the airdock to be with Dexter in New Winchester, the facility was considered reasonably safe as it was heavily guarded as a matter of course and had been reinforced with one of Bonnie's Psi teams. The news of Mina Srivastava's death and the circumstances in which it happened had caused consternation in the Witangemot and the new Highest had promised to join the Da N'tans this evening to discuss future plans, the rest of Sirki's immediate family were still at the dining table discussing Mina's death so Anya Jensen took the grandchildren to the lounge to spare them hearing the adult conversation.

"Bonnie has initiated a Psionic search over the whole of Aengland but you know she can hide from detection just as Freya or I can." Sirki informed them. "If it is Sari then only the Highest or I can hope to stop her, Freya has yet to reach her potential and may not be able to stand against her suster."

"What about Auntie Elli isn't she reckoned to be on a par with Bonnie?" asked Aelf.

"I hate to say this about your suster, Bren, but she isn't powerful enough" confessed Sirki.

"But what will *you* do Sirki, this is our daughter we're talking about?" asked Bren.

"I will try to reach her, she will still be in there just like Madel and I will attempt to bring her out." she replied.

"And if you can't, mum?" asked Aelf.

"I *will* reach her, there is nej other option that I will contemplate." she answered.

"And if Bonnie finds her first?" asked Bren.

"I trust that she will do the right thing, we shall discuss it face to face when she arrives" Sirki hoped the Highest didn't encounter her daughter before then.

As they made their way to the lounge Bern ran out to them "I want my Toki!" he had left his favourite furry bear upstairs.

"I'll get it for him" said Heidi going to fetch the toy.

Sirki smiled, she had been right all along, the ex-*saetere* had turned out to be a good person inside.

As the girl approached the children's room she noticed the door was open and glancing inside saw a figure in a familiar black uniform staring at their beds. It was Sari and she turned her head to spy Heidi looking at her aghast.

"Glaser the traitor!" she snarled.

Heidi turned tail and ran for the stairs only to fall to the floor as pain wracked through her, she tried to crawl screaming and writhing in agony as Sari kept the nerve fire pulsing through her body until finally her heart failed as she went into shock.

Aelf had run up the stairs at the sound of her cries and looked in horror at Glaser's contorted body then at his sister. "Sari, what have they done to you, why did you do this?"

Saying nothing she raised a Draca pistol to shoot him twice in the chest then watched him tumble backwards down the stairs.

Bren had run from the lounge pistol in hand with Sirki following him in time see their son land on the bottom step. Sari floated down the stairwell and stood by his body, her head had been shaved to a buzz cut and metal plates were screwed to each temple.

Bren raised his pistol but could not bring himself to shoot his daughter. "Is it you Sari?" he asked.

"Wassael dad!" she replied before shooting him through the heart.

"NEJ!" screamed Sirki before telekinetically hurling her daughter at the far wall to stun her while simultaneously sending a psionic distress signal.

"Sari?" cried Anya starting from the lounge.

"Anya, stay in there and protect the children." ordered Sirki. "Do it now, Sari is being controlled by the ACG!"

Locking the lounge door the young woman retrieved a Draca pistol from a secret drawer in the tall oak cabinet by the door. "Come on children we're going to play hide and seek" and they took cover behind the large settee in the corner of the room. She primed the pistol and rested the barrel on the back of the couch aiming at the door while dearly hoping she wouldn't have to shoot the woman she loved.

Willa turned to her with a knowing look. "Mummy's very angry isn't she, Ani?"

Sirki squatted next to Bren and tore his shirt open to see the neat round bullet-hole, there was very little blood and she was unable to find a pulse so she cast her mind down into his chest to perceive the bullet lodged in his heart. Sirki concentrated hard and it popped out of the entry wound hot and bloody then after mentally pinching the wound shut, she squeezed his heart and it began to beat weakly.

"Come back you *polho*, I'm not losing you now!" she cried and incredibly his eyes flickered open briefly. His pulse was erratic but as long as she could keep her concentration she could keep him alive.

A sudden wave of pain coursed through her and clenching her teeth she pushed it back to her daughter, who had regained consciousness and was on her feet.

I must keep his heart beating!

"You can't fight me *and* keep him alive mummy!" taunted Sari.

"What do you want?" demanded Sirki.

"I want the children!"

"Nej, you cannot have them they are safe with us."

Sari slitted her eyes and stared over Sirki's head at the locked door. "They are hiding in the lounge and you have trusted my dahling Ani to look after them, she is hiding behind the furniture and has a gun. Aw, she thinks she can protect them, I'll make her bring them here to me, her weak mind won't be able to resist" she said in a mocking tone. "I might even make her shoot you as well."

"You will not have my grandchildren for their evil experiments!" snarled Sirki placing a protective block around Anya and the children.

She was stretching her powers to the limit and Sari knew it. "How much longer can you keep this up, not much I would guess?" she ventured. "I'm bored now mummy, let's finish it!" Sari fired several rounds only to see them splash flat against an invisible barrier before falling onto the floor.

"I'll bet you didn't know about that one, daughter? Bonnie and I have recently developed the technique." Sirki threw a pressure wave at Sari knocking her off her feet, she was weakening *was nej-one coming to help?*

Sari stood and advanced slowly towards her mother who was now trying desperately to hold her back, she couldn't spend more psionic energy without letting go of Bren or lowering her guard over the grandchildren and the effort was draining her.

Sari was pushing forward against the invisible force as if walking into the wind while getting ever closer.

Sirki could see the malice in her eyes. "Sari *lapsi* this isn't you, you're being controlled by them, break free I know you can!" beseeched Sirki, she could not keep this struggle up much longer.

Her daughter said nothing but raised the pistol once more, this time Sirki could not hope to stop the bullets.

"Sari, I know you're in there! Please, I'm your mother!" she screamed, dragging what she could spare of her power into her charisma.

"Mummy?" she mouthed silently.

"Yes it's mummy I can help you, *lapsi.*"

"Mummy?" a look of anguish briefly crossed her face and she lowered the gun.

Sirki held out her hand and Sari was reaching towards it when the front door flew open and Bonnie entered the house like an avenging spirit. She had discovered the security team dead or unconscious at the gatehouse, several with broken necks, and went straight on the offensive spinning Sari across the hall like a rag doll. Struggling to her feet Sirki's daughter snarled and countered by levitating a table directly at Bonnie who fell back hitting her head.

"Nej!" screamed Sirki realising that all hope of reasoning with her daughter had been dashed by the sudden attack.

Sari momentarily regarded her mother with a tortured look upon her face then rushed from the house. Bonnie stood groggily and looked over the carnage in the hall then hearing a flyer starting up, stumbled outside to see a Midge rising from the trees. Visualising the drive units in her head she chose the cooling circuit on the right hand drive and pulled telekinetically at the power cable. The flyer began listing to one side as it flew away, it couldn't go too far now and she could follow it on her Hafoc.

Sirens could be heard approaching. *"Sirki, can you manage till the haelers get here? I have damaged her flyer and plan on catching up with her when she lands."*

"I can cope, Bonnie, please try to not harm her, Sari's still in there somewhere!" begged Sirki anxiously.

"I'm sorry Sirki I can make no promises." As she mounted her motorbike several emergency vehicles arrived to stop before the house, one was a *campscrid* with four *Huscarls* aboard. *"Follow me."* Bonnie path'd to its crew before roaring down the drive pausing only to raise a hand to Freya, who had followed the loose convoy. *"Look to your family!"* she path'd.

With that thought Bonnie rode off in pursuit with the *ferdrinc in* tow.

225

CHAPTER 28 – NO MORE TEARS

Freya entered to chaos in her family home, *haelers* were carefully lifting her father onto a stretcher while her distraught mother knelt by Aelfred's body and on seeing her, Sirki stood to hug her older daughter tightly "Freya look after Willa and Bern, Anya is in pieces and I have to go to the Haelinghus with your father, until he's on life support only my psionic power is keeping him alive."

Freya watched numbly as they took him away with her mother following then with tears rolling down her cheeks she knelt beside her dead brother to place his short *seax* in his hands before cupping her right hand over her heart and throwing it forward, *safe journey my beloved brothur*. Going upstairs she found Heidi's body twisted in its death agonies so Freya laid her on her back and crossed her arms over her shoulders, *poor girl, killed for being Alfie's companion*. She went back down to join her niece and nephew in the lounge and comforted them, choking back tears while Anya sat grief-stricken, head in hands.

Sirki had reached the Haelinghus when Bonnie contacted her. *"I saw the flyer go down on the East Downs, I suspect she was heading for Kenta, Campaeldor Anderson was at the Palace and she's on her way to join me with a tithe of Huscarls, Elli is coming down from London with a Psi' party and back-up from the London Here, we will surround her and endeavour to take her alive."*

Sirki thanked her then contacted Campaeldor Anderson. *"Penni, please be careful, remember who she is."*

"I will try Sirki, how is Bren?" She replied.

"He is in surgery now and the doctors think he has a good chance of recovery."

"I heard about Alf and that poor girl."

"It hasn't sunk in properly yet, I think I'm in shock…Penni?"

"Ya Sirki?" replied Penni.

"I know she can be saved, please don't let her be killed."

"I won't my lover, I promise!"

Bonnie followed the flyer to the southern edge of a heavy wooded area then pulling up she put the Hafoc on its stand to consider her options. The local Ward would be cordoning off the area but miles of woodland lay to the north and somewhere in the midst of it was the Da N'tan's psychotic and very dangerous daughter.

Her head was throbbing and she felt slightly nauseous, hoping it wasn't a concussion she regarded the four *Huscarls* stood before her. "We are going up against the most dangerous foe you will ever meet, she is your physical equal in battle and easily my equal in Psionic power, if we see her let me confront her and take your shots when you can. If you find her and I am not with you, shoot straight away for you will not get a second chance, do not try to reason with her or to make her surrender! Do you understand?"

They nodded gravely and put on the torcs Ashby had issued them with then she led her small team into the woods. Having seen the flyer go down she had a rough idea of where it had crashed, *if they were lucky Sari Jorvik was unconscious or even dead!*

Anderson sat aboard the Flying Beetle with an apprehensive tithe of *Huscarls*, some knew Sari from her time in the Elites and they were not looking forward to the task ahead. She remembered the joy she had felt when Sirki bore the baby she could not and how she had let Sirki bring her up, happy to be known as Auntie Penni but now their genetic progeny was causing mayhem and it was down to her to end it.

The Beetle landed and they disembarked in silence to enter the woods from the west.

Elli Da N'tan was travelling south in a Beetle belonging to the 2nd London Here, it was part of a squadron carrying fifty soldiers with a Psi assigned to each tithe and upon landing they would follow a similar tactic to Bonnie's, she would lead the Psi' and tackle her niece while the Here were to provide firepower if required. The norm soldiers were all equipped with the latest advanced torcs developed by the resurgent ACG which would hopefully give them an advantage should they confront her.

Elli had long been distanced from her half-brother and had never quite accepted the vibrant Sirki. Her sister-in-law was her polar opposite, outgoing and flirtatious where she was awkward and retiring but they were family and had suffered terribly at the hands of their wayward daughter. She reflected on the fact that she was now flying to apprehend her niece, the biological daughter of Campaeldor Anderson who was on the same mission, as well as her oldest friend and recently revealed half-sister Bonnie, *it all felt a little incestuous.*

Along the Northern Road, armoured vehicles belonging to the Wessex *Campward* had set up in battle order along the eastern edge of the forest, if the renegade Psi was driven this way they would be ready for her.

Bonnie found the Midge a mile into the forest. It appeared that Sari had managed to make a controlled landing in a small clearing but blood on the headrest of the pilot's seat told of a less than smooth touchdown. Ashby surmised she had been thrown forward hitting her head on the controls.

A single magpie, disturbed by their approach, flapped cawing into the air as they hiked further in. *"A bad omen?"* thought Bonnie, struggling against her growing nausea. Their quarry was nowhere in sight but a flattened trail through the undergrowth headed north, *towards Kingston possibly?* After following for some distance, it stopped abruptly before a tall tree where bizarrely a bloody streak ran down the trunk.

Gods I forgot she can levitate, I'm not concentrating! She looked up to see Sari perched on a high branch glaring down. "She's in the tree, shoot her!" Bonnie yelled while hurling a psionic shock wave. The *Huscarl*s went into action but it was far too late, she had the advantage and they were flung backwards like rag dolls.

Bonnie heard a brief burst of automatic fire as she blacked out.

Reality came blearily back. "Ma'am, are you all right?" it was Undergealdor Sinfin, "Gods, I thought you'd crossed the bridge when I saw you thrown like that."

"What happened?" Her left shoulder hurt like hell and she couldn't move the arm.

"Your collar bone's broken ma'am and we've lost Burns. He was smashed against a tree but Hwithus and Wilson are still fit for combat" explained Sinfin who, being at the rear had managed to get a few rounds off winging Sari as she fled.

Ferescota Wilson was a *camphaeler* and fashioned a makeshift sling for Ashby's arm but she refused a shot of relaxant as a clear head would be needed to deal with Sari. *Sorry Mina, so far I'm doing a pretty shit job of being Highest.* As Wilson helped her to shakily stand she path'd Elli to inform her of what had occurred, *sloppy, sloppy!*

"Wassael Bonnie, I thought I had killed you." Sari's thought broke into their telepathic conversation. *"Oh well better luck next time."*

"We're coming for you niece," warned Elli.

"You can try Auntie, you can try." she replied menacingly.

There was no point in swapping idle threats so Bonnie set out once again, with Wilson supporting her and the others on point, to follow the trail of blood leading deeper into the undergrowth, *this could make things easier but isn't a wounded animal more dangerous when cornered?* The track headed north which would lead her straight into the path of Elli's larger force.

Anderson, heading rapidly towards the direction of the shooting had remembered Sari's ability to levitate and had her soldiers watching the trees as they pushed on, determined to find her errant daughter first.

Sari psionically closed off the wound in her leg and floated down into a clearing.

"Fucking *Huscarl scunung!*" she snarled to herself while tearing open her trouser leg to examine the bullet wound. She applied an antibiotic and painkiller but as she was taking a bandage from her *haeler*-kit she felt Alphas approaching and one was very different from the rest. Recognising who it was she smiled, *come to me mum I'm ready for you.*

From the cover of the trees, the Campaeldor spotted Sari bandaging her leg and was horrified to see what had happened to the pretty blonde girl who had now called her mum. Penni was sure Sari would listen to her so she walked into the clearing holding her pistol down at her side while the others remained in cover, weapons held in readiness.

"Hei mum, have you come to kill me?" asked Sari sardonically.

"No Sari, give yourself up we can help you."

"Not going to happen, half-mother!"

"Sirki, your birth mother, she can help you *lapsi*.

"It's far too late for that!" she replied scowling.

"Sari, this isn't you, the ACG have done something awful to your brain to make you act like this. Surrender now and you won't be harmed, I give you my oath."

"Your word means nothing to me *scunung*" spat the young woman.

"Please consider it, Sari we can put it right, there is no alternative."

"Go to hell, mum!"

"Then you leave me with no other choice," whispered Anderson raising her arm, at this the *Huscarls* stepped out of cover, weapons trained on the fugitive.

"You can't shoot me!" taunted Sari.

Penni found this to be true, she was immobilised as were all eleven *ferdrinc* who now stood like statues able only to watch helplessly.

"None of you can move unless I want you to and that goes for you two hiding to my left, I know you're there" she announced. "You *scunung* really do not stand a chance against me."

Bonnie's party had heard talking and spotting Penni's futile attempt to reason with Sari they had moved quietly in an attempt to outflank her, Sinfin and Hwithus were now frozen to the spot but Bonnie's mind shield encompassed Wilson and they remained both unaffected *and* undetected by Sari. From their vantage point behind the cover of a gnarled oak tree the new Highest fought against light-headedness to contemplate the worst decision she would ever have to make.

An animated Sari was continuing to mock the transfixed Anderson. "Now I can sense Aunt Elli approaching with her Psi' do they really imagine they can stop me? I will kill her first then I will make your men shoot the *Here* soldiers before I finish you" she aimed a pistol toward the trees waiting for the Psi to appear, *as soon as she stepped into the clearing she would shoot her dead and then the world would be rid of another Da N'tan.*

Bonnie needed to act fast, Sari was more powerful than had been imagined and so gesturing to Wilson to lift her torc the Highest entered her mind *"Sorry to do this but I couldn't think of another way to communicate without her knowing. When I show myself and get her attention, you shoot her, shoot to kill understand?"* Wilson nodded then replacing the headpiece Bonnie took a deep breath before stepping out of cover. "You're not as clever as you think!" she called, sending a psionic shock wave at her. Sari was taken by surprise and lessened her concentration.

A single shot rang out.

Sari staggered, looking at Penni who had fired before Wilson had the chance. "Mum?" she mouthed before slowly sinking to the ground.

Penni, heartbroken rushed to kneel by the dead girl and brush the hair from her bloody face. "Oh my poor baby I'm so sorry" she croaked.

The *Huscarls* observing their Campaeldors distress stood uncertain at what to do next and Elli, emerging at the edge of the clearing, raised her hand to halt the *Here's* approach, her face was a mask of horror. Bonnie sagged to her knees struggling to remain conscious to be caught in Wilson's arms, the effort had weakened her considerably and the concussion was beginning to take its toll.

"Sirki, I'm sorry!" sobbed Penni out loud. "I promised I wouldn't harm our daughter... I've brought this family nothing but trouble... I nearly split you and Bren up... I hurt Freya and now this..." standing she turned to Bonnie. "Tell Sirki I love her!" and with that she raised the pistol to her temple.

"*No!*" pathed Bonnie slipping helplessly into unconsciousness as Penni shot herself in front of the whole assembly.

Sirki was sat next to Bren's bed anxiously holding his hand. "Please Thor don't let him join you, it's not his time!"

She believed she had no more tears left to cry until she felt the deaths of her old lover and their daughter.

BOOK TWO

THE YEARS PASS

What happened to those years?
Why did they have to end in tears?
A promise of happiness that did not have its worth,
A life of love and sunshine stifled at its birth.
Why did it end in tears?
(Excerpt from Lament – music and words by A.S. Vigsdottir.)

FOUR...

Sirki had linked the viewer to the main screen in the lounge where it displayed a picture of Bren, Penni and herself sat on a beach in Kernow and they were each holding a child apiece. Penni was, of course, dandling Sari on her lap and they were so alike it was a wonder her true genesis hadn't been spotted before. Baby Bren started to cry so she plucked him out of his bouncer chair and changed the picture, next along was an official portrait of Dame Hildegard looking stern and formal.

"That is your *mummo* dahling, only we can't call her that because she has to be called grandma, she thinks I'm just a common backwoods Norther but I think she's a *wicca.*" she held him high and he chuckled. "Juu I do *lapsi.*" she cooed.

"Hei Sirk, I hope you're not telling our son tall tales?" teased Bren, he had just returned from a meeting with the Scartho Reeve.

"Only telling him what's so my *rakas*," she flipped the picture back to show the six of them on the beach. "Everything seemed so perfect back then" she remarked, he put his arm about her and they stared silently for a while. The awful events of last year weighed heavily on them, there had been so many funerals directly attributable to their youngest daughter, including her own.

Glaser's family felt antipathy towards the *novae*, the Da N'tan family in particular and had pointedly requested they did not attend her crossing. The Ward, of course, observed at a discrete distance to take note of any ACG sympathisers who might attend, which was a pointless exercise for none came, Heidi was considered a traitor to the cause, her feelings for a *nova* and a Da N'tan to boot were considered unforgiveable.

Sirki had become pregnant a few months after the terrible incident drawing malicious gossip from Aenglish society, some commented on her age while others held that the Da N'tans were coldly replacing one of their lost children and Sirki found this particularly hurtful as she had discussed another child with Bren long before the tragedy occurred. Effie's support of course could always be relied on and she backed her friend to the hilt making public her joy at Sirki's condition.

When little Bren was born with lilac eyes the Psi community was set alight, even the new Highest wondered if her predecessor's ideas about *novae* evolution had been correct.

THREE...

Jocasta Minto had been shopping in Pendinas with her daughter and was sitting under a sun umbrella on Porthmeor Beach which was famous for its surfing. She didn't understand the attraction but Cad seemed born to it.

"Dada, dada!" called Pandora from her pushchair on seeing her father walking from the tideline with his board under his arm and she waved her hands excitedly, Jocasta and Cadoc now lived with their daughter in nearby Helston Base.

Jocasta smiled, admiring his heroic physique as he approached, Cempa Minto was quite old fashioned and had insisted on betrothing the Psi when he discovered she was carrying his child.

"Who's dada's little girl?" he asked before unzipping his wetsuit and kissing Jocasta. "Did you get what you wanted at the shops?"

"I got Pan a new sun hat and this is for you my handsome" she handed him a bottle of cold cider and a bag containing a pasty. "Look at me, a proper little rightwife and mother, who would have thought this my *wyrd*?" she took a drink from her own bottle then spied her daughter throwing her new bonnet on the floor. "Hei, mummy bought that to stop the nasty sun burning you!" Jocasta scolded Pandora, placing the hat back on her head.

She promptly threw it to the floor again, followed by her tippy-cup.

Cadoc picked them up, gave her cup and put her hat back on only for Pandora to laugh and throw them down yet again.

"She needs to keep that on Cad, she has my complexion," observed Jocasta.

"She's got your hair too Cassie and your eyes" he said and looking into them kissed her again. Jocasta's pale blue eyes had begun to change colour early on in her pregnancy and it was no big surprise to either of them when their daughter was born with pale lilac eyes too.

TWO...

The conical white vessel approached Stardock on its pre-programmed course and aligned gracefully with the station's airlock before slowly moving to insert its nose into the docking ring, latches sliding into place as it achieved hard-dock. The vessel was Swan, the successor to Sparrow and it had succeeded in lifting off from the surface to achieve orbit without booster rockets, a sister ship, the Peacock, would be ready for launch later this year and once space-tested it would become the backup vessel for Swan's mission to the moon. The larger star-boat had taken over two years to build and sitting in the pilot's seat, Freya remembered wistfully that it had been two and a half years since the terrible night when she lost two of her siblings.

Stardock was perhaps a fanciful name for what was basically the second stage of a large launcher fitted out to support a small crew in orbit but it was destined to be the nucleus of a much larger station. Freya had wanted to push directly for the moon but Starwing had opted to put a space dock in high orbit as a halfway house meaning her trip to Selene would have wait for at least another year.

Just beyond the station's solar panels, Freya could see Sparrow with its cabin docked to the far airlock, heatshield covered by a protective blanket to prevent deterioration during orbit.

Unbuckling herself from the seat, she grinned at her co-pilot before flying down to the airlock to check it was seated firmly. "Seal is tight, ready to open inner door."

"Check, Flytgealdor, we confirm seal is good and outer doors secure" a familiar voice came over her helmet communicator. The starfarers would keep their suits on until safely aboard the station in case the closure should fail. Hard-docking was a new procedure and it had never been tested in orbit before.

The station's two-man crew had been aboard for over a month and were eager to see new faces, they would swap with Flytgealdor Da N'tan and Lyftgealdor Changying Hua to return to Nerth in the Swan, the smaller Sparrow would now only be used as the station's tender or lifeboat and would stay in orbit indefinitely. "I wish I had your Psi skills" complained Hua as she caught up by pulling herself along an internal ladder. Freya had, of course, levitated to the airlock.

"Sorry about that Ying, so how's your first trip to the void?"

"I feel a bit queasy," she confessed.

"Don't be sick in your helmet whatever you do because you'll be cleaning it out!" Freya laughed but she was only half-joking, in freefall this could be very dangerous.

They entered the station and as they removed their helmets Dexter Sartorius handed Hua a bag. Grabbing it quickly she put a foot on the hatch and pushed away to the far end of the vessel.

Freya sniffed at the ripe atmosphere "It really stinks in here, I may throw up myself."

Dexter grinned. "Better get used to it lover, you've got thirty days of not being able to wash properly ahead of you. Hei, it's a shame we weren't up here together Fri, we could have tried a line of experimentation that isn't on the program."

"Hmm, I'll see if Ying's alright" she replied and flew to join her companion at the other end of the station.

"I hope she's not going to be a puker or neither of them is going to have a pleasant stay." opined Rhys who was Sartorius' fellow starfarer. "You know if we can generate antigravity fields why can't we generate our own gravity up here?"

"Knowing our luck it would pull us straight into the ground" replied Sartorius retrieving his helmet. "We, er, ought to start bringing the supplies in" he suggested on hearing a retching noise from the other end of the space station.

A week later Hua, having got her *space-legs*, was on down-time idly world-watching as the station orbited then spotting something strange called Da N'tan to the view screen. "Freya, something is going on in Neo Kampuja!"

Freya joined her to see a pall of smoke over a large area of the jungle covered land then there was a vivid flash to the south of it. She contacted the *steorhus* at New Winchester. "Stardock to Control, hei down there, do you know what's going on in Neo Kampuja?"

"Flytgealdor, we were about to let you know, it's all over the news. We're receiving reports from the Dominion saying Ket refugees are flocking to the border begging for shelter. From what we can gather there's a civil war going on and the ruling cabal has sent clones against its people!" came the reply from the controller.

"What's the Reignweald's response?" she asked.

"Gugnir has been put on amber alert and forces stationed along the Dominion's borders are on high alert, they have been told to make refugees welcome but Psi' have been deployed to vet them in case Ket saeteres are taking advantage of the situation. First reports from the displaced people say it's pretty bad and the Dominion is itching to spill clone blood, they suffered a lot in the border war. There's a widespread feeling that if they go in we may well be dragged into it?"

"Oh shit!" replied Freya.

"One thing of interest, the Ket people refer to themselves as normals and the government clones as abhorrence's, that's an unfortunate coincidence don't you think?"

"Hell yeah!" replied Freya *this could put the Selene project on hiatus!*

ONE...

Sirki held a party for Dame Hildegard's ninetieth birthday in the main hall at Scartho. Some of the ante-chambers were opened up for food and drink and she contacted Adie to arrange a *respectable* band to play on the night, knowing only too well Hilly would not want her singing. Freya and Sirki committed the unforgivable social sin of wearing identical black dresses and with their similar looks, mother and daughter could have passed for twins which caused great hilarity.

"I really am beginning to hate you, are you ever going to start ageing?" Effie's hair was grey now but hidden under blonde colourant and there were fine lines around her eyes, by norm standards the Queen looked younger than her years but apart from a silver streak at her left temple Sirki would pass for thirty.

"Can't help it Effie, it's in the genes, mami is nearly as old as Hilly and she's still beautiful. That reminds me, I must visit soon it's been months since I was last in Soomi." Her mother had lived with her uncle's friend Axel until his death two years ago before selling the remaining Takala estate and moving to Jyvaskyla to share a house with Adi, her late brother's partner, who was a hundred years old herself.

Bren made a long speech recalling how Hilly had not just been a mother but the backbone of the Da N'tan family and the solid foundation from which his father had run the Thegnweald.

Elli said a very brief word while Bonnie thanked Hilly for taking her in and treating her as one of her own. Sirki thanked Hilly for putting up with her for years then Queen Ethelflaeda paid a special tribute to the Dame who was respected and feared by everyone, *including the social elite who were still trying to come to terms with the novae infiltration of society.*

The guest of honour then made a short speech thanking everyone for the compliments and joked she hoped to see them all again in another ten years, even making a special mention thanking Sirki for organising the event and admitting how she had been unsure of Bren taking up with the infamous celebrity but how Sirkku had proved her wrong.

With the speeches over the band struck up and Bren dutifully led his mother out to dance while the throng joined them on the floor.

Dexter Sartorius was bored, he didn't enjoy this sort of formal occasion and upon seeing Freya go into one of the ante-chambers he followed her in. The room was empty apart from her stood at a table and pouring a drink with her back to him so he crept up behind her, grabbed her hips and whispered into her ear. "Let's nip off early and have a night of unbridled passion."

"Well it's nice of you to make the offer but won't my daughter be a bit put out?" she turned around in his grasp and to his horror it was Sirki, lilac eyes wide and an amused look on her beautiful face.

"Oh gods, forgive me Fro Scartho, I thought you were Freya, I, er, I mean you two look so alike and from behind well…" he spluttered, the woman was so beguiling this close to and had an alluring musky perfume. His hands were still on her hips and realising this he quickly removed them.

She fluttered her eyelashes. "I'm flattered a handsome young man like you would make such an offer but don't worry, I will never speak of this" she smiled again and sashayed from the room, drink in hand. Dexter realised he was watching her shapely rear as she strutted away and guiltily turned back to the table.

"Oh, there you are" said Freya who'd passed her mother on the way in. "I'm bored so I thought we might cut out early, go to our room and shag like bunnies."

"Yes, I'd like nothing better." he agreed, trying not to think about her mother's behind or how it moved when she walked.

The lady herself sidled up her husband who put his arm around her waist to remark. "Do you realise it's been four years now..?" he didn't finish.

"I know, I wish they were all still here." she touched his chest to feel the bullet scar under his shirt and sniffed

ZERO...

Freya regarded her home planet, a bright blue disc against the black of space and shining like a jewel in comparison to the flat grey of the lunar landscape. *Nerth seems so tiny!* She held out a gloved hand to cover it easily with an outstretched thumb, *all I've ever known is up there, or is it down there?* The Selene project had advanced well, so well that in spite of the situation in Neo Kampuja the RAF had sanctioned an early launch and Freya, along with Sartorius, Rhys and Hua had crossed the vastness of space to land on the moon six months ahead of schedule. From her vantage point on the ridge she could see Dexter standing by the small exploratory flier they had brought with them, it was basically a pair of seats mounted on an AG engine. *Time was running out, they would have to leave soon.* Her thoughts turned to those she had lost. *Alfie, Sari, Aunt Penni, poor Heidi. All dead and gone, had it really only been four years ago?"*

Dexter's voice came over the radio breaking her pensive mood. "Hei Fri, we need to get back to Swan, we've only got two hours of air left in our suits!"

"On my way Dex," replied Freya levitating down from the promontory. They had achieved their objective of landing at the north pole of Selene and locating the old Russ base. It was deserted and lifeless, of course, but a core sample had showed most of the sub-surface ice field was untouched. It was the perfect place to establish a new colony on the satellite.

"Fri!" called Sartorius urgently.

"Check Dex, don't fret so!" Freya Da N'tan reluctantly hopped in slow motion to her partner waiting in the grav-scrid. *"Mum, I'm coming home"* she path'd.

The fat man looked through the glass at the long blond hair floating in front of the perfect face. "She is ready you say?"

"Yes indeed Craeftwice, we could keep her in vitro longer but she has achieved optimum growth." replied a white coated *craeftwitan*.

"She looks like a sleeping *Nixe*" he remarked, *with the Reignweald looking nervously to the east there could not be a better time.* "Drain the vat and crack it open, time she was born!"

"Aye sir" said the white coated man waving over his assistants.

The fat man regarded the face again and smiled. "You've a task ahead of you!"

CHAPTER 1 – CUCKOO!

Anya Jensen woke suddenly and thinking she'd heard the back door opening went cautiously downstairs to check. Upon entering the kitchen she gasped in recognition, shocked at the sight of the figure illuminated by the moonlight through the window but before the young woman could run or call out, the intruder stepped forward and knocked her to the floor where she lay motionless. The figure stooped briefly over the unconscious housekeeper to feel her pulse before leaving the dark kitchen and advancing stealthily towards the stairs.

Dexter put his hands on Sirki's hips pulling her to him to kiss her passionately and she responded by flicking her tongue into his mouth.

"You are a very naughty boy" she purred before putting her hand down the front of his pants to grasp his erect penis.

He pulled at her dress and it came off in one to expose her supple body. He cupped her breasts, her skin felt like silk.

"Well what are we waiting for?" she asked, licking her red lips before sinking to her knees and unfastening his trousers …

He sat up in horror, he'd dreamt about Sirki again!

"Dexter are you alright?" asked Freya.

"Yes my love, just a dream that's all" *how could he tell her what it was about?*

"Will you still love me when I'm fat?" Freya was expecting his baby. Shortly after returning from the moon her contraceptor had inexplicably stopped working and she had conceived immediately.

"Of course, do you love me?" he returned, she had never admitted as such.

"I do feel very close to you Dex", they had started off as friends when they joined the space programme years ago and it had spiralled from there. She liked him a lot, constantly telling herself it was not just sex, *but love?* Freya had inherited her mother's old selfish streak and though she wanted the child she did not necessarily want a husband.

She straddled him and put his hands on her abdomen. "Soon my belly will be swollen with your son."

"How do you know it's a boy, it's surely too early to tell?" she was here *that was enough he supposed.*

"Because I know, just as mum knew the sex of all of us." Freya felt a little sadness at this, recalling that not all of her siblings were alive.

Feeling his ardour growing she moved back lowering herself onto him and started moving her hips before freezing in shock.

"What's wrong Fri?" asked Dex.

"No, no it's not possible!" she cried in horror feeling an all too familiar resonation, the bedroom door burst open and there stood Sari, blank-faced, dressed in black and holding a gun at her side.

"Where are my children?" she demanded in a flat monotone.

"You're not my suster, you're a fucking clone!" shouted Freya leaping out of bed while preparing to launch a psionic attack. *This has got to be a nightmare!*

"Give the children to me and I will let you live" continued Sari, her voice emotionless then she regarded her sister who was making no attempt to hide her nudity. "You are with child, you are now required too."

"Go fuck yourself *bicce.*" spat Freya.

Dexter's uniform was on the floor next to the bed, his pistol was in its holster and he was wondering how to get to it.

Sari shuddered and light returned to her eyes "Cuckoo! Cuckoo! Fri, kill me before it's too late, I can't control…"

Dexter, picked his moment and snatched up the pistol.

"No, Dex, leave this to me!" cried Freya but he fired wildly, missing his target.

"Too late" remarked Sari almost casually before shooting him in the chest.

Freya screamed and telekinetically hurled Sari out of the bedroom pressing the clone against the wall until she passed out.

It was almost a rerun of the attack on her mother and father four years ago.

Freya sent an urgent message requesting help then bent over Sartorius to see his glazed eyes staring at the ceiling. "Oh Dex please don't be dead, I never told you I loved you." emotion built up inside her as tears ran down her face. A crashing sound came from below as the gatehouse guard broke down the front door to rush up the stairs. "Where were you, why didn't you stop her?" she sobbed bitterly.

The *Huscarl* Undergealdor found a robe and draped it over Freya to restore her dignity then asked quietly. "Ma'am is there anyone else in the house?"

"Loge, yes Anya! I hope the bicce hasn't killed her too!" she pointed to a drawer. "Put a flat hood on the creature, there's one in there."

One of the *Huscarl*s went to find the housekeeper while another placed the hood over the clone's head. The cloned Sari, now totally submissive, was manacled and dragged roughly to her feet and on impulse Freya snatched her *seax* from her clothes then rushed at the clone in an attempt to stab her.

"No ma'am!" shouted the Undergealdor, grabbing Freya and snatching the weapon from her hand. "She's our prisoner now, it doesn't matter what she's done we cannot let her be harmed in our custody!" he instructed one his soldiers to carefully lay Dexter out, covering his body with a bedsheet. "We have been instructed to take you to the Kingshall where her Majesty will personally look after you until your family arrive" he explained while Freya sat on the bed staring dazedly at the sheet covered body. Dexter had no close family, his elderly parents had crossed the bridge three years ago within a short space of each other, *that bicce was going to pay for this!*

But as she was driven to the palace, a thought struck her, *she asked me to kill her before it was too late, too late for what? She had said cuckoo,* something Freya teased Sari with as a child, *would a clone know that? Was there a real person in there?*

Anya Jensen was found comatose on the kitchen floor while an abandoned *scrid* was discovered a mile away with the clone's fingerprints all over it.

Sari's double was taken to New Winchester and incarcerated in a special cell at the Palace Research Wing, a cell which had been designed and built in case the unthinkable ever happened.

Avril North, who was still under loose house arrest at the PRW, found herself woken up to be informed her skills would be required. The scientist had refined her technique over time and had high hopes for success as the submissive clone was strapped into a chair for de-programming. The craeftwitan attached the electrodes and adjusted the settings then initiated the reversal procedure.

When completed the clone just sat impassively.

"Nothing!" snapped Bonnie, who had rushed from London to see the duplicate "She's no different to all the other bloody ACG clones."

"What did you expect? I can only retrieve a personality if there was one there to begin with." North informed her. "If she's just a clone she will only have basic functionality once the programme is erased."

"But Freya Da N'tan seemed to think her suster was in there somewhere?" stated Bonnie.

"Well we'll remove the implants next and see what happens" said the craeftwitan.

"Implants, there's more than one?" asked the Highest in surprise.

"Yes, I took a scan of her head, there was no evidence of surgery to the brain but two implants were clearly visible in the nasal cavity and they look quite different to the models I'm familiar with." The clone was tranquilised and a pair of streamlined implants removed. "I'll get these to the laboratory and have a look inside once the anti-tamper mechanism is deactivated" explained the *craeftwitan*.

Bonnie waited impatiently by the bed until the clone woke up and opened her eyes then she ordered. "Get off the bed and stand up!" The clone obediently did as asked and stood there in her gown. "Sit on that chair!" she barked and it obeyed once more. "What is your name?" there was no response so the Highest slapped her hard her across the face. The clone did not flinch so she swung again but this time the duplicate grabbed her hand to prevent the blow. Bonnie wrenched it free as dull eyes turned to regard her. "So you are alert at least."

Waving away the Huscarls who had dashed forward to assist she decided it was time to be more intrusive so turned to the Mystagogue who had accompanied her. "I'm going to enter her mind, be ready in case something goes wrong."

Bonnie entered the clone's thoughts, such that they were, to find the expected basic functional level but further into her mindscape there was something unusual, a barrier. Bonnie gingerly prodded at it with her mind then recoiled in shock, quickly withdrawing from the clone's thoughts while fighting the urge to scream.

"Are you alright ma'am?" asked the Psi taking Bonnie's arm as she sagged.

"The pain, the revulsion!" she regained her feet then rushed to the sink and vomited.

CHAPTER 2 – I AM NUMBER ONE

The Thegn of Scartho arrived in New Winchester later that morning to fetch Freya but on hearing what she had to say decided to see the captive for himself.

The special *cacaern* was in the basement of the PRW building. Its single cell had a powerful psionic suppression field, the door was solid steel and its thick walls were built using aggregate from a flat zone mixed into the concrete. A monitor gave a view of the interior allowing Bren to watch keenly as someone who looked like his dead daughter walked slowly round and round.

"She's done that for hours." explained the *Cacaern* Tithengealdor. "She will sit down for a few minutes then get up and carry on, she eats, shits, sleeps and obeys orders just like every cursed clone we've captured and deprogrammed and that's about it."

"You told me you saw something interesting when we spoke earlier?" asked Bonnie.

"Wait a moment ma'am, I think she's about to do it."

The clone stopped and stared at the wall intently before continuing her pacing.

"There you go, stops and looks at the concealed door every now and then" the TG commented.

"Concealed door?" asked Bren.

"It opens into an area with real grass and a window to the sky, we call it the garden and it has an armoured glass walkway around it so you can visit in safety."

"Have you opened the door yet?" asked Bren.

"No, but nonetheless she seems to know it's there, quite bizarre?" remarked the Tithengealdor.

Da N'tan had made up his mind. "Let me into the walkway."

"Sir is that *witan*?" asked Bonnie.

"Let's see shall we?"

Next to the cell entrance was a door with several heavy locks and when it was opened Bren entered the L-shaped corridor. The glass wall ran down and along two sides of a small patch of lawn and on the adjacent wall, clearly visible from this side of the cell, was a door. A chair in the corridor faced the door between two lines drawn on the floor, here the glass was not two-way but formed a frame in which anyone sitting there could be seen from the other side. A heavily bolted door at the dead-end of the corridor gave access to the *garden* and signal wires running across the ceiling allowed use of a wired headset for communication while speakers and microphones were mounted in the *flat-painted* walls.

Da N'tan put on the headset then stood to one side of the framed area so he could not be seen and informed them he was ready.

The Tithengealdor operated the door and it opened silently, folding flat against the outer wall, to reveal the *garden* to the prisoner inside. Da N'tan saw a shadowy figure appear in the opening to look first at the grass then at the dark glazed wall surrounding it.

Bren watched as the figure removed the soft shoes she wore as part of her prison uniform then step on to the lawn to feel the grass with her toes. He was taken aback, *Sari used to do that as a child!*

Now she was out in the daylight he could clearly see the clone was a virtually identical copy of his daughter, *but it's not her is it?*

As she stood regarding the sky through the transparent roof Da N'tan stepped into the viewing area to sit on the chair.

The duplicate stared at Da N'tan curiously then walked to the middle of the lawn to sit cross legged in front of him.

"That's incredible, Bren, she seems to recognise you!" exclaimed Bonnie over the headset.

"Can she hear me?" he asked.

"We'll turn on the internal speakers and microphone."

"Sari is that you?" he asked.

There was only silence.

"Do you recognise me?" more silence, he looked into her blue eyes seeing no sign of recognition, just a blank stare. Bren produced an old print he kept in his wallet of Sirki and their three children and holding it close to the glass, pointed to each one in turn leaving his finger on the young Sari. "Do you know who this is?"

Again there was just the blank stare.

He sat for nearly ten minutes with no response then with a heavy heart decided it was hopeless. "I'm so sorry *lapsi* I thought I could reach you?"

As he stood and made to leave she uttered a single word. "Dad?"

"What?" Bren couldn't believe his ears.

Silence once more, he waited and was about to leave again when she spoke for the second time.

"One father, two mothers" with that she stood and walked back to her cell pausing only to put on her shoes.

"Did you speak to it?" Freya asked her father as he climbed into the Midge.

"Yes, I spoke to her." he replied.

The pilot started the grav drivers.

"She has to die, she killed Dex."

"Fri, my daughter, you said yourself that you thought Sari might be inside her head somehow?" he could see the suffering on his oldest daughter's face. "She was your suster."

"That thing is not my suster and it never will be!" Freya snapped back. "You just want it to be her."

"Of course, I'm her father what do you expect?"

Freya didn't respond but just stared silently out of the cabin window as the small flyer lifted off.

Abridged report from Craeftwitan North regarding implant removal from the clone of Sari Jorvik – *Restricted Access*.

Having previously ascertained there had been no surgery or any kind of control device attached to the frontal lobes of the brain (re; Report on mind control of Sari Jorvik #1), the subject was placed under sedation and two implants discovered at the top of the nasal cavity were investigated and removed via the anterior naris on each side.

Some slight abrasion to the soft tissue and the septum was incurred by the procedure but it has been treated and is not considered to be detrimental to the subject's health.

The implants are slightly larger and more streamlined than any type I am familiar with.

The device extracted from the left side of the nasal cavity was examined and found to be a very advanced version of the standard ACG psionic control implant with the explosive charge removed to accommodate new circuitry.

The right hand device is an entirely new transmitter/receiver unit that, I surmise, utilises the body as an aerial and would seem to indicate that the clone can be sent new orders or reprogrammed at distance and conversely send data back to its controller.

This advanced *boccraeft* is something I have never encountered before and would suggest to me that the ACG still retain a considerable research facility somewhere.

Avril North – Craeftwitan.

MOST SECRET: For the attention of; Her Royal Majesty Queen Ethelflaeda III, the Foreladtwa of Aengland, the Thegn of Scartho.

Report on the Clone of Sari Jorvik by the Psi Highest Ashby:

I will begin by trying to describe the process of entering an individual's mind, something that may be difficult for a non-Psi to understand.

The conscious mind has a sort of landscape within it made from patterns of thought and as we enter the outskirts random or unguarded thoughts will be encountered. These can accessed with very little effort and quite often that may be all that is required. Names and trivial information can be acquired in this way, and some Betas or even sensitive Alphas are able to do this as an individual can reveal information merely by the act of trying to conceal it.

As a Psi progresses deeper, a person will experience the sensation that some refer to as "someone walking on their grave," an individual who has experienced this before will recognise it for what it is and unless willing to allow us into their mind will resist. All individuals are capable of resisting to a degree and it can become a battle of wills which even a high level Psi may occasionally lose.

Further in we will find a more ordered thought structure through which we have to tread carefully, this is generally where the more sensitive information will be found and due to the danger of mental trauma to the subject a Psi may only attempt this after extensive training.

Changing an individual's thought pattern requires a much deeper thrust into their subconscious mind and since this can cause serious psychological or even neurological damage it should only be attempted by an experienced 5th level Mystagogue or above.

Having outlined the basic procedure I will describe what was discovered in the mind of the clone, no resistance was encountered upon entering the mind which was to be expected as prior experience has shown clones to be submissive and responsive, unless programmed for a specific purpose.

When attempting to enter the ordered structure deeper within I encountered an unusual pattern, which, if a visual simile could be ascribed to thought, was like a bright blinding white light. Upon probing it I was subjected to pain resembling nerve-fire coupled with an extreme repulsion the like of which I had never felt before.

I was forced to withdraw immediately and was physically sick, for some reason an aggressively resistive barrier has been set up in the clone's mind and this is an enigma I cannot yet explain.

Audrey Ashby – 6th Level Psi.

Sirki turned up at the **PWR** building in New Winchester the very next day and the Highest, anticipating this, was waiting for her. "Good morning Sirki, I know why you're here."

"Splendid, then you can show me straight to my daughter," asserted Sirki.

"I'm not sure that's a good idea, where is your youngest?" asked Bonnie.

"With his dad, he can cope well enough" answered Sirki. "Now can I see her?"

Knowing it would be almost impossible to refuse, Bonnie personally escorted her to the *cacaern*.

"This is bit special, I didn't know this place existed?" mentioned Sirki in passing after examining the set-up.

"Mina laid down instructions for this to be built" she replied. "It's totally proof against Psionic power, I've tried it myself and it cuts you off completely, it's quite unsettling."

"How come I didn't know about this, I thought I was in her trusted circle and *yours* come to that?"

"Er… because it was built to hold you" replied Bonnie, clearly embarrassed by the disclosure.

"What?" Sirki was shocked.

"Mina was afraid you were growing so powerful that if you ever became dangerous… well she felt we needed some method of neutralising you if it were to happen, especially after the incident with the psychotropic drug."

"Wow it's nice to be trusted, I thought you were my friend?" she replied angrily. "I would never turn against the Reignweald, it would mean turning against Effie and Bren, how stupid are you people?"

"I was against the idea for what it's worth but it was already half built when Mina died and since it was her wish it seemed correct to finish it, I apologise Sirki."

"Hmm, let's see my daughter's clone then" replied Sirki, none too convinced by the Highest's excuse.

They stood at the monitor watching the clone patrolling her cell. "So she had those implant things up her nose?" asked Sirki.

"Yes, Craeftwitan North removed them after de-programming her" replied Bonnie.

"North, she's your pet ACG creature isn't she?"

"She works for us now and is one of the cleverest norms I've met. She can write an algorithm that will allow an atellan to read thought patterns and change them as required, we're lucky to have her working for us" replied Bonnie.

"Using *boccraeft* to control people's minds? That's wrong!" ejaculated Sirki

"She's only doing what we do but by using *elektroncraeft*!" retorted The Highest.

"Are you going to let me see her properly?"

"You will not attempt anything and there will be a guard with you at all times, Sirki, do you understand that?" Bonnie laid down her conditions.

"Joo, I under-stand!" she drawled sarcastically in an affected Soomi accent. The door to the corridor was opened and Sirki stepped in followed by a *Huscarl*. "Oh Loge, I've left my handbag on the desk, could you be a dahling and fetch it for me?" she asked sweetly and the *ferdrinc* obligingly went to retrieve it.

"What are you doing?" Bonnie looked in askance at him. "Don't leave her alone!"

It was too late, the door swung itself shut and the locks clicked into place. The Tithengealdor attempted to re-open them but the controls would not respond.

Sirki had shut herself in the corridor.

"Sirki open the door now!" demanded Bonnie as on the monitor she saw her take off the headset and drop it to the floor. "Get in the cell and manacle that bloody clone!" she ordered.

Huscarls moved to the cell door but it proved to be just as unresponsive, on the screen she saw the hidden exit opening.

"How can she control the doors like this, the bloody things are coated in flat paint?" asked the Tithengealdor, the clone was now moving towards the *garden*.

"Get a team down here with cutting gear, turn on all cameras and microphones and record everything!" shouted Bonnie, *so much for Mina's clever idea,* the special holding cell was proving itself woefully inadequate against its proposed inmate.

Sirki was now sitting cross-legged in the viewing area with the clone similarly posed on the other side of the glass. She regarded her face closely spotting Sari's genetic mother Penni Anderson's beauty, there were some slight differences but it was her *lapsi* in every other respect apart from the blank stare. "Sari, dahling it's mummy, please say you know me?"

"Sirki, it is not your daughter!" Bonnie's voice came urgently over the speakers.

"Shut up Bonnie or I'll turn it all off, speakers, mikes the lot!" she looked directly into a camera and smiled wryly. "This place was built to hold me eh?"

An odd look came on the clone's face and she silently mouthed something that looked like "mummy".

"Do you see that Bonnie? She recognises me."

Sirki attempted to enter her mind only to be thrown back retching, *I need to get closer!*

Sirki looked at the access door and it unlocked with a series of clicks to swing open.

"No Sirki, do not go in there!" begged Bonnie, *the clone could kill her and they could do nothing to stop it.*

Sirki entered the enclosed area removing her shoes and feeling the grass under her feet as her daughter had done, the clone stood up to face her.

Sirki took her hands. "Sit down *lapsi* I'm going to help you."

"Don't do it, it will hurt!" announced the clone unexpectedly.

"I went through pain to give birth to you and I'm quite willing to do it again" she entered the clone's mind to probe at the white light. The pain was excruciating, the feeling of revulsion and disgust intense but she kept pushing against it fighting back the agony until a calm pink patch seemed to develop in the white glare. Sirki path'd through the break to the mind hidden beyond. *"Lapsi, this is so hard but if you push from the other side we could do this together."*

Bonnie could only watch helplessly, the suffering on Sirki's face was clearly visible and she could only guess how she must feel. The clone grimaced, hissing through gritted teeth then after a minute Sirki screamed out loud and both sank slowly to the grass.

All locks clicked open simultaneously and Sirki lost consciousness just as *smithcraefters* finally arrived with cutting equipment.

Soldiers rushed into the garden followed by the Highest who gently lifted Sirki as she came to. The clone meanwhile was dragged harshly to her feet and her arms forcibly restrained.

"Don't hurt her" mumbled Sirki weakly.

"I am not in pain" stated the clone.

"So you can talk now, what is your name?" asked the Highest.

"One" replied the clone.

"One is not a name" said Bonnie.

"That is my number I am merely One, I was not given a name" stated the clone in a flat emotionless voice.

"You're my daughter, Sari!" asserted Sirki.

"No mummy, I can remember being Sari Jorvik but I am not her," replied the clone enigmatically.

"Then why call me mummy?" Sirki was confused.

"Because that is how you are called." One replied.

The clone was taken to the interrogation room and sat at a table with torc wearing *Huscarl*s positioned on either side.

"What do you remember about Sari Jorvik?" asked Bonnie.

"Everything to the point of being captured, the last thing I can recall is a firefight on the road from Cambrycge" she replied.

"You do not remember attacking your family in their home?" Bonnie inquired.

"No."

"But, you killed your brothur and his partner and you tried to kill your parents?" she continued.

"I don't remember that."

"You tried to kill me twice and killed several *Huscarl*s."

"No!" this time her response was more animated.

"Your progenitor was shot by her genetic mother who then took her own life! Do you have any memory of that?" Bonnie pushed more.

"How could if I was dead, how could I? It wasn't me!" One stood clenching her fists before being grabbed and pushed roughly back into the chair. "… it wasn't me" she whispered.

"You attacked your suster and killed her partner two days ago and you assaulted her housekeeper!" the Highest kept on at her.

"Yes" she admitted sadly. "I tried to warn them, I told them to kill me but the programming overrode my will."

There was a hushed word from Sirki sat at the back of the room. "Why?"

"I was instructed to acquire the children of Sari Jorvik and any other useful genetic material pertaining to the Da N'tan family, when I noticed Freya Da N'tan was carrying a child it was communicated to me that she was now to be considered an objective and I was to eliminate anyone who stood in my way" confessed the clone. "Since your woman erased my programming and removed the control implant I no longer have any compulsion to do this."

"You didn't kill Anya Jensen, wasn't she in your way?" asked Sirki.

"She was special to… to Sari."

"I know she was *lapsi*" said Sirki quietly.

"That's as may be but it doesn't change the fact you killed Dexter Sartorius" stated Bonnie. She had been carefully probing the edge of the clones mind and could find no malice, just an overwhelming feeling of regret and sorrow. There was something else as well, something with a very familiar resonance. *"There is a new block in her mind Sirki, one with your signature?"*

"Bonnie, I am reckless but I am not stupid, her Psionic ability has been locked off." replied Sirki.

"You can do that?" the Highest was astonished.

"It was far easier than breaking through the barrier in her mind."

"I fear for the world should you ever turn on us!" exclaimed Bonnie, Fro Scartho's abilities were scaling new heights. *Perhaps I should step down and offer my position to her?*

"One, why did you not use your Psionic abilities when you attacked your suster and her partner?" asked the Highest.

"I had not been instructed in their use, my creators were very eager to send me out and did not leave time for it" she replied. "You have stopped these powers in me now."

"One, please, could you tell us the first thing you can remember?" asked Sirki.

"Waking in a brightly lit room naked and wet on a hard surface, there were strange smells and noises. I was cold and shivering then a warm blanket was put over me. I was on a trolley in a room with three large glass tubes, the nearest had its hatch open and this was how I entered the world. I was taken to another room and bathed then I slept again for a while. Walking and moving were difficult at first but my body seemed to remember how to function properly. Eventually they put me to sleep for implantation and after being programmed I was sent to fulfil my objective. Sari Jorvik's old home in New Winchester was unoccupied and so I went to where I remembered my progenitor living and growing. It made sense that I might find them there, you know the rest."

"Why were you sent to retrieve the children?" asked Bonnie.

"I have no idea. I acted only as my programme dictated."

As the clone was returned to the cell the Highest informed her. "The door to the garden area will be opened upon request and you will remain there until your fate is decided."

Sirki took the clone's hand. "I will visit again soon, I know deep inside you're my Sari."

"I'm sorry to disillusion you, I could pretend but I'm just a clone grown from your daughter's ova" then she walked into the cell. "Could you close the door please?"

Sirki bit her lip in sorrow as it shut. "What will you do with her now?"

"Further interrogation, a more stringent physical examination" replied Bonnie.

"And then?"

"She will probably be euthanized and dissected for study" answered the Highest coldly.

"You can't do that to her, it's not right!" Sirki was horrified.

"She is not your daughter, she said so herself."

"One couldn't kill Anya because Sari loved her and she only shot Dexter in self-defence." snapped Sirki. "She has become self-aware and is a human being not a sick animal to be put down. You felt her suffering, I know you did!"

"Is a human being grown in a glass tube?" retorted Bonnie.

"My ancestor was, and have you forgotten the ancestors of all the *novae* began life in glass dishes. By that reckoning are any of us really human?" she spat. "Perhaps the norms are right, perhaps we are abominations?"

"My, Fro Scartho how you've changed? I remember a certain Sirkku Vigsdottir and how frightened she was of her power and how she *so* didn't want to be a Psi. Look at you now passing judgement on us all, what will happen if you don't get what you want?" asked Bonnie, thankful that despite the power Sirki could wield her peaceful nature outweighed her aggressive side.

"I ask, nej beg of you, let me try and find out if Sari is in there!" she pleaded.

"It will be for a special tribunal to decide her fate, until then you may attempt to reclaim her." answered Bonnie.

"*Kiitos* Highest" she said respectfully.

"Sirki, don't build up your hopes, even if you recover something of your daughter it may not be enough to save her life!" warned Bonnie.

CHAPTER 3 – REHABILITATING A DEAD DAUGHTER

One, wearing a short red dress that had belonged to Sari, was escorted out to a waiting *campscrid*. It was a warm day and she blinked in the bright light, realising that the glass roof over her prison garden was tinted before she was sat in the rear with a *Huscarl* guard and manacled to the roll cage of the vehicle for the journey to the palace.

The Tiger pulled up at the rear of the building where Sirki, who was waiting for them, looked at the chains in dismay. "Nej, she will not wear these, unshackle her immediately."

"Ma'am, the Highest has determined that we must not remove her restraints!" answered one of her escort.

"Very well, you do not have to remove them, I will," the manacles unlocked themselves and fell to the floor. "Now you may wait for our return, I believe the guardhouse can furnish you with refreshments."

"But Fro Scartho, we are to remain with the…" started the *ferdrinc*.

"Hush *polho*! Do you think I cannot handle this by myself, she is to meet her children and what would they think of three hulking great *heremenn* dragging their mother in chains to see them." replied Sirki.

"Ma'am this is a Royal residence, she is categorized as dangerous and has killed already!" he pleaded.

"So have most of you I imagine, I need nej escort!" Sirki was adamant.

As they walked into the palace, One turned to her. "You certainly know how to get your way."

"It's a bad habit of mine I'm afraid, don't you remember?" she asked. Sirki had brought the children from Scartho with the intention of introducing them to her.

"No mummy, Sari may have done but I do not" she replied. "Why are you bringing me to her children, isn't it going to be traumatic for them?"

"You are concerned for the children and yet you say you are merely a clone?" Sirki answered with a question of her own.

One gave in and followed Sirki into a lavishly furnished room where three children and their nanny were playing and she immediately recognised two of them as her... as Sari's. The other, a toddler, had lilac eyes and could only be Fro Scartho's youngest child.

The girl, noticing her, gave a puzzled look before asking. "Mummy?" the older boy looked up then both ran to the clone putting their arms around her and One was surprised by the warm feeling inside her.

Then the girl stiffened. "You're not mummy!" she stated crossly. "You look like her but you're not her."

"I don't care Wil" said Bern "We haven't got a real mum anymore."

"Bern, come here now! She's not our mummy." ordered Willa moving away from her.

"Sorry" he said meekly obeying his sister.

"Willa, some nasty people kidnapped your *mami* and were horrible to her and that's why she seems different, she's only just escaped." *it was only half a lie* thought Sirki.

Wil pointed angrily at One. "No *mummo,* you are not telling the truth, she is thinking that we can tell she is a clone!" at eight years old Willa was at the level of a Neophyte Psi.

"It's rude to listen to people's thinking, Wil" argued Bern. "I like our new mummy."

"She is not our new mummy and she is not our old mummy!" with that Willa strode off pulling Bern with her to stand with their nanny, Soli.

Little Bren smiled at the clone who was surprised to find tears running down her cheeks. "Please, I want to go back to my cell!" she cried, Sirki was crestfallen, she had been certain the children would recognise her as she had. One's wyrd now hung in the balance.

That night the clone dreamed for the first time in her short life and was greatly disturbed by it, faces and events pressed down on her from a mind that wasn't hers and she woke to find her pillow-case sodden with tears. Memories belonging to a dead woman taunted her and the knowledge she was just a mere copy tore at her heart, even worse was the emotional agony she had felt after Sirki's attempt at bluff was so easily seen through by the real Sari's daughter. She felt alone and unwanted.

One had been given an atellan with limited network access and was sat in her cell brooding morosely over it when the door opened to admit Freya wearing a blue dress with a thigh split displaying her Mjolnir tattoo and looking almost the double of Sirki. "Suster, I'm surprised they let you in here?" remarked the clone.

"I inherited more than just looks from mother, no-one knows I'm here, no-one noticed me arrive, the desk Tithengealdor isn't watching the monitor and he won't until I decide he can!" Freya informed her before snarling. "And do not call me suster, creature!"

"The recording devices, can you prevent them from seeing you too?" asked One.

"I could but in truth I don't give a shit!" Freya retorted angrily.

"So are you here to kill me then?" One enquired.

"What do you think, murderer?"

"Then get on with it and leave, I will not stop you" she stated.

Freya drew a short *seax* from the thigh sheath under her dress and advanced on her uncertainly. "Why?"

"Your mother is desperate to prove I am Sari, she half convinced me the children would accept me but Willa saw straight through the deception. I am not a real person just a thing pulled from a glass tube." she lamented.

As Freya shakily held the *seax* out in front of her the clone could see there were no runes on the shining blade. "You have never used it to kill have you?" asked One. "Have you ever killed anyone before?" Freya said nothing as a single tear ran down one cheek. The clone moved the point of the *seax* to her breast and closing her eyes held her arms outstretched. "Push hard Freya and make it easy but please place the *seax* in my fingers when it is done so that I may cross Bifrost."

Freya shaking badly and racked by sobs, turned and ran from the cell leaving the door open. A minute later the Desk TG peered in curiously and on seeing the clone standing there gave a puzzled look before shutting it.

Bonnie sat in her office watching the recording showing Freya Da N'tan walk into the cacaern unopposed then she watched the conversation between the two women with interest. The clone knew the significance of kill-runes and the importance of crossing Bifrost weapon in hand. *True, she had an instruction book of how Sari's mind worked in her head but the reactions seemed instinctive, what did this say about the persistence of genetic memory? Was Sirki onto something after all?*

Freya's ability to walk unseen into the cacaern was a surprise, she had managed to conceal how advanced her abilities were as Sirki had once tried and the clone carried the same genetic material, perhaps she ought to be allowed to live?

Should she argue for its continued existence?

There was also 4th level Psi Minto, nee Blane to consider. She maintained a physical relationship with an Alpha and after giving birth to his child her irises had turned lilac, were the other missing descendants of the group 3 Betas potential Omegas?

Out of curiosity she sent a discrete request to the Psi community asking if any had tried a sexual liaison, anonymity guaranteed. The results astonished her, nearly half of the Psi' admitted to having had physical relations with Alphas, norms or even their fellow telepaths, some out of sheer curiosity, others from pure desire. *Why had Mina never asked this?*

Then there was Sirki's youngest child, so far the only male Omega in existence, *what would he be capable of?*

Bonnie decided the time had finally come, time to do something she had put off since succeeding Mina as Arch Psi. She sat back, relaxed and closing her eyes sent her consciousness out into the Helm actively seeking the entity her predecessor had spoken of.

In the four years that had passed since Mina's death she had not yet dared to do this.

"So you are the new Highest?" the reply came almost immediately, gently caressing her mind. *"We have many things to discuss."*

Fro Scartho had one more trick up her sleeve. One was summoned from her cell to the Kingshall once again and Sirki ushered her into a room to leave her there and standing before the clone was Anya Jensen. She had fading bruises on the left side of her head and her eye was still slightly swollen.

"Hei" said the young woman in a croaky voice.

A memory of warmth and affection rose up in her. "Ani?"

"You hurt me Sari. They told me I was lucky you didn't fracture my skull."

"I bitterly regret that Anya, I was being controlled by them but held back as much as I could!"

She moved towards the clone and touched her face gently. "Is that really you Saz?"

"I want to say yes, Ani, but I can't."

"I still love you, even after all this time, even after what you did!" tears were in her eyes.

One put an arm round her. "Sari loved you very much Anya, I feel it."

"Why did you do those awful things?" Anya embraced her tightly.

One felt something welling up inside her but wrested free and stepped away. "This must stop, I am not the woman you loved." she turned to the door shaking and shouted. "I demand you take me back this instant!"

Sirki comforted the disappointed Ani while the clone was driven back to the cacaern, *curse it I thought it might trigger something in her!* Sirki had lost yet again but was determined not to give up.

One stared miserably out of the Tiger's window on the journey back to the cell. She *had* felt something stir in Anya's presence but was scared it could spiral out of control. Part of her was still locked away, *what if it was the part that made her a killer?*

CHAPTER 4 – DEFINE A CLONE

Sari's clone was retained in custody while the special tribunal convened to decide her fate. The jury comprised of representatives from the government, the PRW, the armed services and the Huscarl Folctoga, *all of them novae*. It was chaired by the Queen's Reeve with the Highest herself representing the Psi Wing.

After the tribunal had discussed all the relevant data, Bonnie stood to present her final analysis. "After much study I have come to the conclusion that this clone, while not actually Sari Da N'tan retains a great deal of her traits and memories and I am of the opinion that she should ought to be considered a person in her own right," the entity had convinced her of the necessity to ensure One's continued existence.

"But was the clone not bred as a weapon to use against us, particularly the Da N'tan family?" inquired the Hame Cancelar.

"Remember how she killed Fro Freya's partner?" asked the Lyftcampaeldor representing the RAF.

"But it was while she was been controlled by the enemy and isn't Scartho supporting her case?" suggested the Folctoga.

"After the removal of the implants the woman has shown no aggression whatsoever and has since proved to be capable of emotion and independent thought, this in itself is unparalleled as no freed clone has ever achieved these heights before and Fro Scartho, the First Omega, believes that the full personality of Sari Da N'tan may yet be recoverable" she continued.

"I do not doubt the Thegnestre of Scartho's sincerity or the strength of her belief but she can hardly be said to be unbiased." stated the Reeve.

"She is still a clone is she not?" asked another.

"What defines a clone?" Bonnie regarded the members of the tribunal and paraphrased Sirki in her response. "Sirkku Da N'tan is the descendent of the clone we know as Isolde yet no-one doubts her humanity, and were not our ancestors cloned foetii, have you forgotten that? All of them began life in glass dishes so by that reckoning are any of us not cloned in some way?"

"That is indeed true, Highest" replied the Reeve.

"We have all met this clone individually and have questioned her, have we not?" asked Bonnie.

"We have indeed" asserted the Reeve.

"And did you find her very different to any other human being whether they be *Novae* or norm?" she continued, most shook their heads. "So are we going to condemn a person to death in their absence?"

The members of the tribunal looked from one to another before making their decision.

CHAPTER 5 – DREAMS

One lay on a trolley shivering with cold while a round fat face hovered over her.

"I don't think she's ready after all," said the face. "Flush her away with the waste."

"We'll take her," announced Sirki, clasping a large glass jar in which floated a foetus.

At the other end of the room a figure with blurred and indistinct features could be seen slowly squeezing itself from a small aperture in a tall glass tube.

"Do you think she'll make a good daughter?" asked Bren, blood pouring from a bullet hole in his chest. "Who will kill her now Penni's dead?"

The figure had left the flask and was advancing menacingly towards her. She could almost make out its features.

"Don't worry dad I'll do it!" yelled Freya wielding her *seax*. "Cuckoo, cuckoo!" she laughed before thrusting the blade into One's chest.

The clone sat up in bed, heart pounding. *"There had been three incubation tubes in the room!"*

Jocasta woke on the sand to the sound of breaking surf, *when had she fallen asleep on the beach?* Realising she was naked she sat up quickly, covering herself with her arms as best she could. The beach looked familiar, it was somewhere in Kernow and thankfully deserted. Standing slowly she began looking for her clothes while wondering how she got here and saw three deckchairs in a line but no other sign of life. Jocasta noticed the moon was shining in a sky full of stars yet everything was lit as if was broad daylight, and it dawned on her.

"This this place isn't real!" she exclaimed aloud.

"*Terve* Jocasta, I knew you could reach here" said a voice.

She turned to see Sirki, barefoot and dressed in a long white gown with a feather trimmed shawl, her chestnut hair pinned back by two cat shaped clips.

Jocasta, mortified, attempted to cover herself again.

"Don't worry you have nothing I have not seen before and there is nej shame here, this is not reality you know?" announced Sirki with a reassuring smile.

"Where is this place?" asked Minto.

"This is my refuge in the Helm which remains as long as I wish it" explained Sirki. "I invited you here in your sleep and you came."

"Then I am dreaming all this?" she asked.

"You are here because I called to you, you will eventually be able to reach this place merely by reaching with your mind and you will eventually be able to fashion your own construct."

"I am not as powerful as you, cousin."

"Not yet Jocasta but it will develop and grow as it did with me. My near death was the trigger and for you it was your baby." Sirki related in detail the creation of their great-grandmothers and the other prototype Betas.

"What about the others?"

"I'm not sure we'll ever know unless they develop as we did. Mina Srivastava believed I was the next step in psionic evolution but I think we'll have to wait and see about that."

"So what do I do now, Sirki?" she asked.

"I just sort of let it happen."

"It would be nice if I imagined some clothes next time" she stated. "How do I leave this place?"

"You just wake up Jocasta." She opened her eyes to find herself back in their bedroom in the garrison-hus, Cadoc was snoring noisily and after elbowing him in the back she drifted back to sleep, this time Fro Scartho was not there.

CHAPTER 6 –
ONE'S WARNING

"There were two other tubes in the cloning room and I remember people discussing how this one, meaning me I guess, had made it to full term. The tube next to mine was clean and empty but the furthest was still occupied. I believe there may be another clone out there somewhere!" One had been released into Fro Scartho's custody following the tribunal's pardon and she was relating her dream to the Da N'tan family.

"And you only thought to tell us now?" asked Freya suspiciously. "Is this some kind of trick, Cuckoo?"

"I did not remember this until having a nightmare about my own *birth* last night!" she replied.

"This is a very serious business" stated Bren. "Our family… the nation could be in great danger, the Palace must be informed and all Scartho forces put on alert including the Ward. Freya, you must leave the old house immediately and move into the Hall, none of us must leave the Thegnweald without escort and even within the burh extreme care must be taken *and* that includes you Sirk."

"Bren, I'm not a helpless little *sangestre* anymore, I can take care of myself" said Sirki. "I took care of you a few years ago, remember?"

"Sorry dahling but I consider the safety of my family more important than the freedom to come and go as we please," he replied.

Elli spoke up. "If this supposed other clone exists then we must assume she has Sari's psionic ability. Sirki, since you believe your daughter's personality resides inside One will this second copy retain Sari's character too and would you try to save her?"

"Of course I would to save her, but she cannot be Sari because that is you!" avowed Sirki to the clone, who sat impassively.

"What do you expect me to do Bren?" asked Queen Ethelflaeda when he contacted her. "I can't panic the country by saying there's a dangerous Psi clone roaming around, it would undo all those years of building up goodwill. I *have* put the Guard on alert and the Thegnwealds have been informed, if she's in the Reignweald we'll find her."

"Thank you ma'am but if this second clone exists she'll almost certainly come after us first, we need to find this last bastion of the ACG and destroy it before then" stated Da N'tan.

"Do you have any idea where she is, Bonnie?" the queen asked the Highest who was presently with Bren's family.

"No your majesty, as you know Sirki and her daughters can cloak themselves from visual and psionic detection, the only thing we can rely on are the monitors but, of course, any Psi above level three could deactivate them" she answered.

"So even if she does exist, we can't find her, fucking great!" Effie swore out loud. "Do you have any idea on the whereabouts of the ACG base?"

"My guess would be in the Home Shires, probably Kenta or Essex, anti-*nova* feeling is still openly expressed there!" said Bren.

"Without any proof my hands are tied, the Foreladtwa is on our side but she will need evidence to use against them." replied Effie.

"I'll find something somehow" promised Bren.

One was watching the afternoon news in the lounge when Freya entered and glared at the clone, her bump was beginning to show.

"At least you don't pretend to like me" remarked the clone.

Freya scrutinised her face. "Are you really in there, Cuckoo?"

"As I have told so many, I have access to her memories but there is something missing" she replied.

"You killed the father of my child, I don't trust you and I'm waiting for you to do something wrong!" asserted Freya.

"I am truly sorry for that, I was a different person then," asserted One before asking. "This Dexter, did you love him?"

"I am having his child!" retorted Freya.

"That's not necessarily the same thing"

"What are you trying to do pig, make me want to kill you again?"

"You can't sus, you're all goody-goody like Alfie and mummy, I'm a cempestre like my mum" replied the clone in a more animated voice than usual.

"Where did that come from, your voice lost that flat quality for a moment?"

"Huh, it's from her memory?"

"You sounded just like her!"

"Really?" asked the clone.

"It won't stop me hating you Cuckoo, you killed people I cared for in both of your incarnations."

The clone put her head down. "I don't blame you."

Sirki walked into the lounge later to find the clone alone with puffy red-rimmed eyes.

She put her arms around her. "What's the matter *lapsi*?"

"What am I?" she put her head on Sirki's shoulder. "A duplicate pulled from a glass tube with the memories of a dead woman! Not a human being just a creature bred by *boccraeft*, Freya should have killed me when she had the chance!"

"You are my Sari you just haven't made the connection yet. You are upset and full of remorse and that makes you very human in my eyes."

"Thank you mummy but you are the only person who believes it, the man I know as dad is uncertain of me, the children don't like me and Freya hates me with very good reason, even I don't share your belief" she continued. "What if deep inside I'm still an ACG killing machine?"

"I would know believe me and little Bren likes you" said Sirki, trying to find to some light to counter her darkness.

"That's only because he hasn't learned how to hate me yet" she half smiled.

"I believe in you, you are Sari-Ednew."

"Sari renewed? It's a fitting enough name I will have to try and live up to it."

"Now dry your tears let's go and find the children."

Willa, who had been eavesdropping, ran to join her brother. "Ber, our pretend mummy is crying, she thinks we don't like her"

"You don't like her!" he replied. "I do!"

"I don't not like her but she's not our real mummy! P'raps we could be a bit nicer to her though?

CHAPTER 7 - A FAILED ATTEMPT

One week later Jocasta Minto was pushing her daughter up Fore Street in Pendinas, Sirki's comments had plagued her mind and now this second clone was rumoured to be stalking the Da N'tan family.

"Mummee look!" Pan was pointing to a pink dancing rabbit in a toyshop window.

"Not today sweetie" replied Casta. "It's your birthday soon, look there's daddy's *scrid*."

A Tiger with the Chough of the 5th Elites on its doors was illegally parked outside the Kernow and Wessex Bank, *my husband abusing his authority again but at least I don't have to push Pan up that cursed hill to the station.*

They crossed the busy road to Minto who took his daughter in his burly arms. "How's my favourite little girl?" he asked.

"Lo dada!" answered Pan brightly.

"Your mam sends her love Cad and wonders why you didn't come with us?" asked Jocasta pointedly as she folded the pushchair, she had taken a rail*waegn* to visit her mother-in-law as Minto had been *conveniently* busy.

"I will next time my lover" he replied sheepishly. His mother still treated him like a little boy in front of her.

Jocasta regarded him with her lilac eyes. "Hmm, I think you most definitely will, no matter how uncomfortable it makes you feel."

Cadoc strapped his daughter into her seat and got in the driver's side.

"A child's seat in a hulking great camp*scrid* does look a little incongruous" remarked Casta.

"Don't give a toss my lover." he replied. "Pan's safety comes first."

"And don't forget your lovely rightwife!" Casta jibed.

"Of course my handsome." he replied with a grin and brushing her red hair aside gave her a kiss.

As they drove out of Pendinas on the R30 a white Maxim that pulled out behind them. "That's odd?" said Jocasta. "It feels like we're driving through a flat zone."

"You know there are nah flat zones in the shire, Cassie, and we've driven across the spine of Kernow plenty a' times before" he answered then after looking in the rear view mirror frowned. "What's wrong this this tuss? He's practically trying to get in the back door."

Jocasta looked back at the Vanward Maxim which was drawing closer, the windows were tinted but on close inspection the driver appeared to be a blonde woman.

She had a bad feeling. "Cad I think we're being targeted by the ACG, that woman driving the *scrid* might be the second clone!" she said in alarm.

"Clone, what're talking about, *moren*?" Cad was not in on Psi secrets.

"Sirki's dead daughter has been cloned, possibly twice. The first one went after her own children."

"Why did it want the children?"

"Who knows? We are talking about ACG slime."

"Why would she be following us?" he asked then caught sight of Pandora in the mirror, her lilac eyes shining. "Oh nah, not my little girl!" he growled feeling his anger rising.

"She's supposed to be really powerful, I hope I can stand against her!" exclaimed Jocasta as the Maxim slammed into the back of the Tiger making Pan cry.

Cadoc gunned the motor and pulled away. "That thing can't stand up against a *campscrid*, is she bleddy mad?"

"I can't read her at all and I should be able to feel resonation at this distance even if my telepathy is being blocked. It must be her!" she cried.

"Right then my lover, hang on, I'm sorting this!" Minto swerved into the other lane baking heavily and as the pursuer shot past Cadoc accelerated ramming the Tiger violently into the Maxim. The vehicle left the road to hit the rocky hillside but as the vehicle came to rest there was a massive explosion that threw the campscrid over rolling it twice before scraping to a halt on its side. Pandora was screaming fit to burst and Jocasta lay up against the passenger door. "Cassie, *moren* are you alright?" he asked in concern.

"Yes Cad just shaken up, get Pan out!" she answered.

Minto climbed out of the driver's door and reached in to retrieve Pandora before ducking down behind the *scrid*. Jocasta jumped down beside him and thankful that his military vehicle was armoured, he handed Pandora to her, then drew his pistol. His assault rifle was out of reach in a clip next to the driver's seat.

He could see pieces of the Maxim that had landed behind their temporary shelter and dotted here and there were scraps of something grisly. After glancing quickly from the cover of his upturned vehicle, he informed Jocasta they seemed to be alone before cautiously emerging to examine the devastation.

Little remained of the vehicle as a whole *or of the driver* and what was left was still burning. A thick acrid smoke hung in the air and the roof of the upturned *campscrid* was dented and peppered with shrapnel. As Cadoc walked into the road, he heard a vehicle approaching and a grey-blue Tiger hurtled around the corner to screech to a halt. A pair of grey uniformed figures emerged and the *Huscarl* pointed his Draca pistol towards them while moving his left hand to the hilt of his *seax*. The aircrew raised their hands.

"Hei steady on Cempa, we're on the same side!" cried the officer, a Lyftestre from the RAF base at Culdrose. "What happened here?"

"Some Tuss tried to run us off the road!" replied Minto.

"Loge, ain't never seen a power cell go up like that before" remarked the Lyftmann who had been driving.

"That's not a bleddy power cell done that my cock, that's a parcel of high explosive for sure!" stated the Cempa.

Jocasta joined them holding Pan in her arms. "Cad, whatever was blocking my power was in that *scrid*. I've been able to contact Helston, they're sending a Beetle to pick us up and the Ward is on its way."

The aircrew stared obviously at mother and daughter's lilac eyes but said nothing.

Bren sat at Campaeldor Rika's desk listening to the report from the Kernow garrison. The Ward had found traces of *Thunorblaest*, a powerful explosive generally only available to the forces.

The Palace Research Wing had taken possession of what was left of the body and forensic reports showed it be an exact genetic match with One, it appeared the alleged *other* clone was a reality but had failed in its attempt to kill Jocasta and her child. Upon receiving this information Da N'tan alerted Campaeldor Rika, instructing him to keep his men on alert for the time being, *this was a new tactic by the ACG, what would they do next, launch a missile attack on Scartho?*

The Kernow *Huscarl*s clamped down their new Thegnweald tightly, they were proud to have an Omega married to a local boy and were not going to let her or her family be exposed to danger again, causing Jocasta to complain to her clone cousin that she was being wrapped in a blanket, Sirki assured her it was for her own good and was only a temporary inconvenience before buttonholing her husband for the exact same thing in Scartho.

"So if this other clone is dead we can relax now can't we?" she suggested. They were in the morning room.

"Let's give it another week or so Sirk, we need to wait until we can be certain." replied Bren.

"Certain of what?" asked Sirki. "The ACG are never going stop plotting against us while they exist."

"I don't want to let you out of my sight until they're completely eradicated them this time!" emphasised Bren.

"Dahling?" she pushed herself against him, her lips were parted slightly, her dress clung in all the right places and her lilac eyes were shining.

He gathered his resistance. "Don't try to use your charisma on me, what do you want?"

"Sari-Ednew is getting on well with the kids so I thought it would be nice if we took them to the seaside for a day out?" Sirki cupped a hand around his crotch.

"I disagree!" he retorted quickly. Her touch was turning him on, as usual.

Sirki ran her thumb up his fly. "Pretty please?" she felt something stirring under the material.

"Where to?" he said with resignation, he could never hope to win at this game.

"Thorpe Sands, it's not far from Scartho." she found the zipper pull.

"What's wrong with Scartho, it's got a beach?"

"Call that a beach? It's mainly quicksand and from it you get a lovely view of the ugly gun-forts in the estuary. Thorpe is a quaint old-fashioned place and so, so much nicer" she stroked the bulge in his trousers with a free finger.

"It's in the Weald, I suppose I could organise *Huscarl* protection?" He reached down to the hem of her dress and began to raise it as they kissed.

"We'll leave from the Hall and meet our bodyguards at the landing pad there, check?"

"Check." Bren could feel bare flesh under the dress. Sirki was, as usual, bereft of underwear. "You are such a tart" he said with a grin as she pulled down the zip.

"Our deception didn't quite work as planned, they are still maintaining a state of high alert" the Cempa related to Milby.

"Not to worry, the remaining clone has exceeded all expectations and is now in place, all that is required is the opportunity" he replied.

Scartho-Palace communications had been intercepted and the ACG had been alerted to the fact that their enemy suspected a second clone. Upon hearing this, Milby had devised an ingenious plan, Clone Two had expired in vitro at almost full term and had been stored for future research. The body was thawed and sat in a remote controlled vehicle packed with explosives then sent to attack the other lilac-eyed abhorrence and its child.

If the Kernow dryicge and her spawn were killed, all well and good, if not, it would at least convince the Scartho hore and her family that this copy of her scunung daughter was dead.

Now, unbeknown to the *novae* the third clone, very much alive, was ready to strike.

Sari-Ednew was actually beginning to feel she belonged, the children had even referred to her as mummy on one occasion but Freya, forced to live at the Hall during the emergency, kept her distance as much as possible even to the extent of not dining with the family. If they met by accident she would simply glare and walk by, Sari-Ednew had attempted to talk to her on one such occasion but received a snarled warning by way of reply.

Later this morning she was going on a trip with her family *as she was now beginning of think of* them and having some time to kill, finally got around to viewing the records of Experimental Group 3. Her mother Sirki had roots here but the views of the cloning chambers gave her a chill *it was all very reminiscent of her own beginning.*

Thinking it all looked rather too familiar she called up the records of the expedition led by Cempa Da N'tan into the ERW bunker forty years earlier and again had the uncomfortable feeling of recognition but it was possible that all such installations built before the Q-war were similar. Then she saw the sign on the wall, its peeling paint, barely legible, read.

← Flythall East   Boccraefthus West ond Livinghus A →

A chill ran down her spine, she had passed that sign many times during her training *and* on the way to the flyer that took her on her mission to New Winchester. The clone now knew where she had been grown and it had to be where the secret ACG base was located.

CHAPTER 8 - I AM NUMBER THREE

Sirki was overjoyed. Thorpe Sands, being inside Scartho's borders, was considered a safe destination and better yet, Willa and Bern now accepted Sari-Ednew as a friend and she too was looking forward to the trip. Seeing the Midge sat on the apron at the front of the Hall Sirki waved to the clone sitting at the pilot's seat wearing Sari's favourite red dress. Curiously there were no guards by the main door.

Sari started the Midge and waved back cheerily.

"Wait for me" laughed Sirki jumping in.

"You took your time mother." laughed the clone.

Sirki glanced into the back where her son and grandchildren appeared to be fast asleep, *that didn't seem right and she called me mother, not mummy?*

Realisation came too late as a trank was jabbed fiercely into her arm. "You're not Sari-Ednew!"

"Quite right *wicca*, I am Number Three!" Sirki heard her say before slipping into darkness.

Da N'tan sat at the Campaeldor's desk watching the view-screen, and his heart sank, the cameras by the main door had recorded everything and he watched Sirki climb into the Midge then slump down before the flyer lifted off. "This is it, this is all we have?"

"Sorry Bren, there's nothing else. We have everyone we can spare out looking." Hal Rika had organised a search the moment he found out.

The missing guards had been found sitting in the gardens with no recollection of how they got there and after Elli examined them she deduced they had been subject to mind control.

"It has to be that bloody clone, she must have broken the lock Sirki put on her mind" thought Bren on hearing this.

The Midge had been detected flying towards Cambrycge before disappearing off the map, the Anglian Ward was scouring their shire but Bren knew it would be a waste of time.

He was certain where they had been taken.

"Bren, I can't force the Kenta Reeve to fingertip search the entire shire, we still have a serious situation in East Frisha in case you've forgotten. They have alerted their Ward and it's the best we can expect for now" replied Effie.

"This is Sirki and the kids we're talking about! Curse it, Effie, she's your best friend can't you do anything?" he asked.

"I will ask the Foreladtwa to put pressure on the Kenta Reeve," she replied. "We have rules for a reason, Bren."

"The ACG are illegal and if Kenta is hiding them the *Huscarls* will take action. The Thegn of Jorvik has already sent me word he is willing to assist if necessary" he warned, *hardly a surprise as Jorvik mistrusted everyone south of Scartho and east of Brythony.*

"I cannot condone the deployment of *Huscarls* within the country without sanction from the Witan!" she replied anxiously. "Kenta has the largest contingent of *Here* in Aengland let alone their enlisted *Fyrd* and they could make things very difficult if they wanted, the last thing we need is another bloody civil war!"

"Then get permission from the fucking Witangemot and get them to put pressure on Kenta! Are the Home Shires part of the bloody Reignweald or not?" he snarled ending the communication abruptly.

Tiw knew how many conventions he had just broken, Effie would have to understand.

As Sari-Ednew stepped out of the door it felt as if she'd walked headfirst into an iron bar then as she reeled back a fist was driven into her stomach. Falling to the floor she saw her own face looking down at her and realised the truth.

"Hei One, guess who I am?" said her twin.

"Fucking *bicce!*" she had gasped painfully.

"Try Number Three, traitor!" the third clone punched her again and stars seemed to explode in her head as everything went black.

Sari-Ednew slowly came to and gingerly felt her painful face. There was a massive swelling on her cheek, her right eye was partially closed and her stomach hurt like hell. She became aware of someone standing over her and tried to stand but pain coursed through her body like electricity, *nerve fire!* "Please stop." she gasped as an unseen force lifted her off the ground to hold her in mid-air, toes dangling downwards.

"Where are they, *bicce?*" demanded Freya, a look of fury on her face.

"Where are who?" her head was splitting.

"Don't play the innocent with me!" she snarled. "I'm not mum I won't fall for your lies so easily."

"Please, Freya, I'm in pain here!" begged the clone.

Her sister studied her bruised face. "Mum must have put up a hell of a fight, what have you done with her?"

"I don't know what you're talking about?" then it dawned on her. *Three was behind this.*

"Well let me remind you, Cuckoo, mum and the kids flew off in a Midge with you and it vanished off the radar, now an hour later I find you here wearing ACG uniform and..." realisation interrupted the flow of her conversation. "If you flew off with them how did you get back here?"

"Because I didn't leave, it was the other clone, she knocked me out and changed clothes then left me here to cause confusion!" she examined her arm to see a needle mark. "The *bicce* even tranked me just to make sure I stayed out, please put me down Freya, we're wasting time!" her sister almost reluctantly released her hold and she dropped to the ground.

"So how did she get in here?" Freya was not convinced as yet.

"You walked into the Palace Research Wing without being seen, if she has Sari's psionic ability it would be easy for her."

"Gods, we have to find her. I'll tell dad, he's looking for them now" started Freya.

"Wait, I know where she's taken them!"

"Where, how?" demanded her sister.

"The Kenta in the old ERW bunker, it has to be there, that's where I was un-tanked. I recognised it when I watched the atellan recordings!"

"We must tell dad!"

"Agreed, I'm going after them Fri and I need a fast flyer with stealth boccecraeft."

"I'll requisition my Dragonfly and fly you myself." she replied.

"But you're mid-term, is that wise?"

"We're talking about my family and you'll need me to cloak you from the ACG's scanners once we're inside, I'm coming with you!"

Freya path'd to the Psi on the duty desk, informing her where to find the abductees but did not mention she was going herself. "It'll just give dad something else to worry about" she informed her cloned sister.

Da N'tan received the message from Freya and immediately contacted Queen Ethelflaeda. "They're in the old fucking ERW warren in Kenta, I'm going there right now and if they want to shoot at the Thegn of Scartho so be it!"

Effie shook her head resignedly and contacted the Foreladtwa's office again.

Connor had just boarded the Flying Beetle when a Tiger screeched to a smoking halt on the pad. He stepped down onto the concrete to see the Thegn wearing full combat dress and hefting a Sterlinger. "Cempa, I'm looking for a ride to Kenta, got any room in that crate?"

"Aye sir, I was just taking a tithe out on another search of the Wolds?" he gestured inside the vessel.

"Don't waste your time Ed, I am going to rescue Sirki and the kids, I have no sanction to do it and it's going to be bloody dangerous, are you with me?"

"Need you ask sir?" he called to the *ferdrinc* inside the vehicle. "Did you lot hear that, what do you say?" a chorus of ayes was returned.

"Let's get going we've not got time to waste" asserted Connor, they climbed aboard the Beetle and it lifted off at full power.

Upon clearing the Thegnweald's border Bren received some welcome news, word had got around and a scratch *cohort* of volunteers was leaving to support their leader. The message also came that Jorvik was *beating its shields,* openly threatening to attack Kenta if Da N'tan was downed. All they had to do now was cross half the country without air clearance, trespass in a shire that was openly anti-*nova* and carry out a raid on an underground bunker with Woden knows what facing them inside. It wasn't going to be a walk in the park but he did have one advantage, a forgotten entrance they'd used all those years ago. Bren told himself if he pulled this off it would the last time he would go *wiking,* although he knew that given half the chance it wouldn't be.

Unknown to Da N'tan a small airship had already landed at his exact destination. "Are we nearly there yet?" Freya shouted from under her hood. It was raining heavily and she was having a very uncomfortable trek down into the hidden valley.

"Nearly, it's just behind that little waterfall." answered One.

"Waterfall?" cried Freya in dismay. After negotiating the narrow path they arrived at a small cataract which cascaded into a fast flowing stream on the valley floor and hidden behind it was a small metal door.

"See, just as in dad's report!" stated Sari-Ednew. "There's an emergency release handle just here" she said sliding her hand into cleft in the rock. "It's a bit, stiff, there got it!" the door creaked open slightly.

"Still working after forty years, that's a bit convenient?" Freya mused as the clone wrenched the sturdy door open.

"Perhaps they use it occasionally?" replied One then hefting their Sterlingers the pair entered the unknown. A short distance in they encountered a second heavier blast door that had fortuitously been jammed open, beyond that was a large square opening in the floor. It was the service lift shaft and the twisted gantry above had once held long fallen winch machinery.

"That's quite a distance" remarked Freya, her voice echoing in the gloom. They were laying on the edge peering into the darkness and using their infra-red vision to reveal the depth of the shaft.

"It was last used when they were fitting this place out before the war. Tunnels leading to the surface are on the next level down and below that is the main bunker. There are several smaller working lifts in the occupied area for access to the outside world and the hangar is there too!" explained the clone scanning the sides. "I can see ladders built into each side of the shaft and we'll have to use them to reach the bottom but I'm afraid it'll be quite a climb."

Freya stepped out into the void to hover in mid-air. "I'll make my own way down thank you."

"Incredible, you can lift me into the air and hold me up, but not levitate us both down there?"

"Sorry but I don't have the Psionic strength, I would probably drop you." she confessed.

"Let me go down first in case there are any hostiles about!"

Freya cocked her weapon. "I can use one of these you know?" and with that she floated down into darkness.

Sari-Ednew climbed down one of the ladders hearing it creak and groan ominously but eventually reached the wreckage strewn floor without incident.

"Which way now?" asked Freya, the doors at the bottom of the shaft had been cut through as if by an energy weapon and from here corridors went off in three separate directions.

"Straight across leads to the auxiliary power area and storage, there used to be a comms' room there too. The left tunnel leads to derelict laboratories and the other will take us through the hangar to the occupied zone."

Freya looked down the right hand corridor where a distant glow could be seen. "So we go this way?"

"No that will take us right into them, if we go directly ahead that will lead us through the auxiliary area. We can get to the cacaern block from there and that will be the most likely place to find them."

"You seem to know a lot about this place" said Freya.

"I studied the reports made after dad's expedition and don't forget I lived here while being *re-educated*. Now as I remember it these corridors are patrolled regularly so we had better be careful!" she led the way past a sign which read, in peeling paint. "Ciethehus 1-4, Auxilium Communicare ond Elektrikhus A – B➜"

The unconscious Da N'tan family had been taken to the aforementioned cell block where a torc and a suppression hood had been put on Sirki before she was handcuffed to the bench.

Milby smiled as he looked over the prisoners. "Well done Three, you have more than made up for One's failure. We'll leave them here for a while and when they wake up I'll have a little chat with them, I am especially looking forward to *interrogating* the *hore* of Scartho."

An *offestre* was left to look after the children with a clone to keep watch over Sirki while more guards were stationed outside before a gloating Milby, followed by the

CHAPTER 9 - BACK TO THE BUNKER

The Beetle had crossed into Kenta without incident and was now heading south. Bren, wearing a painted war face for the first time in many years, brooded over what was to come. He had just twelve *ferdrinc* to go up against an entire ACG installation, true, the volunteer *cohort* was on its way but they would arrive first to face who knows what?

"Crossing the R262" announced the pilot. They were flying over the road where he had been ambushed all those years ago, the very spot where Faedra had died. He was returning here after all this time and having lost one love in Kenta he was determined not to lose another.

They were now approaching the mined out hills of Wealden, below which was concealed their target. *In hindsight it was so obvious, the ERW bunker was only twenty miles from Denge Marsh the site of the ACG's original research establishment and it was in a flat zone totally impenetrable to psionic probing and opaque to radio signals. Hadn't past experience told them this was a place where the ACG were likely to hide? This time they would wipe the bahstards off the face of the planet, although they would no doubt be hiding behind an army of clones.*

Besides their Sterlinger assault rifles the tithe wielded a Bladesung *liegswaepn* and a Fire-axe LMG, *they would create havoc if nothing else,* his plan was to enter the base through the old service lift shaft just as he had years before and hopefully it would still be accessible. *He had to find Sirki and the children before anything bad happened, how could Clone One turn on them like this after the hospitality they had shown her and how had she overcome Sirki so easily?*

The Beetle circled the target area allowing Da N'tan to see the Dragonfly with a Cormorant insignia already landed there. That was odd, the clone had stolen a Midge and the only Dragonfly registering as booked out from the Hall's hangar was his daughter's personal flyer?

Oh Gods Freya, surely you haven't followed her here on your own?

The flyer dropped low, the floor hatches opened and thirteen *ferdrinc* jumped to the ground before the airship gained altitude to keep station overhead. The rain slowed to a light drizzle as the soldiers made their way down to the small waterfall where they found the concealed entrance invitingly ajar.

"They've left the back door open, that's very kind of them!" remarked Connor sardonically.

"I have a horrible feeling another one of my family has put themselves in danger!" replied Da N'tan.

"There's one way to find out, Sir" stated Connor making for the entrance.

Da N'tan watched as the tithe filed past, this was the first time he had been here in more than thirty years, *what awaited him inside this time?*

The *Huscarls* blurred through the access door and finding no opposition approached the lift shaft to peer into the darkness. Da N'tan noticed two wet rain-cloaks lying nearby, *who had accompanied Freya here?*

"That's quite a drop" observed Tithengealdor Berton surveying the dark shaft.

"There are ladders set in the walls all the way down but I wouldn't trust them" pointed out the Thegn. "It's been forty years since I was last here and it's even more dilapidated, we need to be careful."

The soldiers roped up then abseiled down two at a time to secure the area. Upon reaching the bottom Da N'tan pondered for a moment before deciding they should make towards the dim light.

Sirki, now fully awake, concentrated through the pain of the torc and the flat hood's distortion to discern Willa and Bern huddled next to her on the bench while her son was in the arms of a norm. She also felt the presence of the single clone standing guard over them.

Sirki psionically killed it, which she hated doing even to an ACG creature but the children's lives came first, then holding the nurse in a state of immobility she called to her granddaughter. "Willa, take the hood off mummo's head please."

The offending item was removed and she saw Willa's tear stained face.

"*Mummo?*" said the girl.

"Now, take this horrible thing off my head but be careful it can sting so pull your sleeves over your hands first." even the touch of flat metal was painful to a Psi. The girl gingerly lifted off the hateful torc.

"Right!" Sirki, now free of the pain, telekinetically unlocked her chains while freeing her hold on the *offestre*. "Give me my child!" she snarled and after taking little Bren back stunned the enemy nurse. Now free of any psionic restraint Sirki could tell they were in a major flat zone, *no point in calling for help*. She regarded the cell door which opened itself and the clone guards outside fell lifeless to the ground before they could even move.

The inmates emerged from the cell and after quickly looking about Sirki led them into the darkest of the tunnels that stretched away.

"I know the way to the airships" piped up Willa. "I saw it when they brought us here."

"Then lead on *lapsi* but we must be as quiet as mice. You too my sweet!" she whispered in little Bren's ear and he put his finger to his lips to shush softly. When they reached the hangar she would charm an enemy lyftfara to fly them out, *they had luck on their side at the moment but where was Clone Three? She was more dangerous than all of the ACG heremenn put together.*

The Craeftwice received the news with a stony face and after staring silently for a while finally spoke. "So she escaped despite all our precautions? I should have had the *dryicge* killed immediately!" he turned to Three stood impassively by his desk. She was still wearing Sari's bright red dress but with a pouched weapons belt as a most unconventional accessory. "There can be no more mercy for her! Find them, kill the lilac-eyed *hore* and bring the children to me here, preferably alive" the clone turned and left without a word, *she even frightens me!* Milby turned to the guard commander. "Cempa put your men on high alert, the Scartho *bicce* is very dangerous so issue orders to shoot her on sight and hope that Clone Three finds her first."

Milby sat back in his chair. *Curse the woman I should have had her killed straight away!*

The communicator on his desk shrilled "Craeftwice Milby, *Huscarls* have been spotted by monitors in the abandoned zone. They are in corridor 4, a clone detachment has been sent to intercept them.

"That's too close to the hangar for comfort, they must be stopped!" he ordered, alarmed by this further revelation.

Several minutes later more came bad news from the comms room. "The northern lookout post has spotted a fleet of airships heading this way."

"A fleet of airships?" exclaimed Milby.

"Several Flying Beetles with two larger lifters probably *hereflota,* their recognition signals identify them as being from Scartho" answered the comms room.

"That's *cohort* strength! Da N'tan has no jurisdiction here, this is an unauthorised action, get on the landline to Maidstone and find out why the Reeve hasn't ordered them to turn back!" he shouted angrily, *they could rely on Kenta for air support, surely?*

"They have orders from the Palace apparently, sir!" the response came.

"The Queen couldn't have done this without the Witan's permission?" *the scunung bicce of a Foreladtwa must be in her pocket,* without Kenta to protect them they were in serious trouble. Milby had the awful feeling he had been here before.

The four fugitives had arrived at a cavernous hall full of old and dilapidated machinery, columns and girders stretched from floor to ceiling and rotting cabling hung everywhere. A sign by the doors read "Elektrikhus A – Unpermitted Ingang Forbaden!" this place had been a power generating facility, long abandoned since the end of the Q-war.

"This isn't the way surely?" asked Sirki.

"I think we took the wrong turn, mummo!" cried Willa in panic.

"It's alright Wil, we'll go back and find the right way," said Sirki in a voice more calm than she felt.

They had hardly taken another step when a familiar voice echoed around the room to taunt them. "I know you're in here *dryicge,* did you honestly think you could escape from me?" it was Clone Three.

Quickly screening herself and the children from detection Sirki attempted to locate their pursuer but the clone was likewise blocking her. On the plus side, the banks of generators formed quite a labyrinth meaning the clone would have trouble finding them too.

Sirki gently entered the fringes of her granddaughter's mind. "*Willa, take little Bren and when the nasty woman appears you and Bern must run in different directions.*"

"*But mummo, what about you?*" thought Will, her lip trembling.

"*I will stop the horrid lady, check?*"

"*Check mummo*" answered Willa reluctantly.

Seeking shelter in a metal cabin they waited for Three to make her move, even little Bren, seeming to understand the gravity of the situation, was very quiet.

"Contact dead ahead" yelled the leading *ferdrinc* as the clones appeared and a fierce firefight broke out in the rough-hewn corridor. The *Huscarls* laid down suppressing fire with the Fire-axe but the enemy were advancing steadily behind improvised metal shields made from heavy steel doors. Bullets were ricocheting everywhere and Connor's soldiers were forced to find what meagre cover they could find, *this called for drastic action.*

"Bladesung wide spread!" ordered the Cempa above the clamour and the Ferescota wielding the weapon altered the weapon's aperture to launch a brilliant blue fan of energy buckling the metal shields while incinerating those sheltering behind them. Da N'tan could feel the heat of the blast in the close confines of the corridor and several of the Elite received singed eyebrows and beards, thick greasy smoke was roiling around and the smell of ozone and burned flesh hung in the air.

"Press forward and take the room ahead! We need to get out of this fug and secure the area!" yelled Connor.

They emerged into a large brightly lit hangar with several berthed flyers including a pair of stipple painted Flying Beetles and the stolen Scartho Midge. A small group of black uniformed soldiers gave token resistance before retreating through a gated exit while several overalled figures, obviously non-combat staff, fled into another corridor. "We've hit the jackpot, we've captured their bloody transport!" yelled the Tithengealdor.

The hangar had a wide sloping ramp that led to a pair of heavy doors to the outside world, and upon seeing this an idea occurred to Da N'tan. "Cempa, are any of your men flight trained, we could do with one of these Beetles to cover our backs and enable our reinforcements to get in safely?"

Connor grinned widely. "You want us to arm one of these buggers up?"

"You got it Cempa, open the hangar doors, and make lots of smoke and fire so our chaps outside can see it then keep a watch on our arses. I doubt they have anything heavy enough to take out a Beetle down here?" answered Da N'tan.

"Berton, you heard the Thegn!" shouted Connor to his Tithengealdor. "Get yourself and Ifans in one of these flyers and get cracking." then turning to another soldier yelled. "Find the door controls and get them open, soon as!"

There were two corridors leading from the hangar and Da N'tan led the group after the unarmed figures as they made their escape. They were only a short way down when one of the armoured flyers could be heard powering up, several loud explosions followed and a hot breeze caught up with them. The Beetle had launched a salvo of flares to explode in the forest that sprawled down the hillside then turned on its axis to concentrate on the ACG soldiers who were returning in greater numbers. In the sky above, the circling fleet spotted the smoke and began spiralling down towards the open hangar doors. The Scartho Elite Guard was coming to support its Thegn.

Connor's small force fought its way into the research area encountering only slight resistance but ACG craeftwitan and their subordinates were surrendering to them in such numbers they had little choice but to wait until reinforcements arrived to help marshal their captives. With just a tithe of soldiers they had managed to take almost a third of the installation, in the hangar men were debarking from the first *hereflota* while more troops streamed in through the open doors to give battle to the defenders.

Of the whereabouts of his family or of the treacherous clone who had betrayed them, Da N'tan had no clue.

Sari-Ednew lowered her weapon, its muzzle still smoking. "We're clear!" this was the second clone patrol they had encountered and as before, Freya had psionically prevented a warning being sent while Sari dealt with them.

"Are you sure this the right way?" asked Freya as they stepped cautiously over fallen bodies.

"This will take us to the cell block and beyond that is the cloning facility where I was *born*" she answered.

"I'm sorry I doubted you" said Freya, a little out breath.

"I can live with that Freya, but we need to find mummy and the children." she regarded her sister who was pale and sweating. "You really shouldn't have come in your condition, it was because you didn't trust me wasn't it?"

"Yes, sorry again," she admitted.

Gunfire could be heard in the distance and both women stopped to look quizzically at each other. "Dad?" asked the clone. Rumbling detonations followed.

"Dad!" affirmed Freya before giving a shudder. "Did you feel that tremendous psionic surge after the explosion?"

One shrugged, she had no psionic power and felt nothing.

"To feel it in this flat zone it must have been..." Freya faltered, feeling suddenly alarmed. "Mum is in trouble, suster, we must hurry!"

Sirki could feel a faint resonation and instinctively knew it had to be Bren but she still had no clue as to where Clone Three's was. The maze of rusting metal was proving as much a hindrance as help.

"Show your face *dryicge!*" the voice came again, this time it was close by and little Bren, startled by the sudden shout, began to cry.

"Come out Fro Scartho, you cannot escape me now!" taunted the voice and peeking through a rivet hole Sirki could see the clone, not far from their hiding place.

Saddened to hear her daughter's voice speaking in that way, Sirki whispered. "Remember what I told you children?" before stepping out to face their pursuer.

"Get out of my head *dryicge!*" yelled Clone Three as Sirki entered her mind. Neither could use avatars in the flat zone.

"Where are the children?" snarled the clone, forcing away the mental attack.

Sirki gave no answer but instead telekinetically lifted her daughter's double into the air to launch her bodily against the side of a large container and the noise reverberated like thunder.

"Run!" she shouted before blurring away. The clone, unharmed, picked herself up and after making a mental note of the direction the children had taken went after Sirki, firing her pistol.

Sirki threw up a pressure wall and as the bullets flattened against it she ducked through a gap in the pipework to temporarily gain some distance from her pursuer.

The children reached a corridor outside the power hall and Willa finding a metal door opened it to discover a small locker room. "Get inside and keep uncle Bren safe!" she ordered handing the toddler to her brother.

"But *mummo* said to run?" he protested.

"I want mummy!" cried Bren.

"Shh, I'm going to help *mummo*." Willa replied.

"But…"

"Just do it Bern!" she interrupted and closing the door blurred back into the generating hall.

Sirki was picking her way cautiously through the metal labyrinth unaware that the clone, having spotted her prey, was now quietly stalking her.

Hearing distant explosions Sirki paused, and with her attention taken the clone chose this moment to step out and thrust something into her abdomen. Sirki screamed as she felt an agonising pain right through to her back and sagged, held up only by the combat knife in Three's hand. After twisting the blade to cause further injury, the clone pulled it out ripping Sirki's stomach open and she dropped to the ground like a rag doll.

She could taste blood in her mouth and breathing was difficult, it felt as though she'd been cut in two and there was no feeling in her legs.

The clone squatted to peer into her face "I've destroyed your portal and your powers are gone *dryicge*, now the question is, do I let you bleed to death or shall I put you out of your misery?" through a haze of pain Sirki saw a face like her daughter's face twisted in sadistic mirth.

"Mercy I think, after all I do owe you something for giving birth to my progenitor!" but as the clone held the bloodied blade close to Sirki's throat something bounced off her head.

"Leave *mummo* alone you *haeg*!" Willa, using her burgeoning psionic power had levitated a heavy metal pipe at the clone who, turning slowly, gave her an unpleasant grin.

"Run!" croaked Sirki.

As Willa blurred away the clone looked down at her and sneered. "Very well mummy, enjoy your slow painful death" and she set out after the girl who was attempting to lead Three away from the boys.

Now alone, Sirki found she had some power from the portal cells in her wamb and used it to staunch the blood flow but she found could no longer move. The knife had been driven in with such force that it had not only split her

Helm node but severed the spinal cord paralysing her, and worse still *something* was protruding from the gaping wound. *I'm going to die here, where are you Bren?*

The two sisters were approaching at the power hall from the corridor side. "If we find the *bicce*, leave her to me, check?" ordered Clone One.

"Three'll beat you easily she has all her abilities, we'll have to work together" replied Freya.

"Your baby… I can't let it be threatened."

"If she kills you she'll come after me next, we have no choice."

One reluctantly agreed and they continued until they reached a wide chamber with a set of double doors at each end. Marks in the dust revealed the doors to the left had been recently opened.

"Looks like someone might have come this way?" ventured Freya regarding the small footprints on the dirty floor. "I can feel resonation. It's your son and our little brothur!" she exclaimed pointing to the locker room. "And there's someone else nearby, it feels like mum but it's very weak."

They opened the door to discover two frightened boys hiding inside. Clone One clutched Bern tightly in her arms while Freya scooped up Bren to comfort him.

"Mummy, there's a horrible lady who looks like you and mummo was fighting her and now Willa has gone!" he cried.

"Freya stay here, protect the children and your baby at all costs and do not attempt to follow me!" ordered the clone before heading for the open doors.

As Sari-Ednew entered the power room she could hear laboured breathing somewhere in the darkness, and assault rifle at the ready she followed the sound to find her mother lying curled up in a pool of blood.

Sirki's eyes flickered open at her approach. "Have you come back to finish me off after all?" she croaked.

"Mummy, what's happened?" Sari squatted down next to her.

Sirki, her mouth bloody, managed to gasp. "Three."

"We'll get you help, I'm pretty certain dad's here!" she gently moved Sirki's arms then tore open her dress to examine the gaping wound.

Sirki whimpered and Sari-Ednew almost retched. Loops of intestine protruded gorily from her stomach, in her previous life she had seen worse on the field of combat *but this was mummy!* She knew this would be fatal unless treated soon.

"No... she's after Wil... Three..." Sirki moaned again, the pain was excruciating.

One remembered Sari's battlefield training and took the haeling pouch from the leg pocket of her ACG uniform. Removing a one shot syringe she injected her mother, easing the pain slightly.

"Demetol," thought Sirki recognising her old drug of choice, *it's hardly likely to harm me now.*

"I'll stop her mummy, I promise" affirmed Sari-Ednew. "This is going to hurt I'm afraid!" she unfolded a large plas and gathered up the protruding mess then carefully rolling Sirki onto her back, brought her knees up slowly.

"I can't feel anything now Penni" said Sirki weakly.

"I'm your daughter Sari" One corrected her. *She may not survive what harm would a lie do now?*

After looking in the kit again, Sari gently covered the wound using the last large plas then settled it down sealing it as best she could. She gave her mother a shot of antibiotic and yet more pain relief.

"Come closer daughter," husked Sirki focusing her waning power on the clone.

As she bent down to her mother's face Sari-Ednew felt something release in her mind with a snap and sat back in shock. Her mother was resonating feebly and she could feel her sister *and* the children nearby, *her suster?* Yes, it was her sister Freya and she was Sari Jorvik who had two children and had once been kidnapped by the ACG! Sirki had not only unlocked her psionic ability but in doing so had released her daughter's personality from its mental prison.

Memories had meaning once more. "Mummy I'm me again!" she exclaimed before staring in horror. Sirki, having exhausted her remaining power was no longer able the staunch the wound and began bleeding heavily, the plas lifting at one side.

Sending her mind into the wound Sari quickly clamped blood vessels shut but her mother's life was slowly ebbing away. She tore a strip from Sirki's dress and folding it into a pad pressed it over the wound in an attempt to stop the blood flow causing her mother to whimper in pain. "Sorry" said Sari.

"Leave me and find Wil, Three… you're able to face her now…" Sirki's thoughts tailed off as she faded into unconsciousness.

"No, no! Freya, get in here now!" she yelled.

"One, what…Oh gods" her sister had rushed in holding Bren and she turned quickly away pulling her nephew with her. "Don't look Bern!"

"Bern, be a big boy and look after uncle Bren, don't let him see mummo like this" path'd Sari to her son, then *"Fri, mummy has given me my psionic power back!"* she handed her sister the medical pack then sent a flash thought instructing her how to staunch the wound with her mind. *"Look after our mother, keep pressure on the wound and keep her alive, I'm going to get that fucking clone bicce!"* With that Sari blurred away following a trail of bloody footprints leading from the gory pool where her mother lay.

Da N'tan was sitting at a desk in a room he remembered all too well, it was the office where he had discovered the stasis bubble containing the truth of their creation.

Milby had been found hiding in a broom cupboard and was now standing before Da N'tan, *the aberration was sat at his desk,* and the *scunung* was regarding the Craeftwice with its evil blue gaze making him feel as if he was in a waking nightmare.

"I know who you are, you're Da N'tan, husband of the lilac-eyed *hore* and father of abominations!" he spat.

"You don't know me at all *galdrea* but you, your unpleasant reputation precedes you!" he retorted.

"Doubtless the traitor, Avril North, gave you my name to save her own worthless life!" retorted Milby insolently.

"You seem to have forgotten a certain Psi who remembers you only too well!" Bren leaned forward to address him closely. "We will shortly be in control of this base, *galdrea* and I wish to know only one thing, tell me where to find my rightwife and the children and you will be treated fairly."

"Go fuck yourself *scunung!*"

Da N'tan sighed. "You people are always so brave to start with, I really haven't got time for this," he turned to Connor. "Cut one of his fingers off."

A *ferdrinc* held the struggling man's right hand on the desk while Connor drew his *seax*. "This is not a weapon of surgical precision and it may be hard to take just the one but I can assure you that it will hurt!" stated the Cempa before swinging the blade.

Milby shut his eyes and feeling the rush of air as it flew past his face screamed. "No!"

"Stop!" commanded Da N'tan.

Milby opened his eyes and dared to look at his hand, the blade had stopped just above his little finger.

"Changed your mind?" asked Bren.

"They escaped from their cell so I sent the clone after them, it is possible she may have found them already," he admitted quickly.

Da N'tan fought back the urge to thrust his own blade into the man's heart and growled. "I just hope for your sake she hasn't!"

Connor looked at him then at Milby. "Just give me the word Thegn" he said threateningly.

"Release him Cempa. *Galdrea,* you will show me where they were held." Bren pointed at the wall map.

The *craeftwitan* shakily pointed out the cell block on the plan.

Da N'tan nodded grimly. "An old acquaintance of yours wants to see you again. I'm sure you'll remember her, a pretty blonde girl by the name of Madel and she's so looking forward to meeting you again, on her terms! Tithengealdor, take this piece of shit and lock him up before I forget I'm a decent man" Bren felt a growing anxiety.

"Connor, get some men together and we'll start at the cell block!"

After running along a dark corridor Willa had taken refuge in a long rectangular room which had served as a cable store when the original installation was active, tall shelves and cabinets stretched from floor to ceiling providing hiding places aplenty but unknown to her Three had followed the child's warm footprints using her night vision. "Where are you my child?" she called in mock concern as she entered the room. "Come to mummy."

Willa crept quietly behind the shelves furthest from the entrance but her pursuer, aware of her presence, was following her every movement. The girl paused and the clone did likewise waiting patiently like a predatory beast.

Willa took her chance and blurred towards the doorway as the clone dived, snatching at her to grab a leg, the girl fell heavily and after kicking her pursuer in the face pushed herself away and struggled to her feet in an attempt to escape.

"You aren't going anywhere child." snarled the clone, advancing slowly towards Willa and backing her into a corner.

"Hej, Three, frightening little children now are we?" asked Sari-Ednew, brandishing her Sterlinger.

"One, so they let you go? I should have finished you when I had the chance" snarled her twin. "I've already killed the Scartho *hore* and now it's your turn to die!" the weapon was snatched from Sari's grasp by invisible hands to land on the floor with a clatter some distance away. "Is that the best you have?" she asked mockingly before attempting to incapacitate Sari with nerve fire, only to be taken by surprise when it was deflected back at her.

"Sorry to disappoint you *bicce* but I'm back to my old self again!" Sari flew forward and knocked Clone Three to the floor. "Run and find Auntie Freya!" she ordered but Willa, transfixed by fear, just stood and stared.

Three sprang up drawing her pistol only to have it dashed it from her hand by Sari who swung her fist back to strike her across the head. Three reeled but quickly retaliated, kicking Sari in the stomach before hitting her with a doubled handed blow, she staggered briefly then head-butted her assailant and the fight descended into a brutal brawl with each clone fighting for advantage. Three briefly gained the upper hand and pulling back her duplicate's head drew her bloodied combat knife intending to slit her throat but Sari grabbed the hand holding the blade and twisted it as they both fell to the ground.

Willa watched with uncertainty as one of the clones slowly struggled to a kneeling position while the other lay lifeless with the knife buried in her chest.

"Don't move, don't even think about moving!" ordered a stern voice, it was Da N'tan with Cempa Connor and several *Huscarls*, all had their weapons trained on his daughter's clone.

Bren took in the scene before him, there were two identical copies of Sari, one dead on the floor stabbed through the heart, the other on her hands and knees beside the body. One wore a red dress and the other a black ACG uniform.

"Grandad don't shoot mummy!" cried Willa, running to stand in front of him.

Sari turned her battered face to look at her father, her ACG uniform torn and bloodstained and indicated to her dead twin. "Hei dad, this is Clone Three, she swapped clothing with me to steal the children and... mum..." her eyes widened in horror. "Dad, we have to get to her before it's too late!"

"Saz she's slipping away I can't keep her alive!" cried Freya upon their arrival, an ACG *rihtleech* had been pressed into service and was tending to the dying woman.

Sari had thought of something radical on the way back and path'd her intention to her sister, who, suitably astounded at the idea asked. *"Will it even work?"*

"I don't see that we have a choice for even if, by Woden's will, mummy survives, she'll be paralysed for the rest of her life." replied Sari then kneeling by her dying mother touched her face pathing. *"Mummy, you're coming with me."*

In the falling darkness of her mind Sirki was confused. *"Sari I don't understand, I'm so tired?"*

"Don't worry mummy, just let me take you." Sari had sat down cross-legged, a little distance from the group, to enter a trance-like state.

The haeler halted his attempt at treating Sirki and scanned her again before announcing sadly. "I'm sorry ma'am, there is no cerebral activity, she's gone I'm afraid," he was familiar enough with psionic power to know that Freya was keeping the heart beating and reached forward to touch her hand gently. "Ma'am, you're wasting your effort."

Bren wanted to scream in rage at the gods in Asgard, his love lay with a peaceful look on her beautiful blood-smeared face but Sirki was undeniably dead.

Freya path'd to him. *"Dad, this may seem odd, but we must get mum out of the flat zone as quickly as possible and get her body to the PRW in New Winchester!"*

Then she explained the outlandish plan in full.

CHAPTER 10 - HALFWAY HOUSE

Sirki was wearing her old white dress with its feather trimmed cape and glancing down at her feet saw bare toes, the sun was warm on her face while overhead a glorious rainbow arched across the blue sky. *Had she crossed Bifrost, was she now in Fólkvangr the meadow of Freya?*

She was standing on a ridge overlooking a pretty glade and in the distance a familiar house was visible through the trees. Sirki knew this place well, these were the woods that surrounded her old family home in Soomi but she knew that no matter hard she tried it would impossible to reach it. Sirki set off down a well-worn path into the woods, feeling the soft grass under her feet, and arrived in a pretty little glade where she could hear a burbling stream, *as she knew she would*, the air was crisp and clean and birds sang in the trees while large butterflies fluttered over a carpet of vibrantly coloured wild flowers.

It was perfect, too perfect, like something from a child's imagination and it was all so familiar but she knew this was a construct made from someone else's dreams. After walking a little further Sirki spotted a small green roofed cabin with a swing outside and smiled, Uncle Bear had built it for her and she used to bring childhood friends here to play, the roof had originally been red but her uncle had repainted it for *her* children. Sirki remembered how much larger it had seemed when she was a child but now it was so small that she had to bend down to enter the door.

Inside the cabin it was much roomier, as things often are in dreams.

"Hei mummy!" said a voice, and there stood Sari wearing Soomi national dress complete with knee high fringed boots.

"This is your construct isn't it?" asked Sirki, it all made perfect sense.

"Yes, I created it in a dream like you did. I used to hide here as a child when Freya and Alfie teased me so this was the obvious place to conceal myself when the ACG did awful things to my mind. I could return occasionally only to watch in horror while I killed and hurt people and when Aunt Penni shot me I retreated here managing to maintain my presence as a disembodied consciousness. When my first cloned foetus reached the right stage of growwth I became connected to it but slumbered here until reborn" replied Sari. "I brought you here to prevent you from crossing the bridge."

"Then I am dead *lapsi*?" enquired Sirki nervously.

"Your body is long gone but your mind is safe and sound here. The PRW have harvested your ova and are confident they can clone you."

"And you believe I can return to a cloned body?"

"Of course, I did, didn't I?"

"I'm frightened *lapsi*." confessed Sirki.

"I know mummy, I had to do this on my own remember? I was terrified when they put those bloody things in my new head so I sealed myself away behind a barrier of pain and revulsion, horrified at what I had become. I could reach out from it but rarely until you set me free."

"I understand. Sari, how long will it take to grow a new me?"

"Four or five years to reach adult stage, the PRW have little experience with the technique but some ACG personnel have offered to assist in exchange for leniency and we already have one of their best Craeftwitan working for us, a certain Avril North."

"But this is your construct and it relies upon you to maintain it. You can't stay with me for years?" Sirki was concerned.

"I was going to have myself put in a coma and kept on a drip just to keep it going but the Highest believes it can't fold up with a mind as powerful as yours residing in it. I survived for years without a physical body so it should present no problem to you." she explained.

"This is really scary stuff."

"You'll be safe enough." Sari reassured her. "Think of it as a halfway house between your old life and the new."

"Four years seems such a long time Sari."

"Time runs differently here, you'll be back with us sooner than you know and I will visit often to make sure you're alright. It helps if you sleep."

"I do feel very tired. Sari, you're doing this to me, aren't you?" asked Sirki.

"The time will pass quicker this way" replied Sari.

"But I can't sleep for years on end *lapsi*?" she yawned. A carved wooden bed had appeared in the corner of the cabin and it looked so comfortable.

"Think of it as hibernation, like when animals slumber through the winter" suggested her daughter.

"When will my winter end?" asked Sirki.

"Have a nap mummy and you'll be back with us before you know it…"

CHAPTER 11 –
SIRKI-EDNEW

The woman came back to reality laying in a foetal curl on a hard wet surface and after briefly opening her eyes she screwed them tight shut against the harsh white light, every sound assaulted her ears like gunshots and a smell like haelinghus antiseptic mixed with something organic was in her nostrils.

There was a brackish taste in her mouth and breath came in bubbling gasps but did not seem to cause any distress, nor did the salty liquid that foamed from her lungs with every cough. As a tube was put into her mouth to draw the fluid away the woman tried vainly to push herself up but her limbs were too weak to respond.

"Fro Sirkku, don't exert yourself" a calm voice came from somewhere.

Fro Sirkku the name sounded familiar and she attempted to speak but could only manage a bubbling clicking.

"Don't strain your throat, you haven't remembered how to talk yet" the voice reassured her.

"Disconnecting the umbilical" said another.

There was a stinging sensation at her navel and she started to cough again but this time retched at the awful tasting liquid that came up, the tube was returned to suck it away once more.

"You're over the worst, that was the last of the amniotic fluid," said the first voice. "You'll be cold now you're out of your nice warm tank but we can do something about that."

The voice was right, she was shivering. Hazy figures in white surgical gowns helped her to sit up then something was wrapped about her hunched shoulders and she began to feel warmer.

The bright light still hurt but her vision was slowly coming into focus and she was becoming accustomed to the noises around her, a pleasant fuzzy face looked into hers and smiled. "Welcome back Fro Scartho, my name's Avril North. We'll move you out of here in a moment and clean you up then find you a nice warm bed, you won't have proper use of your limbs just yet and you'll find it hard to do things you used to take for granted but it will all come back in a day or so. You will tire easily to begin with but don't worry, this is all perfectly normal." Her head dropped forward limply and hair fell over her face, it was very long and had the organic smell to it.

"There are some people here who you know" the nice face with the brown eyes had come into sharp focus now but the woman did not recognise her. Some people were standing at a long window watching her intently, a young woman with lilac eyes stood with a tall blond girl who had eyes of vivid blue and they were flanking a tall man with a neat beard but she could not bring any names to mind.

She was then lifted into a grav-chair and pushed into a white tiled room as she sank into torpor...

Memories of bright lights and faces hovering over her, of half familiar voices speaking but she had been too unfocused to understand. They had put tubes in her arms and there had been a catheter, *had she gone back in time, was she back in Slote Haelinghus?*

Nej, her throat didn't hurt.

The woman woke again in a comfortable bed with crisp white sheets, the tubes and monitors had been removed so she lay listening to the birdsong outside the window to gather her thoughts. She was Andra Sirkku Vigsdottir and she was the rightwife of... it would come back to her, she had four... no three, no, had had four children. *Was she a sangestre?*

Sirki stretched out her right hand feeling pleased to do even this simple thing and after staring at it for a while she opened and closed her fist several times then repeated it with the left hand, *wasn't something supposed to happen?* Sirki examined the palm and realising there was no communicator lattice there smiled then touched her face and body, *the skin felt incredibly soft and smooth.* She slowly raised and lowered her legs one at a time wiggling her toes before forcing herself to a sitting position with some difficulty.

A door opened and an *offestre* rushed in. "Fro Scartho, it's too soon to try to move on your own!"

But on seeing Sirki's determination he helped her to turn and place her feet on the floor.

"Huh… ow long?" she croaked in a voice that had never been used before.

"You were un-tanked two days ago, Fro Scartho, Craeftwitan North will fill you in on the details when she thinks you are ready" he answered.

"Now!" gasped Sirki.

"I will see if she's available, ma'am but please lie down."

Sirki allowed the nurse to help her back under the covers as she had become fatigued very quickly, *it wouldn't hurt to wait a bit longer?*

She must have dozed off again because there was now a recognisable resonation in the room and opening her eyes saw Sari sitting next to the bed.

Her daughter got out of the chair crying and throwing her arms round her. "Welcome back mummy I'm so glad to see you!"

"And I you *lapsi!*" she held her daughter as memories came flooding back.

"Craeftwitan North thought it best that one of us filled you in" said Sari through tears then taking a breath, composed herself. "You were in the growth tank for four years and thirty days."

"How do I look?" asked Sirki, her voice was recovering its normal character.

"You look younger than me, a teenager."

"Oh? And how is my *poikavauva* Bren, and Willa and Bern how are they and Freya must have her son now, I have so much to catch up on."

"Bren is nearly seven now mummy, not so little anymore quite the image of his dad and looking forward to seeing his mummy again, Freya has called her boy Aelf after our late brother" answered Sari. "Willa is nearly thirteen, quite the little madam and Bern is the spitting image of Stig." Sirki held back tears as her daughter continued. "And you haven't even asked about dad yet?"

"I saw him with you when I was reborn, is he here?"

"Dad's been camping outside since you were uncorked but now he's afraid to visit in case you don't remember him."

Sirki laughed hurting her new larynx slightly. "He is such a *polho*!"

"Do you want me to fetch him?"

"*Nej* let me look at myself first" Sari helped her mother to the full length mirror in the room "Is Freya here too?" she asked.

Sari nodded. "She's outside with dad."

"How are things between you now?"

"Better, she lives with dad in Scartho now but we're not close."

"That's very sad *lapsi* but what about you and Anya"

"We're together again and we live in the old house, she's looking after the kids at the moment."

"Good, now let's see the new me." Sirki stared in the mirror which reflected a perfect unlined face. "I don't remember ever looking this young!" she exclaimed, the silver streak had gone from her chestnut hair which had grown so long it reached down her back. Sirki tightened her gown across her impressive new bust with her hands "Where the hell have these come from? I never had tits this big when I was nursing you lot!"

"You shouldn't complain, cloning doesn't produce a one hundred percent perfect copy, I have differences too you know." answered Sari.

"Now you mention it my nose is different" Sirki said.

"Wasn't it broken once?"

"Oh I forgot."

Sirki regarded her neck which was now free of scars and raising the hem of her gown saw the tattoo on her right thigh was missing then lifting it higher she examined her stomach where it had been torn open, there was nothing to see but a plas over her raw navel.

"It's a good job you're wearing pants mummy!" laughed Sari.

"Makes a change for me" she smiled. "And anyway, you lot were there when I was pulled naked from a glass tube, I don't think I have any secrets from you now. There's one other thing, did something happen while I was in the Helm?" Sirki had a vague feeling her long sleep had been disturbed.

"That'll keep for later, check?" replied Sari mysteriously.

"Check, now bugger off and give me five minutes before sending your dad in."

With Sari gone Sirki reached out to contact Freya by telepathy and was almost as delighted to discover she had retained her psionic ability as she was to contact her oldest daughter. They exchanged emotional greetings with Freya stating she would come in with her son as soon as Bren had visited.

Sirki decided she would work on Freya to make it up with her sister then standing unsteadily in front of the mirror stripped off her gown and pants to admire her new body. With her hair this long she looked like a maiden from a saga and Sirki realised she literally was a maiden again, a *koskematon!* She would look forward to her second deflowering, *there's a job for Bren* she thought and smiled as she picked up his resonation approaching the room.

Da N'tan entered uncertain of what he would find and was astonished to see the unclothed vision stood there. "Sirki?" he asked uncertainly

"Hei *Lufiend!*" she replied stumbling into his arms. "I haven't got this walking thing right yet!" she confessed. They kissed and embraced. "*Minä rakastan sinua!*" asserted Sirki.

"Sirki my *rakas*, I've missed you so much" Bren managed to croak and they stood holding each other for a long time.

The entity, or the Vanir Freya to give her proper name, sat in her green meadow contemplating the situation. *There is still plenty of time and Sirkku will have no choice but to come to me eventually.*

The Ende?

GLOSSARY

Language Guide
Most words are a form of ersatz Old English with some Celtic and Scandinavian.

Adjo – farewell
Aegflota – sailor
Aeldor – a senior official
Aelfland – lit. Fairyland, a popular amusement park in Scartho
Atheling – prince or princess
Bifrost – the rainbow bridge to Asgard
Bicce - bitch
Bicynne – bisexual
Cailin – girl (Erin)
Cempestre – a female warrior
Cwene - queen
Cyning – king
Daege – bread maker, kneader of dough (used as a euphemism for lesbian)
Dottir – daughter
Demend – Umpire, referee
Demetol – an opiate used by Haelers as a painkiller but highly addictive if over used
Diolch – thank you (Brythonic)
Emmet - ant
Ende - end
Farvel - farewell
Ferdrinc –warrior

Folcwen – Popular queen, mighty queen
Gast - ghost
Glaem – gleaming, right, correct, 'Great'
'Grim' – nickname for Woden or Odin
Haeg – hag, witch
Haerfest - autumn
Hafoc – hawk
Hei or Hej – hello or hey
Heilio – hello (Erin)
Hej kaunis – Hey beautiful (Soomi)
Hel – hell
Helm –an inter-dimensional energy field and the source of Novae powers
Helbore – witch, demon
Heremann – generic term for a soldier
Helmward – Pilot
Hore - whore
Hou – hello (Kernow)
Huscarl – a royal soldier from a Thegnweald
Jaa, juu – yes (Soomi)
Joiking – to joik, a traditional chanting style of singing from Soomi
Kitty – affectionate term for a cat, used as a colloquial term for vagina.
Kuinka voit – How are you (Soomi)
Kulta – Sweetheart (Soomi)
Lapsi – child (Soomi)
Larboard – port, left
Loge – trickster god, used an expletive
Lost-ones –Frishan people exploited by the Wights
Lufestre – lover, sweetheart (F)
Lufiend – Lover (M)
Ma rakastan sua – I love you (Soomi)
Mancynn – mankind
Merasta – Thank you (Kernow)
Mithran – follower of Mithraism
Micelre – excellent
Moi – hi (Soomi)
Moi-moi – goodbye (Soomi)
Moren – lass, often used as affectionate term (Kernow)

Mummo – grandmother (Soomi)
Nej – no (Soomi)
Nerth – the earth, after the goddess Nerthus
Niflheim – land of fire, Hell
Niwfara – newcomer, stranger
Nixe –water sprite
Omenakakku – Soomi apple cake
Onweald – jurisdiction
Polho – fool (Soomi)
Raet – rat
Rakas – dear, beloved (Soomi)
Ratatoskr – the squirrel who gnaws at the world tree, also a name of a popular gossip magazine
Reignweald – kingdom, the name used to describe the union of nations
Saetere – Agent, spy (one who lies in wait, insidious one, seducer).
Sangestre – female singer
Scota – a professional soldier
Silkie – a water fairy (they live as seals in the sea but can shed their skin to become human).
Soomilek- the language of Soomi Sirki's homeland
Sott – fool, idiot
Suth - south
Terve – hello (Soomi)
The Ket - mysterious eastern people who use clones for labour and as soldiers.
The March - the area of Reignweald influence in eastern Frisha
The Wights - Oppressive regime opposed to the Reignweald
Thegn –equivalent to a baron
Thegnestre – female Thegn
Thegning – son (or daughter) and heir to thegn
Thegnweald – Thegns area of control
Thorian – follower of Thor
Tithe – a tenth, in military use a unit of ten men (a tenth of a company of one hundred)
Tiw – god of war, justice and self-sacrifice
Tuss – 'cock' derogatory term (Kernow)
Waelcyrie – female emissary of the gods

Wamb – womb
Wiking – a pirate, sometimes used by soldiers as a term for a raiding party
Wisgi – Whisky (Brythonic)
Witan – wise, wise man, also used as a word for a politician or to describe government.
Wyrd - fate
Ystävä – friend (Soomi)

<u>Buildings</u>
Aethus – Mess hall, cafeteria
Anwighus – fighting/training arena
Burh – walled or fortified town
Cacaern – Prison, jail
Camphus – War-house, Command-house
Castel – Castle, fortress
Ciethehus – storehouse, warehouse
Cynegold – The Kings Gold hotel in Slote
Ealdorhus – Leader house (officer's quarters)
Feldhus – Tent
Flytworks – Aircraft Manufacturer
Haell – a hall, any large building
Haelinghus, haelinghall – Hospital
Haelingeth – Army hospital or temporary clinic
Hearg – temple, religious building
Horehus – Brothel
Hus - house
Incempahus – Company house (barracks)
Psihearg – Psi 'temple' headquarters
Supaethus – Restaurant
The Cwenes Faethm – The Queens Arms hotel in Slote
Wardhus - Guardhouse
Witanhus – Government house

<u>Vehicles</u>
Cwichscrid – sports car
Flota – a boat or a ship
Hefigbat – Heavy haulage/crane flyer used by military and civilians alike
Hraedwaen – sports car, fast car

Scrid – car
Searuwheol – Motorbike
Scip - ship
Traktori – Tractor
Twinhweol – Bicycle
Waegn – Large car, van, lorry

Military Terms

Bladesung – Portable directed energy weapon (lit. shining lightning)
Campscrid – 4WD car, Land Rover, Jeep like vehicle.
Campwaegn – Lorry like vehicle
Camp-scethewaegn – military ambulance
Draca – a type of pistol
Eagescytere – Marksman
Entaflota – Flying warship (lit. giant flyer)
Fire-axe – a type of Light machine gun
Flying Beetle – Armoured Flyer used as troop transport and fire support
Flygpil – Fighter aircraft (lit. flying dart)
Hereflota – Flying troop transporter
Herewaegn – Army lorry
Liegswaepn – Powerful directed energy weapon (Lightning weapon)
Lyftfara – Generic term for an Aeronaut, a skyfarer
Lyftfloga – dragon flyer
Lyfthere – Airforce
Randcampwaegn (RCW) – A tank like vehicle
Randherewaegn (RHW) – Armoured personnel carrier/armoured fighting vehicle
Randscrid – Armoured 4WD
RSF Sif – Royal Seaforce Flota Sif, a submarine.
Seax – A single edged sword either 1 or 2 foot in length carried exclusively by Novae
Scota – Experienced soldier, a private
Scyfescot – A type of small machine pistol often worn in a large holster
Sterlinger – A type of advanced assault rifle with integral grenade launcher
Syndigbat – submarine (lit. swimming boat)

<u>Command Structure of the Reignweald Defence Force.</u>
Her Highest Majesty Folcwen Ethelflaeda III –
Commander in chief of the Royal Guard,
She is assisted by the Ofer Heretoga of the Huscarls
Wigfruma – War Minister responsible for the Here and the
Fyrd.
Feldwealda – Field Marshall of the Here (Regular army)
Fyrstwealda – First Marshall of the Fyrd (Conscript Army)

<u>Rank</u>
      <u>Commanding</u>
Regnward – Overall Commander
      Army (Not Huscarls)
Heretoga – General
      Field Army
Folctoga – Lieutenant General
      Corps
Campaeldor – Major General
      Legion
Cempa – Colonel
      Cohort
Undercempa/Hundredsman – Captain
      Company/Hundred
Bydel/Fiftiegsman – Lieutenant/Warrant Officer
      Platoon/Fiftieg
Tithengealdor – Sergeant
      Patrol/Tithe
Undergealdor – Corporal
      Fire-team
Ferescota – 1st Class Trooper/Private
      Fire-team

<u>Non-Combat Staff</u>
Reeve – Adjutant officer equivalent to Undercempa.
Sceaweregealdor – Intelligence Officer
Aelicgealdor – Legal Officer
Weregealdor – Personnel Officer
Talugealdor – Communications Officer
Daelbealdor – Quartermaster, logistics officer
Raed-Cempa – Planning Officer

Beaduweorcealdor – Operations Officer
Haeling-Cempa – Senior Medical Officer
Camphaeler – Army medic

The Elite Guards – Royal Household Troops comprised
entirely of Novae
The Palace Guard - Royal Household Troops comprised of
both Novae and norms
The Here – The Regular Army
The Fyrd – The Conscript Army

Reignweald Air Force
Lyftdryhten – Supreme Air Commander
Lyftcampaeldor – Air Commander
Ficteregealdor – Wing Leader
Flytgealdor – Flight Officer
Lyftgealdor – Air Leader
Lyftmann – Airman
Lyftestre – Airwoman
Steorrafara – Star farer, astronaut.

Seaforce (Navy)
Brimwisa – Admiral
Foremost – Commander
Capitan – Captain
Undercapitan – Ship's lieutenant
Frumlida – Chief Petty Officer
Aeglaedere – Leading sailor
Foresteora – Look-out
Lida – Sailor

Psi ranking – (Romano-Hellenic titles used)
1st level - Neophyte
2nd level - Acolyte
3rd level - Magus
4th level – Hierophant
5th level – Mystagogue
The Highest – Arch Psi

Government - Witan

Foreladtwa – Prime Minister
Horderwice – Treasurer
Hame Canceler – Home Secretary
Ellende Canceler – Foreign Secretary
Haelth Canceler – Health Secretary
Wigfruma – War Minister (not responsible for Royal Household Troops)
Discthegn – Minister of Food (Agriculture, fisheries)
Mangungwice – Minister for Trade
Macungwice – Minister for Industry
Craeftwice – Science Minister
Witangemot – Parliament and also gathering of all Witans (wise men)

<u>Public Services</u>
Leech – doctor
Rihtleech – surgeon
Suster – Nursing Sister
Offestre – nurse
Haeler – paramedic
Scethewaegn – Ambulance
Scetheflota – Flying Ambulance
Ward – Police, police officer
Fyrgealdor – Fire chief
Fyrwaegn – Fire engine

<u>Vehicle manufacturers</u>

Austin –
Aurora, sports car
Arrow, sports car

Vanward –
Atheling, small luxury car
Cyning, large luxury car
Maxim, large car
Minim, small car, Aquila, fast sports version of Minim
Ox, lorry
Pony, van

Stallion, van

Rover -
Imperator, large car
Imperatrix, streamlined large car

Sigurd -
Leopard, sports car
Lion, utility vehicle
Tiger 4x4, heavy utility vehicle often used by the forces
(campscrid)

Aelgar Utility -
Brock Randscrid 4x4 (Armoured scout vehicle) carries up to
5
Taurus, large utility vehicle (multi-role) can carry cargo or
personnel
Randherewaegn 75 Stalwart/90 Spearman (Eight wheeled
armoured fighting vehicle) carries 12 including crew
Randcampwaegn Mjolnir (a tank-like vehicle) 4 crew
Randcampwaegn Einherjar (super-heavy tank) 5 crew
Heracles Hefigbat, heavy lifter used by civilians and forces
alike 4 crew
Raven troop carrier/Cygnus airship, 250 personnel
capacity + 6 crewmen.
Flying Beetle, an airborne armoured personnel carrier
carries up to 12 + 2 crew.

Wayland Flytworks –
Wasp fighter, extreme manoeuvrability supersonic
warplane, single seat
Hornet fighter/bomber, supersonic warplane single or two
seat variants
Midge – Small 6 seat flyer used by military and civilians
alike
Lyftfloga (Dragonfly), small supersonic flyer, max 6
personnel
Entaflota, large troop/transport carrier (flying battleship)
capacity 500
Cyning-entaflota, large version of above, capacity 1000
Sparrow, space vessel 2 crew

Swan, advanced space vessel 2 crew + capacity for 10 personnel or cargo

Hereward –
Hafoc motorbike

<u>Science and technology</u>
Andgiete Craeftgemot (ACG) – Research and Science Council.
They are called galdreas (wizards) by Novae.
Novae are called in turn scunung (abomination) the Psi are called dryicges (sorceresses).
Palace Research Wing – Royal household facility which operates independently from the ACG

A-pad – (Atellan-pad) small portable computer
Atellan, Rimcraefter – Computer
Bonecraeft – Medical Science
Boccraeft – Science, technology
Rimcraeft – Arithmetical Science, computing
Craeftwitan – Scientist
Craeftgemot – Scientific research
Craeftsmann – skilled worker/engineer
Elektroncraeft – Electronics
Smithcraeft – Technology
Smithcraefter – Engineer
The Dema – Supercomputer, active during the stasis period.
Uncraeftsmann – unskilled worker/labourer

<u>Sealticgan -The Solar System</u>
Sol – The Sun
Loge, Loki – closest planet to the sun
Freya – Brightest planet in the system
Aerworuld, Nerth - World, earth
Selene, Mona – The Moon
Tiw – moons Angnes and Ege (Fear and Dread).
Odin –the red spot is said to represent his single eye, four main moons Sleipnir, Gugnir, Huginn and Munnin
Thor –the rings are said to represent the world serpent

Eostre – goddess of rebirth
Aegir – God of the sea
Fenris – furthest known planet from the sun.
Planeta– Planet(s) mainly named after deities in the Edda
Steorra – star

<u>Calendar</u>
Monday – Moonday
Tuesday – Tiwsday
Wednesday – Wodensday
Thursday – Thunorsday
Friday – Frigesday
Saturday – Ellisday
Sunday – Solsday, sunneday

Gerebyrth – January
Mudmoon– February
Tiwaz – March
Eostre – April
Blosme – May
Sunweald – June
Passcalm – July
Ripnes – August
Harfaest – September
Winterfall – October
Bloodmoon - November
Geola – December
Festivals - Easter, Harvest, Yule, Eftboren (New Year)

AR = Ante Romani (Before Rome)
IO = In Occupatio (During Roman Occupation)
PC = Post Cadite (After Fall)
PC1 = would equate to 500AD indicating the inhabitants of
the parallel world are five centuries ahead of us.

Other titles by BLKDOG Publishing

Sirkkusaga
By Kyt Wright

Several hundred years after an world-shattering war, two of the surviving nations, the Reignweald and the Dominion have fought themselves to a standstill, both remaining determined to control of what's left of it.

Sirki Vigsdottir, a songstress who performs under the name Freya in folk-rock group *The Harvest* is beautiful, self-centered woman who is fond of drink and a recovering addict to boot, not the sort of girl a boy brings home to mother.

Following an attack from an unexpected quarter, abilities awaken within Sirki, who begins a journey of self-discovery. These new found skills attract the attention of both the Psi, a mysterious group of telepaths headed by the fearsome Mina and an equally sinister government department; the ACG.

Sirki, learning the real truth of her origin, is dragged into plotting between the queen and the Government, finding herself in constant danger as Bren, fighting for the nation, becomes an important part of her life.

As it becomes clear that her life of self-indulgence is over, Sirki wonders if her new-found powers are a blessing or a curse.

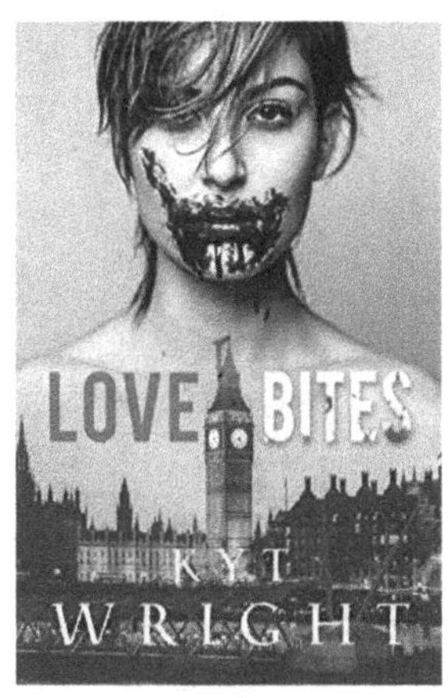

**Love Bites
By Kyt Wright**

Elisabeth Bathory wears a police uniform and patrols the streets of London at night.

Elisabeth Bathory is over four hundred and sixty years old.

Elisabeth Bathory is a vampire.

Elisabeth Bathory enforces the Edict ensuring humans are never killed by vampires.

Humans are starting to turn up dead and it's obvious her people are behind it!

**The Journals of Professor Guthridge
By Kyt Wright**

When a goldsmith is discovered brutally murdered the strange circumstances of his demise lead Inspector Poulson of Scotland Yard to call on a man experienced in investigating the weird and uncanny, Professor Arnold Guthridge of St. Aidan's College, Oxford.

Join the academic as he takes on the case with gusto, accompanied by the feisty Miss Evelyn Poole and a host of unlikely assistants in this rollicking tale of bloody revenge in Edwardian London.

Arthur: Shadow of a God
By Richard Denham

King Arthur has fascinated the Western world for over a thousand years and yet we still know nothing more about him now than we did then. Layer upon layer of heroics and exploits has been piled upon him to the point where history, legend and myth have become hopelessly entangled.

Arthur: Shadow of a God gives a fascinating overview of Britain's lost hero and casts a light over an often-overlooked and somewhat inconvenient truth; Arthur was almost certainly not a man at all, but a god. He is linked inextricably to the world of Celtic folklore and Druidic traditions. Whereas tyrants like Nero and Caligula were men who fancied themselves gods; is it not possible that Arthur was a god we have turned into a man? Perhaps then there is a truth here. Arthur, 'The King under the Mountain'; sleeping until his return will never return, after all, because he doesn't need to. Arthur the god never left in the first place and remains as popular today as he ever was. His legend echoes in stories, films and games that are every bit as imaginative and fanciful as that which the minds of talented bards such as Taliesin and Aneirin came up with when the mists of the 'dark ages' still swirled over Britain – and perhaps that is a good thing after all, most at home in the imaginations of children and adults alike – being the Arthur his believers want him to be.

A Storm of Magic
By Ashley Laino

Being brought back from the dead is an impressive trick, even for magician Darien Burron. Now he must try and use his sleight of hand to swindle modern-day witch, Mirah, to sign her power away, or end up a tormented demon in the afterlife.

Meanwhile, sixteen-year-old Mirah is starting to lose control of her powers. After an incident at her aunt's Witchery store, Mirah is sent to a secret coven to learn to control her abilities. While away, Mirah meets up with a soft-spoken clairvoyant, a brazen storm witch, and the creator of dark magic itself. The young woman must learn to trust in herself before she loses herself entirely to the darkness that hunts her.

Weirder War Two
By Richard Denham & Michael Jecks

Did a Warner Bros. cartoon prophesize the use of the atom bomb? Did the Allies really plan to use stink bombs on the enemy? Why did the Nazis make their own version of Titanic and why were polar bear photographs appearing throughout Europe?

The Second World War was the bloodiest of all wars. Mass armies of men trudged, flew or rode from battlefields as far away as North Africa to central Europe, from India to Burma, from the Philippines to the borders of Japan. It saw the first aircraft carrier sea battle, and the indiscriminate use of terror against civilian populations in ways not seen since the Thirty Years War. Nuclear and incendiary bombs erased entire cities. V weapons brought new horror from the skies: the V1 with their hideous grumbling engines, the V2 with sudden, unexpected death. It was a catastrophe for millions.

The stories in this book are of courage, of ingenuity, of hilarity in some cases, or of great sadness, but they are all thought-provoking - and rather weird. So whether you are interested in the last Polish cavalry charge, the Blackout Ripper, Dada, or Ghandi's attempt to stop the bloodshed, welcome to the Weirder War Two!

Click Bait
By Gillian Philip

A funny joke's a funny joke. Eddie Doolan doesn't think twice about adapting it to fit a tragic local news story and posting it on social media.

It's less of a joke when his drunken post goes viral. It stops being funny altogether when Eddie ends up jobless, friendless and ostracised by the whole town of Langburn. This isn't how he wanted to achieve fame.

Eddie knows he's blown his relationship with rich girl Lily Cumnock. It's Lily's possessive and controlling father Brodie who fires him from his job - and makes sure he won't find another decent one in Langburn. And Eddie doesn't even have Flo to fall back on - his old nan died some six months ago, and Eddie is still recovering from the death of the woman who raised him and who loved him unconditionally.

Under siege from the press, and facing charges not just for the joke but for a history of abusive behaviour on the internet, Eddie grows increasingly paranoid and desperate. The only people still speaking to him are Crow, a neglected kid who relies on Eddie for food and company, and Sid, the local gamekeeper's granddaughter. It's Sid who offers Eddie a refuge and an understanding ear. But she also offers him an illegal shotgun - and as Eddie's life spirals downwards, and his efforts at redemption are thwarted at every turn, the gun starts to look like the answer to all his problems.

Burning Bridges
By Chris Bedell

They've always said that three's a crowd...

24-year-old Sasha didn't anticipate her identical twin Riley killing herself upon their reconciliation after years of estrangement. But Sasha senses an opportunity and assumes Riley's identity so she can escape her old life.

Playing Riley isn't without complications, though. Riley's had a strained relationship with her wife and stepson so Sasha must do whatever she can to make her newfound family love and accept her. If Sasha's arrangement ends, then she'll have nothing protecting her from her past. However, when one of Sasha's former clients tracks her down, Sasha must choose between her new life and the only person who cared about her.

But things are about to become even more complicated, as a third sister, Katrina, enters the scene...

www.blkdogpublishing.com

www.ingramcontent.com/pod-product-compliance
Lightning Source LLC
Chambersburg PA
CBHW011920050726
47591CB00007B/2262